# ANGELS AND OTHERS

# ANGELS AND OTHERS

## Mike Ripley

Published in 2015 by Telos Publishing Ltd
5A Church Road, Shortlands, Bromley, Kent BR2 0HP, UK

www.telos.co.uk

Telos Publishing Ltd values feedback. Please e-mail us with any
comments you may have about this book to:
feedback@telos.co.uk

*Angels and Others* © 2015 Mike Ripley
Please also see the individual story copyright details at the end
of the book.

Cover Design: David J Howe
Cover Background: Gwyn Jeffers

ISBN: 978-1-84583-920-8

# CONTENTS

# Author's Introduction

## ANGELS

### 'Smeltdown'

The first Angel short story was commissioned by the legendary editor of Collins Crime Club Elizabeth Walter as part of the anthology *A Suit of Diamonds* to commemorate the Crime Club's Diamond Jubilee in 1990.

It was an offer I could not refuse, as I would be in very good company in that anthology. Despite being a comparative novice, I would be rubbing shoulders with some great crime writers: Reginald Hill, Robert Barnard, Sarah Caudwell, Gwendoline Butler, Charlotte MacLeod and Patricia Moyes, all of whom, sadly, are no longer with us.

My story, 'Smeltdown', drew on my experiences in my 'day job' with the Brewers' Society trying to get the theft (and smelting) of aluminium beer casks by organised gangs taken seriously by environmental agencies, scrap metal dealers and the police. It was later to form a sub-plot in the novel *Family of Angels*.

### 'Lord Peter and the Butterboy'

In 1990, I attended a lunch to celebrate the one hundredth 'birthday' of Lord Peter Wimsey, organised by the Dorothy L Sayers Society, with the formal address given by P D James. At some point during that lunch, or perhaps soon after, the Chairman of the DLS Society, the late Christopher Dean, suggested that the writers present be asked to contribute to a *festschrift* entitled *Encounters With Lord Peter* to mark the fictional detective's centenary. At the time I was not terribly sure what a *festschrift* was. In fact, I may have misheard '*festschrift*' (a volume of writings that honour a particular person) entirely – it was a very good lunch – and *thought* I heard the words 'short story collection'; anyway, a short story was what they got.

The result was 'Lord Peter and the Butterboy', and while those fine crime writers Jessica Mann, June Thomson, Catherine Aird, Simon Brett, Harry Keating and T J Binyon all made sensible contributions, it was the only short story to appear in *Encounters With Lord Peter*, which was published by the Dorothy L Sayers Society in 1991.

## 'Calling Cards'

In some ways, this story is a piece of social history. It is set at a time when mobile phones were rare and exotic and public phone boxes were common. In most towns and cities, but especially central London, they would be festooned with business cards offering a wide variety of sexual services. Over time these cards got bigger and the artwork better, in fact quite artistic. There was even an exhibition of them mounted in a café-gallery on James Street near Selfridges, which lasted about a week before the police closed it down.

'Calling Cards' was originally written in 1991 as my contribution to a Fresh Blood anthology featuring new British crime writers that did not get off the ground until 1996. The idea was that all members of the unofficial 'awkward squad' of new writers known as Fresh Blood would write a story starting with the words, 'There was fresh blood on …', but it proved impossible, in 1991, to find a publisher.

My story was bought by *Winter's Crimes 24*, published by Macmillan in 1992 and edited by Maria Rejt, although it did get a reprint when *Fresh Blood 1* eventually appeared, edited by myself and Maxim Jakubowski, alongside stories by John Harvey, Ian Rankin, Derek Raymond, Stella Duffy and Nicholas Blincoe.

## 'Brotherly Love'

'Brotherly Love' was written for the anthology *Royal Crimes* in 1994, but set in the year 2000, and is probably the strangest

Angel tale of all.

The anthology was an American initiative, although the majority of contributors were British, edited by Maxim Jakubowski and Martin H Greenberg. The brief was to write a story involving the British Royal Family. I was, at first, reluctant to contribute, but then I came up with the idea of a future-world scenario involving a young prince of the realm (aged about nine at the time of writing) out on the tiles in a London nightlife that now seems ripped off from the film *Blade Runner*. It was probably treasonous, but fortunately few people in the UK read it, at least not until it was surprisingly reprinted in *The Mammoth Book of Comic Crime* edited by Maxim Jakubowski in 2002.

One person was very happy with it: the late Michael Jackson (no, not that one), who was best known as the author of *The World Guide to Beer* and for his TV series *The Beer Hunter*. Michael, a fellow Yorkshireman living in exile in the soft south, was possibly most proud of his authoritative book *World Guide to Whisky* and was delighted when I used it in the story, predicting that it would be in its twenth-ninth edition! I also made him Sir Michael Jackson, which pleased him immensely.

'Angel Eyes'

'Angel Eyes' was my contribution to *Fresh Blood 3,* published in 1999, which was the last of those volumes of stories celebrating new talent, again edited by myself and Maxim Jakubowski – and now famous for including the debut (and for a long time only) Jack Reacher short story by Lee Child.

By this time I had introduced Rudgard & Blugden Confidential Investigations, an all-female detective agency, into the Angel canon, and Angel was to go on to work for them as an unconventional and very reluctant private eye. I was always being asked what Angel looked like, as he's never described, so I thought I'd give somebody else the chance to do that. It's just a pity it had to be Veronica Blugden.

## 'Ealing Comedy'

'Ealing Comedy', my first short story in over 15 years, was written under duress thanks to the threats of Telos Publishing, who have made a splendid job of keeping the Angel novels in print.

Having drawn a line under Angel's adventures with *Angels Unaware* in 2008, I had completed an unfinished (in fact hardly started) novel by Pip Youngman Carter featuring his wife Margery Allingham's famous detective Albert Campion. *Mr Campion's Farewell* appeared in the spring of 2014 and was generously received by critics and fans; so much so that the publishers commissioned a second novel, *Mr Campion's Fox*.

While immersed in the world of Margery Allingham – whose writing I had almost admired since I was a teenager – I came across the fact that she had been born, in 1904, at 5 Broughton Road, Ealing. Although the Allingham house was blitzed during World War II, the address gave me a focal point around which to crystallise a story that had been buzzing around in my tiny brain for a few months. What could be better than an Ealing comedy set in Ealing?

The story was shortlisted for the Crime Writers' Association Margery Allingham short story award in May 2015 and is published here for the first time.


## OTHERS

### 'The Body of the Beer'

My very first short story, 'The Body of the Beer', was written for and published by the magazine *Brewers' Guardian* in December 1988. The editor of the magazine, aware that my first novel had appeared in August, thought it would be a jolly good idea to have a Christmas short story and, naturally, it should be set in a brewery.

I named one of my characters as a nod to my fellow crime

writer the late Robert Barnard. Robert very quickly, if unflatteringly, returned the favour with a character called 'M Ripley' is a short story 'An Exceptional Night' published in *Ellery Queen's Mystery Magazine* in March 1990.

My rather gruesome (if you think about it) tale follows the brewing process in a traditional brewery, which basically starts at the top and drops down in stages, the final drop being the conditioning of the beer when sediments fall to the bottom leaving the finished beer bright and clear. The original magazine story was illustrated by Dr David Long, a scientist at, and later Director of, the Brewers' Society.

'The Body of the Beer' was republished in 1989 in the anthology *New Crimes* edited by Maxim Jakubowski, and once again I was in very distinguished company with, among the contributors: John le Carré, James Crumley, Andrew Vachss, Derek Raymond, Margaret Yorke and even Cornell Woolrich and David Goodis!

## 'Gold Sword'

'Gold Sword' was originally another Christmas story for *Brewers' Guardian* in 1989 but was quickly reprinted in the Crime Writers' Association's anthology *John Creasey's Crime Collection 1990* edited by Herbert Harris, and it holds a very fond place in my heart.

Once again, inspiration came from the day job. I was researching a (serious) historical article on two hundred years of British exports of beer (later to be published in the journal *The Brewer*) when I came across a file containing the minutes of the Beer for Troops committee from the Second World War. The first thing that impressed me was a note pinned to the cover of the file containing the typed instruction that all contents were 'To be copied to Mr Smiley', and although this turned out to be *Norman* Smiley, then company secretary at Whitbread, there was a definite whiff of espionage about that dusty old file.

One matter discussed by the Beer for Troops committee was a request from America asking if British brewers could supply large quantities of canned lager beer for use in Iceland. The

Brewers' Society was not enthusiastic (because they didn't brew lager and all the metal for cans had gone into Spitfire production!) but, significantly, the matter was discussed some months *before* the US Marine Corps conducted a friendly invasion of Iceland in July 1941 – while America was still technically a non-belligerent.

The file was not marked 'Top Secret' or 'Confidential' but it had predicted, through the movement of beer, the American invasion of Iceland. Could the same be done later, in 1944, for the D-Day landings in Normandy – and what would that be worth to an enemy spy?

'Gold Sword' was selected for the Crime Writers' Association's annual anthology that was named after the CWA's founder, John Creasey, and famously published by Gollancz. It was my first appearance in the collection and the last, as the 1990 edition turned out to be the last one published, though I do not think the two events were necessarily connected.

I was inordinately proud when, in 1994, 'Gold Sword' was chosen as Radio 4's Afternoon Short Story on 6 June, to mark the fiftieth anniversary of the D-Day landings.

### 'Our Man Marlowe'

The *John Creasey Crime Collection* may have ended but the CWA's annual anthologies trundled on – they still do – with a new series, *Crime Waves 1*, edited by Harry Keating and again published by Gollancz, in 1991 (although I don't think there was ever a *Crime Waves 2 …*)

'Our Man Marlowe' was one of only three original stories contributed to *Crime Waves 1* and seemed to tickle the fancy of Harry Keating (then President of the Detection Club) who noted (the) 'first spritzer of surprise in the very title'. The story came with a 'Warning to Scholars' that it was 'fundamentally unsound' and profuse apologies to John le Carré (you'll see why) and to that great team of comic writers Caryl Brahms and S J Simon, whose 1941 novel *No Bed For Bacon* provided (uncredited) much of the inspiration for the film (and now West End show)

*Shakespeare in Love.*

The story was reprinted in Maxim Jakubowski's *More Murders for the Fireside*, published by Pan, in 1994.

## 'The Trouble With Trains'

The year 1991 saw another new crime anthology appear, *Midwinter Mysteries 1* (and again, I don't think there was a second …), edited by Hilary Hale and published by Scribners. Once more I was asked to contribute an original story. Given that Hilary Hale, formerly crime editor at Macmillan, had introduced me to Colin Dexter the year before, I decided to have some fun with a thinly disguised version of his Inspector Morse. Despite this, Colin and I remain firm friends almost 25 years on.

I had just discovered Leo Bruce's marvellous 1936 spoof *Case For Three Detectives* and thought that if he could take the mickey out of three famous fictional detectives, then so could I, cheekily throwing in a train stranded in a snowdrift for good measure …

Thus in 'The Trouble With Trains', you have a dapper little Belgian, an Aristocrat, and a morose Inspector – or rather the actors who played them on television. I was not to know, back in 1991, that I would eventually meet them all in the flesh – the late John Thaw (Morse), David Suchet (Poirot) and Edward Petherbridge (Lord Peter Wimsey). All disproved my long-held prejudices about actors and turned out to be absolutely charming.

## 'New Year's Eve'

Yet another new anthology appeared in 1992, *Constable New Crimes 1*, published, logically enough, by Constable and edited by Maxim Jakubowski, who describes me in his introduction as 'the *Eminence Grise* of the Fresh Blood gang of British mystery writers'.

In the company of some rather more hard-boiled practitioners this time – including Derek Raymond, Mark Timlin, Denise Danks, Ed Gorman, Russell James and Ian Rankin – I eschewed comedy and spoofery and tried my hand at the spooky and obsessional with 'New Year's Eve', which was set slightly in the future.

(There is a reference to 'Guardian Angels' acting as peace-keeping vigilantes on the London Underground, as they did on the New York subway. At the time of writing there was serious consideration being given to the formation of a similar blue-beret-wearing corps to control the Northern Line, particularly on Friday nights after the pubs closed.)

## 'MacEvoy's Revenge'

Writing comedy crime fiction usually means thinking up a crime and then trying to make a joke out of it. With 'MacEvoy's Revenge', I started with the joke, a very good joke, told to me by a London cab-driver. It was a joke I told many times at the 1995 Bouchercon, winning from crime writer Russell James the accolade: 'Mike Ripley told the best joke of the convention again – and again, and again.'

The name of the protagonist was my tribute to the charming and extremely generous licensee of The Spice of Life in Cambridge Circus in London's West End, the scene of several infamous launch parties for the Angel novels.

The story was first published in the anthology *Fresh Blood 2*, edited by myself and Maxim Jakubowski in 1997.

## 'Old Soldiers'

'Old Soldiers' was written speculatively in 2002 for the anthology *The Mammoth Book of Roman Whodunits*, which appeared in 2003. I was in the middle of researching my first historical thriller, set in Roman Britain, and this story was part of the 'back story' of a grizzled Roman army veteran – Roscius – talking in retirement about his involvement in quelling the revolt of Queen Boudica (Boadicea). I wanted to show that professional soldiers haven't changed much over the centuries – they just get on with the job – and also to settle on a 'voice' for Roscius. Here he is talking to unseen researchers who might just have been working for the historian Tacitus (who wrote the near-contemporary history of the campaign). The story never made it as a Roman Whodunit but was incorporated almost completely into my novel *Boudica and the Lost Roman* in 2005, which had Roscius as one of the story's narrators.

## APPENDIX

*Angels in Arms:* **The Script**

The script for a full-length TV movie version of my novel *Angels in Arms*, to act as a pilot for a series of one-hour episodes, was written under duress in 1997.

Attempts to get Angel on television had begun as soon as the second novel, *Angel Touch*, appeared in 1989 but had suffered from a severe case of the disease known to writers as 'television development hell'. After six years of dalliance, bad scripts and broken promises, the rights reverted to me in 1996 and were immediately snapped up by a small independent production company.

These new producers (or producer, as I only ever saw one person) were very friendly and enthusiastic and asked me if I would write the script of a pilot episode myself. Having worked on the BBC's *Lovejoy* series and written a couple of scripts for Yorkshire TV, I felt confident enough, and a fee was agreed for a one-hour script to introduce the characters and (I thought) the London setting that was Angel's home turf. For this reason I deliberately ignored *Angels in Arms*, as most of the action takes place outside of London; indeed a fair chunk of it is set in France.

However, within a week or so of starting work, the goalposts changed. The production company now insisted that the pilot should be a 90-minute film with 'all the bells and whistles' (whatever that meant) to show off what the company could do. The producers in their wisdom thought that *Angels in Arms* was the ideal book to adapt, offering location shooting in the Channel Islands, France and a Dorset monastery, and the chance to go on the road with a touring heavy metal band. Budgets, it seemed, were no problem.

I registered my disapproval of the choice of book (by that time there were five stronger contenders, I thought), re-negotiated my fee and set to work. In August 1997 I delivered the completed script – just as the production company announced it was folding and all bets (pilot films and series) were off.

I do not know if anyone ever read the script apart from me. When the television rights were sold (again) in 1998 – to another independent hoping to get a series deal with the BBC – their view was that the series should concentrate on introducing the characters and the London setting that made up Angel's home turf … The *last* book they wanted to adapt was *Angels in Arms* with all its 'foreign', non-London, locations. Needless to say, nothing happened with that idea either.

**Mike Ripley**
**Colchester, 2015**

# ANGELS

# Smeltdown

This all started because Taffy Duck couldn't keep his mouth shut after a few drinks even if he topped his lager with superglue, and Armstrong got belted up the backside by a diesel tanker so recently half-inched that the steering-wheel was still warm.

The truck thing happened first.

I had left Armstrong parked under a street lamp in a respectable, middle-class street in Barking. (Who am I kidding? But that's what would have gone on the insurance claim form.) Now it's none of anybody's business what I was doing in that particular street at 5.00 am that morning, except to say I was in the process of leaving. The lady in question has a husband who works very antisocial shifts (you're telling me – 5.00 am!) in the London Fire Brigade and I'm not about to cross anyone who knows all there is to know about how things catch fire.

Armstrong is an Austin black cab – the London taxi you find on postcards and biscuit tins – and although I and the Hackney Carriage licensing authorities know he isn't actually a licensed cab anymore, you have to look close to tell. Which is why I can usually park with impunity on a variety of yellow lines and, in this case, probably closer to a road junction than I should.

But I'm not making excuses for the tanker-driver, whoever it was, because he simply came round the corner far too fast, lost control and over-corrected, so that while the cab unit missed by a mile, the tanker unit belted Armstrong over the rear offside wheel, lifting him a couple of inches into the air with a scrunch of buckling metal.

My first reaction was to stand where I was about 20 yards away and yell 'You stupid son of a bitch!' as the tanker slowed to a stop at an angle across the street. But then, and I must have had the Fire Brigade on my mind, I thought: petrol tanker – collision – fuel tank – fire. And I did the most sensible thing: I threw myself face down on the pavement and put my hands over my head.

Nothing happened, except it went very quiet.

I uncovered an ear and opened an eye. The tanker blocked the street, but it was still in one piece. So was I, and so, almost, was Armstrong. So was the pair of feet doing a nifty four-minute mile round the corner. He could run, which is good, as everybody has to have *one* thing in life they're good at (Rule of Life No 10) and he certainly couldn't drive.

There was no way I was driving Armstrong anywhere, not with the rear wheel-arch caved in like that, and probably the wheel itself bent. This was a job for my old mate Duncan the Drunken; probably the best car mechanic in the world. But first I had to find a phone and generally get out of sight before an off-duty fire-engine drew up.

I also thought it might be an idea to move the tanker. People notice these things, especially when they are casually parked at right-angles to the road.

The tanker itself was decked out in the colours of an international oil company. It also contained diesel, not petrol, around 33,000 litres, which I calculated to be about £12,000 retail value. I wondered if I could claim salvage.

The driver had left his cab door open and the keys in the ignition, so I climbed up and settled myself behind the wheel. I felt quite at home, as one of my driving licences is actually for Heavy Goods Vehicles, even though I'd never actually moved a tanker before.

I started her up and spun the wheel so the cab came back in line with the bowser, and began to climb through the gears trying to think of a suitable place to park the damn thing in what was, after all, a residential area.

It hadn't crossed my mind then to ask what it had been doing in the area in the first place. But that's what I was asked in the next street when I stood on the brakes to avoid the police Rover and two traffic cops got out.

They had to let me go eventually, although they took my fingerprints so they could eliminate them from those in the tanker's cab, promising – I don't think – to destroy them afterwards.

I could prove that Armstrong was mine and that I was really an innocent victim in all this. In fact, I told them the complete truth, missing out only the reason for my being in that particular street at 5.00 am. Instead, I said I'd been to a party, had too much to drink and slept in the back of the cab, and even had my sleeping-bag (called Hemingway) in the boot if they'd like to check – if they could get the boot open, that was. In fact, I was the one being the responsible citizen in not drinking and driving, I pointed out, claiming the moral high ground.

So they breathalysed me, but didn't get a result and had to believe me. There were a lot of questions before I was allowed to walk. Like had I ever nicked 33,000 litres of diesel before? (Armstrong ran on diesel, so I was fair game.) Did I know anybody who would? Did I know a driver called Gwyn Vivian, sometimes called Taffy Duck? Where had I been the previous afternoon? Had I ever been to a transport café called Spaniard's Corner near Harwich out in Essex?

They weren't happy with all those negatives and were miffed enough not to let me use the phone on the way out, so I hoofed it to Barking station and took a tube into the City, then bus-hopped to Hackney and the house I share with assorted weirdos.

By the time I'd rung Duncan and told him where to collect Armstrong, it was early afternoon. I cooked myself some lunch, popped a can of beer and put my head down for a much-needed kip.

Duncan rang back around five and told me that it would cost up to two grand to fix Armstrong, but surely the insurance would cover it. It would have, if I'd remembered to pay the last premium three weeks before. But Duncan needn't know that. I told him to go ahead, and asked if he had a vehicle I could borrow in the meantime, and he said he would drop something round and put it on the bill.

I had a shower and changed into my shabbiest jeans and second-best leather jacket, having removed Springsteen from it with only a modicum of violence. He was going through a mid-life crisis (say, life number five) where he thought he was possibly not a cat at all, but some furry nesting creature.

Then it was another bus ride and another tube down to Whitechapel and, in an alley just behind the tube station, the Centre Pocket, a snooker club of ill repute where I knew I'd find Taffy Duck.

Oh yes, I'd sort of glossed over the fact that I knew him when the cops asked. In fact, I'd worked with Taffy in the past, roadie-ing for various minor pop groups, although Taffy's heart had never been in it. He was your basic tobacconist/pub/betting-shop/back-to-the-pub man who could take two days to read the *Daily Mirror* and looked on snooker as his version of jogging. One-nighter gigs in Birmingham and then Newcastle weren't his scene.

Taffy wasn't playing on any of the tables in the Centre Pocket, he was sitting nervously on a barstool at the corner of the bar, which had been fitted out by a carpenter who'd had bits left over from the last undertaker's he'd remodelled.

He was watching the door and was obviously relieved when he saw it was only me. He brightened when I offered to buy him another lager, but with typical Welsh foresight he said: 'I can't get you one back, you know. I'm out of work.'

'I know, Taffy, as of yesterday when you let those two lads walk off with your tanker.'

While Taffy did a double-take, the barman gave me my pint and took a fiver from me. He didn't offer any change, but as I wasn't actually a member of the snooker club, I didn't complain too loudly.

'You've picked an expensive place to be unemployed,' I said, smiling.

'Orders. I'm waiting for the boss,' said Taffy, and once he was started he was difficult to stop. 'How did you know about my spot of trouble?'

Before I could answer, he told me the whole story. Hired as a relief driver, he'd hitched his way to Harwich with a pair of false delivery plates under his arm, which is like a free ticket in a car belonging to anyone in the motor trade. He'd collected the tanker and stopped at the Spaniard's Corner café (pronounced 'caff' and, as one of the very few establishments remaining that wasn't a Little Chef, likely to get listed building status soon) for lunch, or 'dinner' as Taffy put it.

On his way to the toilets, in a separate block outside, he'd been tackled – yes, tackled, just like a Welsh fly-half going over the line to score – behind the knees and gone down like a sack of coal. The coal was probably Welsh too. He'd had his hands and feet tied with electrical tape and the keys of the tanker lifted from his pocket and then he'd been dumped behind the rubbish bins, to be found by one of the cooks an hour later. There had been two attackers, both in full motorbiker kit including helmets with dark visors. They hadn't said a word to him or each other, and just after he heard the tanker leave, a bike revved up.

'What could I do, Roy? I was powerless.' He said it like it was a word he'd been rehearsing. 'Anyway, how did you hear about it?'

'The Boys in Blue told me, Taffy.'

Then I told Taffy most of what had happened to me, and he rolled his eyes and tut-tutted until I'd finished, but he made no move to buy another round.

'Now, one thing bugs me, Taffy,' I said, rolling my empty glass on the bar.

'Oh yeah. What's that, Roy?'

'How much do you reckon that tanker rig was worth?'

'Dunno.' He shrugged his shoulders. 'Ninety grand? It was almost new.'

'And the diesel inside was worth maybe 12 grand. And when I found your truck this morning, it was empty. Now who do we know who has a central heating system that requires 33,000 litres of diesel? Or a fleet of about 600 black cabs? Or how about a garage that retails diesel? Or maybe a very thirsty cigarette-lighter for a chain-smoker?'

'What are you getting at?' asked Taffy.

'Who wants that much diesel? Who goes to the trouble of pinching your tanker, draining it and then dumping it?'

'You've got me there, Roy. But the funny thing is, it happened two weeks ago to Ferdy Kyle. I was talking to him about it in here the other night. And he works for Mr McCandy as well. Good evening, Mr McCandy.'

He said it over my shoulder and I turned slightly to find most of the light blocked out by an exhibit from the *Guinness Book of Records*. (Largest dinner jacket ever made category.)

'Who's he?'

'Name's Roy Angel, Mr McCandy,' said Taffy. 'You listen to what he has to say and it'll bear me out, honest it will.'

'Sit. Over there.'

The one who'd asked who I was wasn't quite as big as the one in the dinner jacket, but it was close. He was fifty-ish and dressed in a light brown suit. He had rings made out of half-sovereigns on both hands. (Rule of Life No 85: Never trust anyone who has rings made from coins. If they do it because they think it's fashionable, then they have appalling taste. If they do it because they're good as knuckle-dusters, keep clear of them anyway.)

'I'm Donald McCandy,' said the suit. 'They call me Big Mac McCandy, but not to my face.'

I wasn't about to break the habit.

'And this –' he waved a ring at the huge dinner jacket '– is Domestos.'

He waited for a reaction but didn't get one from me. 'That's right,' said McCandy, tempting us to laugh, 'Domestos, like the lavatory cleaner because he's –'

'Thick and strong?' offered Taffy, and I winced and closed my eyes, so I didn't see exactly where Domestos hit him, but I heard it.

'Good. Now that's out of the way, the rest of the evening's your own,' said Big Mac pleasantly. 'Let's have a drink.'

We sat down, Taffy scraping his chair across the floor and staggering slightly, his eyes full of tears. I noticed that the few snooker players there were in the club had moved to the table furthest away.

The barman came to take our order. We were honoured.

'Good evening, Justin,' said McCandy. 'My usual, a Perrier for my colleague and whatever these gentlemen are drinking.'

'Large brandy,' said Taffy. He was game, I'll give him that.

'Whatever these gentlemen were drinking last,' smiled Big Mac.

'It's Julian,' said the barman, and we all looked at him. He was about 19, his hair fashionably short, and there was a faint sneer on his lips.

'Julian,' he said again, 'not Justin.'

'Whatever,' said McCandy and let it go at that. The kid had either loadsa nerve or no brains at all.

'Now let's talk shop, gentlemen.'

Big Mac had obviously got the outline of Taffy's tale already but he was very interested in what I had to tell him. At the end of it, McCandy said: 'So where does that leave us?'

I didn't like the 'us' one bit, so I kept quiet.

Taffy, of course, couldn't do that to save his life, or in this case, mine.

'Roy's got a theory, Mr McCandy.'

'Then let's hear it, son. What did you say your name was?'

'Angel, and it's not much of a theory.'

'Angel, eh. I don't think Domestos here has ever met an angel before.'

'But I bet he's helped create a few,' I risked, and McCandy grinned.

'Nice one, son. Now, in your own time …'

'Can I just get one thing clear? What exactly is this to do with you, Mr McCandy?' I was as polite as pie. 'And I'm not being chopsy, I just don't get the whole picture.'

McCandy raised an eyebrow, which I hoped wasn't code for Domestos to stomach-punch me from the inside.

'Well, Mr Angel, the picture is this.' He sipped on his 'usual', which looked like *crème de menthe frappé*, but I bet nobody ever said anything about it. 'I run an integrated business. Garages are my core business, but also a few pubs, this club and a couple of others. The secret is to have cash-flow and channel it properly.

'Now, just at the moment, my garages, like most others, are having a big push on unleaded petrol. It's the in thing. At the same time, there's a rising demand for diesel due to the increase in private cars with diesel engines. Okay? Right. What this means is the small operator like me buys fuel on the spot market, but because the oil companies are running around like headless chickens supplying unleaded, there's a shortage of tankers and drivers. I have to use what talent is available.' He looked scathingly at Taffy. 'To top up my regular supplies, that is. One of my garages goes through two tankers of diesel a week, easy. Only I'm going to run short again this week, and that means I lose customers, 'cause those bastard black cab drivers take their business elsewhere.'

If Taffy breathed a word about Armstrong, he wouldn't have to worry about Domestos.

'Taffy said this has happened before,' I said sympathetically.

'This is number four in two months.'

Taffy looked astonished.

'And were all the tankers recovered?'

'Yep. All bone dry. And anywhere from here to Dover, just left at the side of the road.'

'Did they travel the same route?'

'No. Ferdy Kyle got done on the M1 at Northampton.'

'At a café?'

'Yeah,' said Taffy. 'Ferdy knows all the caffs and truck stops.'

McCandy and I looked at each other. Domestos looked at Taffy, judging the distance between them.

'Ferdy's not the villain,' said Big Mac. 'He got badly hurt in the kidneys.'

'During the hijack?' I asked.

'No,' said McCandy, all matter-of-fact. 'Afterwards.'

'He wasn't too chipper the other night when he was in here,' said Taffy, thinking he was helping.

'And I suppose you discussed your route for your tanker?' I asked him.

'Sure. I've been out of the game for a bit, Roy. Ferdy suggested the Spaniard's Corner place as having good nosh, as well as giving me a coupla short cuts.'

'Who else was here when you and Ferdy were rabbiting?' I asked.

'Nobody. It was early on. Just me and Ferdy. No customers. Young Justin said it had been quiet all morning.'

'Julian,' McCandy corrected him softly.

'Do you find all your drivers in here, Mr McCandy?'

'Most. If not here, then in the Jubilee down the road.'

'One of your pubs?' He nodded at me. 'And do your bar staff do relief work in all your establishments?'

I thought he'd like that – 'establishments' – but he just nodded silently again and then said, even quieter than before, 'Julian.'


Which is how I came to be following young Julian for the next three days. Big Mac had thought it a good idea as I was on hand and Taffy was a known face. And I had an incentive. Do it right and I'd never see Domestos again.

Duncan had supplied us with relief wheels while Armstrong was laid up: an ancient Ford Transit van that had been so badly resprayed you could still read 'WILLHIRE' down the side. The clock said it had done only 8,000 miles, and charitably I assumed it had gone round only once.

Big Mac had convinced himself that the spate of diesel thefts had been engineered by a rival to sabotage the legitimate parts of his business empire. To me, that seemed like putting a toothless flea on a Rottweiler, but I did as I was told. Mr McCandy has that effect on people.

For two nights running he had pairs of his drivers meet in the Centre Pocket and discuss their tanker routes for the next day in earshot of Julian. I was to wait outside in my Transit until closing time and then see where Julian went and who he met. Nothing happened except I managed to get half-way through Paul Kennedy's *Rise and Fall of the Great Powers*, a paperback big enough to use as a weapon in case of trouble.

Julian would usher out the last snooker players, lock the front doors, presumably wash the last of the glasses, then emerge from a side door, put three or four empty beer kegs out on the pavement, lock up and walk home. In his case, and I followed on foot twice to make sure, that was the Jubilee, one of McCandy's pubs, where he lived in the staff accommodation above the bar. Most big pubs in London have to offer rooms to their staff nowadays in order to keep them longer than a week. McCandy had leases on a dozen pubs and, by asking around during the day, I discovered he had about fifty youngish staff, mostly Irish or Australian, living in.

On the third night, I followed Julian in the van after he'd gone through his lights off, kegs out, lock up routine. He arrived back at the Jubilee and entered through the back yard, where he chatted with one of the pub's barmen who was going through the same ritual, putting out empty kegs for the delivery dray to collect next morning. Then they disappeared inside and lights came on in the upstairs rooms, followed by the faint strains of a Wet Wet Wet record.

'This is getting bloody silly,' Big Mac said the next day when we met as arranged in a café/sandwich bar across the road from one of his garages in Bethnal Green. 'I've now got more diesel than I can sell and this is not helping my cash-flow situation at all.'

As my cash-flow tended to be all one way, I found it difficult to empathise, but I pretended.

'Maybe we're wrong about Julian,' I said.

'I have a feeling in my water about him,' said McCandy, turning his killer look on me. 'And I told Nigel that when he hired him.'

'Nigel?'

'My son. He runs all my licensed properties.'

Well, somebody had to. With Big Mac's record he wouldn't have got a licence.

'Bright lad. Did Business Administration at university.

Likes to help out his old mates, and I think that's a good sign. You know, the mark of a considerate employer.'

I'd assumed that the mark of a considerate employer as far as Big Mac was concerned was leaving somebody with one good eye, but I said: 'Er … I don't follow, Mr McCandy.'

'Nigel. And Julian. They were at university together. Julian couldn't get a job, so Nigel took him on until something turned up. I have to be fair; we've had three or four of his old cronies through the firm and they've done okay. Two of Nigel's buddies are managers in my pubs right now. And it gives the organisation a bit of class to have all those degrees after the names on the letterheads.'

'So Julian's got a degree, has he?' I sipped some milky coffee and put the brain out of neutral.

'Two, as a matter of fact,' said Big Mac proudly. 'A BSc and an MSc. What's that got to do with anything?'

'Probably nothing.' I took a deep breath. 'Look, Mr McCandy, we've got to think logically about this.'

'Go on, then,' he said.

'You think this is somebody getting at you. You personally.'

'Yeah,' he said slowly, thinking about it.

'But it's not – in itself – going to put you out of business, is it? Just filching the odd drop of diesel.'

'Over a hundred thousand bloody litres to date,' he snapped. 'That's not chicken feed.'

'No, I know,' I said soothingly. 'But it isn't the way to really screw you, is it?'

'So?'

'So that can't be the main reason for nicking the fuel, can it? It must be because whoever's doing it actually needs the diesel.'

I licked my lips, which had suddenly dried out.

'Mr McCandy, what would you use all that fuel for *apart* from putting it in engines?'

'I haven't a fucking clue.'

'I have.'

That afternoon I drove across town to Bloomsbury and parked in a side road off Gower Street. The place I was looking for was the rear quarter of a 1930s office block converted into a laboratory and a small lecture theatre. It was part of London University, but since the upsurge in the activities of the animal liberationists a few years ago it hasn't appeared on any map of university buildings and the phone number is ex-directory.

Zoë had worked there on secondment from London Zoo for five years, lecturing and demonstrating on wild animal physiology and behaviour, but we went back longer than that. She used to get away from her parents overnight by telling them she was going badger-spotting, and even though she lived in a part of Tooting where they hadn't seen a tree since George III got out of his carriage to swap small talk with it, they believed her.

I had to blag my way past an ancient security guard who would have stood no chance against a libbers steam team, but the key to their security was that no-one knew of their existence. He reluctantly got Zoë on the internal phone and she reluctantly told him to let me in.

She was sitting in an empty lab cataloguing a tray of 35mm slides, and she looked up from under huge blue-framed glasses to say: 'Well, a rave from the grave. Mr Angel. What are you after?'

'Now, Zoë darling, we had a pretty steady relationship once,' I said, showing the good teeth.

'Just remember,' she said, pointing a pencil at me, 'it was purely sexual. There was nothing platonic about it.'

'You do remember.'

She pretended to think for a second, then smiled, swivelled on her bench stool and opened her knees so she could pull me in close. I pushed her glasses up into her hair and fumbled a hand inside her lab coat.

Between kisses, she murmured: 'So you just happened to be in the neighbourhood, eh?'

'Sort of,' I whispered into her ear, my hand trying to find the place on her lower spine that I knew was The Spot so far as she was concerned. 'And I just had a thought about that experiment you ran with the squirrels in the New Forest.'

'Squirrels? What are you after?' She tried to push me away but I held on and then started to gently rub the spot on her back. She gave a startled little 'Oh', then sighed.

'You know how you tracked them, followed their habits, with those little radios on collars.'

'Mmmm. That's my job. Mmmm. Don't stop.'

'How effective are those transmitters? What range do they have?'

'A ... mmmm ... mile and a half. Why?'

'Got any kicking around? Any that could conveniently go missing?'

This time she did lever me away.

'It'll cost you,' she said, looking me in the eye.

'How much?'

She took off her glasses, laid them on the tray of slides and shook her hair out, then put her arms around my neck.

'Did I mention money?'


I took Domestos with me because he was better than a warrant card. Norman Reeves, the manager of the Shadwell Arms, the farthest-flung pub in the McCandy empire, was also the longest-serving employee of Big Mac. Without Domestos there he would have had me out on my ear for asking questions, let alone demanding to go into the pub's cellar.

The Shadwell was a backstreet boozer within a stone's throw of the Tower of London, but few tourists were encouraged to find it. The cellar floor was cleaner than any flat surface in the bar.

'How many kegs do you get through in a week?' I asked Reeves.

'Usually two or three kils or 22s and, say, six firkins or 11s or tubs, whatever we've been selling most of,' he answered carefully.

I knew enough from my own days as a barman to decode what he'd said. Strictly speaking, beer came in casks, and a pressurised keg was a type of container – not a type of beer, as many think. They were known by the size of their contents: a 'kil' was a kilderkin (18 gallons) and a firkin was half that, all the imperial measures being in multiples of nine up to a barrel (36 gallons). Metric containers were measured in hectolitres, but just to confuse the foreigners, publicans referred to them by their imperial equivalents: 22 or 11 gallons. A 'tub' was slang for anything that wasn't a regular imperial or metric size, say ten gallons, and you'd get low-volume beers or cider in those.

'Are they all collected when the draymen deliver?'

'Yeah, we leave them out back. I don't have room to store empties down here.'

'And when do you get deliveries?'

Reeves looked at Domestos, who nodded, before he answered. 'Mondays, Tuesdays, Wednesdays, whenever ...'

I frowned at him.

'Whenever the wholesalers deliver.' He shrugged.

'You don't buy direct from the breweries?'

'No, we shop around.'

'And do the wholesalers charge deposits on the kegs?'

'Nah,' he chuckled. 'We'd get a new wholesaler if they did.'

'How many do you deal with?'

'Four or five. What's this all about?'

'Mr McCandy's called me in as a sort of efficiency expert. But we don't talk about it, okay?'

'Sure, sure. Never seen you.'

'Good,' I beamed, enjoying my newfound sense of power. 'Do you have a rota for barmen for Mr McCandy's pubs?'

'Yes. Mr Nigel sends one round every week so we can swap staff if there are any gaps.'

'Just what I need. Get it, will you?'

He got the nod from Domestos and disappeared upstairs.

'I need two of those in the back of the van,' I said to Domestos, and pointed at a row of kegs. Then I picked my way carefully through puddles of spilt beer to have a look at the damp-rotted noticeboard tacked to the cellar wall near the hatch doors that lead on to the street.

There were regulation safety notices about carbon dioxide, no heavy lifting and electrical circuits in cellars, and one other that I stole and folded into the back pocket of my jeans.

Domestos was grunting up the stairs to the bar. He had to move sideways as he had an 11-gallon keg under each arm. I could see that they still had green plastic caps on the siphon unit where you plugged in the beer pipe.

'No, Domestos,' I said gently. 'Empty ones.'

A day and most of a night later I was seated in the Transit again, watching the back door of the Centre Pocket club. This time I had Big Mac McCandy next to me, and in the back Domestos snored gently.

'You sure this thing'll work?' He prodded the radio receiving unit on the dashboard.

'Up to a mile,' I said, hoping Zoë had been straight with me. 'Watch.'

I flicked the on-switch and the centre one of the three orange lights began to flash. I'd had Duncan the Drunken solder the tiny squirrel collars to the underside lip of the two kegs I'd borrowed, and right now they were about 50 yards away on the pavement, in a stack of about a dozen, outside the Centre Pocket. It was nearly five in the morning and we'd been there since three.

They came round the corner at about half five, in a box-backed truck with no markings. It stopped outside the Centre Pocket and two guys in jeans and zipper jackets with the name of a well-known London brewery stencilled on the back got out.

'Cheeky buggers,' breathed McCandy as we watched them roll up the back of the truck and start loading the kegs.

The snooker club had obviously been the last hit on their run, as they were lucky to get the Centre Pocket's kegs on board.

'How many do you think they've got there?' McCandy asked me, thinking along the same lines.

'Dunno. Forty? Fifty? They reckon you need about sixty to smelt down a ton of aluminium. Scrap value, 12 hundred notes a ton.'

'You know a lot,' he said suspiciously.

'I asked around.' Then I saw the look in his eyes. 'Discreetly,' I added.

'They've left a couple,' he said suddenly and loudly, but we were well away and they couldn't have heard. 'They know you've bugged those two.'

'Relax. The two they've left are stainless steel kegs, not aluminium. There's no smelt value in them, but if you stick them in the back of an old car and put it through the wrecker, they add to the dead weight scrap content.'

I wondered if I'd gone too far, showing off like that, but McCandy let it go.

The truck pulled away and turned left around the corner. I started the Transit and flicked on the receiver. The flashing light alternated between the centre bulb and the one on the left. 'It's crude, but effective,' I said. 'And we keep out of sight. With so little traffic this time in the morning, I figured that was important.'

McCandy weighed the receiver in one hand.

'If we lose them,' he said, looking straight ahead, 'you'll need surgery to remove this.'

I put the pedal to the metal.


The smelter turned out to be in no-man's-land between Barking and Little Ilford, though there are people who live in Ilford who don't know there's a Little one.

It was tucked away in the corner of an old factory site that the developers called a prospective industrial park and the local residents called waste ground. We found it when the receiver started blinking right but there was no obvious right turn. Doubling back, it was McCandy who noticed something wrong with the shabby picket fence, but he told me not to stop but see if we could get round behind.

They'd been very clever, you had to give them that.

A whole section of ten-foot-high fence had been fixed so it could be slid aside to provide access to the site. The drivers of the box truck had literally driven off the road, then replaced the fence, and nobody would have been any the wiser if we hadn't had the transmitter bugs. The smelter itself was a good 300 yards from the fake fence. The giveaway was its chimney – it usually is – though these guys had given the problem some thought and had kept it to no more than ten or 12 feet high and had fitted a fan on top to disperse the smoke. There were enough other old buildings, piles of scrap iron and even broken-down caravans to screen the place from casual passers-by, not that there would have been many of them.

Right next to the smelter – a one-storey brick building with double iron doors – was a black fuel tank, perhaps the remains of some heating plant.

'That's where your diesel went,' I said to McCandy.

I had parked the Transit at the south end of the site, around the corner from the hole in the fence. Big Mac and I were standing on the bonnet looking over the fence and I had given him a pair of binoculars that were no bigger than opera glasses but 20 times more powerful. I'd got them from a passing acquaintance who didn't use them for bird-spotting. Well, not in the conventional sense.

'They nicked your tankers when their tank was running low. Drive it in there, transfer the fuel and dump the rig the next day.'

McCandy grunted and handed the glasses back.

The two guys we'd followed were unloading the truck, adding their haul to a rack of kegs already there. It wasn't only McCandy's pubs getting ripped; this was a well-organised operation, probably buying kegs from freelance chancers at a couple of quid a go. To the side of the smelter, there were two cars, one a Porsche, and a motorbike parked.

'Let's get closer,' said Big Mac, and he put his hands on the top of the rickety fence and side-jumped over.

I hesitated just long enough for Domestos to feel the need to cough discreetly, and then I followed.

We picked our way through the mud and over the junk until we were within a hundred feet of the smelter; so close I imagined I could feel the heat. We could certainly hear voices and the clanging of empty kegs, and they were so confident that they even had a radio on, tuned to the World Service.

Big Mac led the way around a burnt-out caravan and then stopped short. I almost bumped into his shoulder, but halted myself. Physical contact was not advisable, I reckoned.

Then I saw why he'd stopped dead: a big, sleek, brown Doberman bitch was coming at us at Mach 2, ears back in attack mode.

I looked around frantically for a weapon, and despite the junk all around, couldn't decide on anything likely to stop the dog. McCandy still hadn't moved, except to go into a fighting crouch. I did the sensible thing and moved back to give him room to get on with it.

'Hello, Louise,' he said, holding out a hand. 'There's a good girl.'

The dog skidded to a halt and rolled over, exposing her stomach and extending her tongue to wrap around Big Mac's hand.

'How long have you had this strange power over dogs?' I asked.

'Ever since she was a puppy and we gave her to my son Nigel,' he answered without looking up. Then he said: 'Louise – stay.'

The dog stayed. We moved nearer the smelt.

From behind a pile of building rubble we could see at least five men working. One had what looked like a homemade wrench that undid the pressurised seal on the top of the keg. That way the steel spear that fed carbon dioxide into the beer could be removed. It had to be unsealed or it would have blown up as they put it in the furnace. One of the others had the job of collecting the seals and lopping off their tubular spears with a power saw. I'd heard that most smelting operations were given away when people found hundreds of discarded steel spears. They hadn't found a way of making money out of them. Yet.

McCandy and I could see right into the crude smelting oven they had constructed. Not that you need anything fancy. If you have enough diesel to burn, once you hit the right temperature, the aluminium kegs just collapse in front of your eyes. It was almost as if a giant invisible hand crushed them. One minute they were there, shaped and intact against the flames; the next minute they'd folded and turned to liquid, which the smelters ran off to cool in moulds made out of kegs cut lengthwise. That was a bit of a giveaway if you ask me, as it was a none too subtle hint as to where the aluminium had come from.

One of the smelters pulled off a pair of asbestos gloves and sauntered out of the smelt and over to the Porsche. He opened the boot and took out an insulated cold box, the sort you take on picnics. He opened it and handed out small bottles of Perrier. It was thirsty work.

'Is that Nigel?' I asked McCandy softly, and he nodded. The two guys who'd brought the truck began to load it with the half-keg-shaped ingots.

'Do you want to follow them, Mr McCandy? Find out where they're selling the stuff?'

Big Mac shook his head. He was still staring across the site at the back of his son's head.

'Griffin Scrap Dealers in Plumstead, south of the river,' he said without turning round.

'Oh. Er ... one of your ... er ... businesses?' I stood back a bit, just in case.

'Yep,' he said grimly. 'Got it in one.'

'You want me to *what*!'

'I want you to grass my son Nigel.'

'You want me to turn him over to the Old Bill? Your son?'

'And his mates. The whole shooting match,' said Big Mac, reasonably. 'Well, I can't, can I? I'm not a grass.'

'Neither am I,' I protested.

'But everybody knows I'm not. I have my position to think of.'

We were back in the front of the Transit, back in the City. Domestos had been sent to pick up McCandy's Jaguar from the car-park of a well-known firm of solicitors.

'They send people down for smelting nowadays, Mr

McCandy. The breweries have got together and they press for prosecution. It's not just a slap on the back of the legs with a ruler anymore.'

'I know that,' Big Mac said philosophically. 'Prison was an education for me. It taught me how to manage people, how to plan ahead, watch your stock control, expand your options and diversify in a static market. I think of it like other people think of school: maybe the best days of your life. Doesn't mean you want to go back, though.'

He lit a small cigar, and I regretted that I'd given up smoking again.

'When I think of all the dosh I've spent on private education for Nigel and he's still daft enough to think he can cross me ... A spot of stir will be the making of the lad.'

I had a nasty feeling he was right.

'He'll thank me for it one day, but he mustn't know it was me. That's why you've got to do it. I don't care how. I need 24 hours to clean out the Plumstead yard. Make sure we don't have any of his – my, I should say – metal there.'

'But ...'

'I'm sure you'll think of something, Roy. You seem a resourceful lad to me. And that old taxi you run about in. Send me the bills for having it repaired. In fact, I'll open an account for you at one of the garages and put some credit behind the counter for you. Have a year's free diesel on me. How's that?'

'Very fair, Mr McCandy. But are you sure about this?'

'Absolutely.'

'I'll need a few expenses.' It was worth a shot.

He produced a wallet and dealt me ten ten-pound notes onto the dashboard.

'What about Mrs McCandy, Nigel's mum?' I tried. 'Won't she be upset if he goes down?'

A slow smile lit up his face.

'Mortified. Absobloodylutely gobsmacked. She'll have to resign from about 500 committees and stop putting on airs and graces.' He opened the door of the Transit and made to climb out. 'Get it done,' he added.

Then, when he was standing in the road holding the door, he said: 'Or you will be. Done, that is.'

Later that morning, when I'd worked things out, I visited one of the few genuine ships' chandler's left in London and spent some of McCandy's money. Then, just short of opening time, I called at the Shadwell Arms and, using the McCandy name, got the landlord, Norman Reeves, to take me into his cellars again.

'I need a couple more kegs, Norman,' I told him. 'And I want them in the back of my van now without anyone seeing us.'

'What's going on?' he asked irritably.

'Why don't you ask Big Mac himself?'

'Will these two do?' He dragged two 11-gallon lager kegs toward the hatch that led to the street.

'Fine. One more thing, What do you use to unscrew the spears?'

Reeves pretended to look stupid. He was a gifted impressionist. 'Don't know what you mean. Them's sealed containers. You can't tamper with 'em.'

'Not even when you want to recycle some old beer, or maybe water down some good beer? I know. Now where is it?'

To my surprise he gave in before I could invoke Big Mac's name again. He reached behind a stack of boxes containing crisps and cleaning materials in equal proportions and produced a long-handled tool adapted from an adjustable wrench.

'Just lock on to the pressure seal and turn anti-clockwise,' he said.

'Thanks, Norm. Shall I get Domestos to return it when I've finished?'

'Don't bother. I've got a spare.'

The balloon went up, so to speak, at ten past seven the next morning.

It wasn't a balloon, of course. It was a large cloud of noxious orange smoke that even the fan they'd fitted to the smelter chimney couldn't cope with. It blew back and out of the oven itself, the smelters on duty running blindly out onto the waste ground, one of them, blinded, even tripping over the back bumper of the Porsche. I hoped it wasn't Nigel. He had enough to worry about.

Short of a big arrow coming down from heaven and pointing 'Here They Are', there wasn't a better way of spotting the smelter. And the assembled hordes of policemen and brewery security men took the hint, smashing through the fake fence and surrounding the choking, crying smelters.

I was watching from the far end of the site through my binoculars, standing on the Transit as Big Mac and I had done the day before. It had all gone according to plan. McCandy had made some excuse to keep Louise the Doberman at home, and the naval distress flares I'd packed into the empty kegs had worked a treat once they'd been pushed into the oven.

It had taken me a couple of dry runs in packing them with sheets of plastic so they didn't rattle or fall out when the smelters took the spear out. And they were so light, the extra weight wouldn't have been noticed. When I was satisfied, I'd called the hotline number on the notice I'd stolen from the cellar of the Shadwell Arms on my first visit. The notice had explained that keg theft was illegal and gave a phone number for anyone spotting anything suspicious.

I'd done it that way, and let the brewery guys call in the cops, so I could stay out of the action.

After all, I had my reputation to think of.


Watching people getting arrested must give you an appetite. That, and the fact that I owed her for a couple of squirrel collars and had to return her radio receiver, led me to drag Zoë out of her lab for an early lunch,

Over a bottle of Othello, a fine head-banging red wine, in a Greek restaurant off the Tottenham Court Road, I told her some of what I'd been up to. (Rule of Life No 5: Always tell the truth, but not necessarily all of it or all at once.)

She seemed most concerned about the damage to Armstrong, but I told her not to worry, he was being well looked after. That reminded me I owed her for the transmitter collars, and I reached into the back pocket of my jeans for the remains of Big Mac's folding money.

As I pulled out my depleted wad of tenners, something else came with it and fluttered to the floor under the table.

Zoë bent over and picked it up. It was the notice about keg thefts I'd pinched from the pub and it was folded so that the pay-off line, printed in red, was clearly visible. It said: 'KEG THEFT HOTLINE – TO CLAIM YOUR REWARD', and there was a number.

'What's this?' she asked, handing it over.

'Think of it as extra car insurance,' I said. 'You can never have too much.'

# Lord Peter And The Butterboy

'I had that Lord Peter Wimsey in the back of a cab once.'

'What?'

I hadn't meant to snap at the old man, but he'd caught me on the raw.

'Lord Peter, the detective. And gent. Oh yes, he was a gent.'

What was the old fool on about?

'Er … t'riffic. Excuse me, pal, but I'd like to get home before the monsoon lets up.'

It was raining so hard you could hardly see the Islington streets getting cleaner. If it kept up, they'd been privatising the Highways Department.

'Twice, actually, if the troof were known. Once when I were a Butterboy.'

Just my luck. Half-way home on a Saturday evening, having carefully plotted a route to Hackney to avoid the football grounds where there were home matches. The plan was: get home, get changed, get fed and get out to meet an old flame called Fly, as I was on a promise down in Ponder's End after her film club's latest offering in its Warren Oates retrospective season. No hassle, no problems. Then it started to rain and rain hard, and then I had the flat in the rear nearside tyre.

One of the benefits of driving round London in a delicensed FX4S Austin black cab is that, normally, nobody notices you. One of the disadvantages is that when it rains, especially on a Saturday, they not only notice you, they follow you like wild dogs tracking wounded prey. I had been a good boy and turned down all the hailed offers I'd had from women loaded down with shopping and men staggering out of the pubs having decided they'd missed the football anyway.

All those good intentions and I get a flat tyre.

And it was slating it down, the rain seeping inside the collar of my bomber jacket and running down the arms and into my gloves as I struggled to get the jack set up.

And I had an ancient onlooker, an old wrinklie with an umbrella and a long raincoat and galoshes. And I just knew he would start giving me advice.

'I remember these things coming out in 1958,' he said, leaning over me so that more rain dripped off his umbrella and onto my head. "Course, the FX3 was introduced before that.'

'Yeah,' I said under my breath, 'that would make sense.'

"Course, I'm talking 'bout long before this FX model, yer know.'

Oh God, I had a taxi nut. Where do they come from? Why do I attract them?

'That's nice,' I said, ignoring him. He ignored me ignoring him.

'Beadmores,' he said.

'Naturally,' I agreed, adopting the well-tried policy of keeping smiling and not turning your back.

'Beadmore Motors,' the old geezer went on. 'That's who used to make cabs, the old black cabs before this lot.'

He flicked his umbrella at Armstrong, my trusty chariot, even if no longer a legal Hackney Carriage, and showered me with even more water. My hair was already plastered to my skull and I was standing on the wheelbrace, having learned long ago that the best way to undo wheelnuts on a flat tyre is before you jack it off the ground.

From my vantage point, a foot in the air, I gave him my killer look. Like the rain, it bounced off.

'I had a Beadmore Mark I De Luxe when I first picked him up,' he droned.

'That'd be the one before the Mark II,' I grunted, shifting one of the nuts.

'First new cab after the Great War. Came in in 1919. Four cylinder, 16-horsepower engine, interior light and starter motor. Pretty good schmutter in them days. Six hundred and ninety quid new. 'Course I got mine from an uncle, second-hand. He was too bleedin' lazy to work the West End, but I always said that was where the money was.'

'Some things haven't changed, then.' I had the last of the nuts loose now and started to fumble the brace into the jack, swearing as my wet gloves slipped on all the sharp edges I'd never noticed before.

'That was how I came to meet him; cabbing for him. Twice, like on two different occasions.'

'What? Who?' I asked before I could stop myself.

'Lord Peter Wimsey, the great detective, like I said.'

'Oh yeah, him.'

I didn't say any more, honest. I didn't encourage the old man; I didn't even look at him.

I just went on changing the wheel and cursing as I got wetter, and really took only about half of it in ...

Like I said, it was a Beardmore Mark I. That was my first cab, and the first one that became known as the black cab or the London cab. There were still horse-drawn ones before the War, you know.

Anyway, I picked him up outside the Savile Club and he asks me to take him to Brocklebury's, where there's a second-hand book sale or something. We only get as far as Piccadilly Circus and, blow me, he says he's left his catalogue and can't go to this hop without it.

I hadn't put him down as a travelling salesman, mind you. No, he was obviously a real toff, so I didn't know why he was carrying a catalogue, but mine's not to reason why, so I says 'Back to the Savile Club, sir?' and he says, 'No, make it 110A Piccadilly instead.' We get there and he dives inside and I wait. After a while, another gent comes out and gets in.

This is a gent's gent, if you know what I mean, but very well spoken, and he says he's going to Brocklebury's instead of 'is Lordship. And he tells me I've just driven Lord Peter Wimsey.

Of course, all us mushers got to know Lord Peter in the '20s. Familiar sight he was, and more than once one of us would get him out of a scrape – out of a fountain or down from a lamppost sometimes – and get him home safe. He was always very generous, mind, and if he didn't have company with him in the back of the cab, he'd always have a word or two for the driver.

And then there was the time he looked after Harry Hill. That became famous in cabbie circles. It would be about 1925, 'cos Harry was driving a Beardmore Mark II and Lord Peter was already calling us 'Butterboys' then.

There'd been this big trial at the House of Lords involving Lord Peter, and as it broke up when the jury got a result, there was 'undreds of people – if not farsends – milling about outside the Houses of Parliament. Then this big bearded geezer, who had it in for Lord Peter's brother, pulls out a gun and starts taking pot-shots at all and sundry. He does a runner and poor old Harry Hill, who's coming over Westminster Bridge looking for a fare, is headed straight for him. He panics and shoots out one of Harry's front tyres. The cab throws a wobbler, out of control, and Harry careers into the bloke with the gun and pins him up against a tram, then crashes into the end of the bridge.

There was nothing he could have done about it – an honest accident – but there was an inquest and suchlike and it worried Harry sick so he couldn't work for months. It was Lord Peter who sought him out and told him not to worry and stood by him. He looked after Harry's family as well. Dead generous he was.

So we all kept an eye out for Lord Peter after that.

He called us cabbies 'Butterboys' because of the Yellow Cabs that had appeared in America in 1924. Yellow Cab mushers were called butterboys because of the yellow colour, you see, and Lord Peter spread the habit. All newly licensed drivers after that were 'Butterboys'. Of course, if you'd been around a bit, or done 'the Knowledge' like you have to these days, then you were a proper 'musher', but only real cabbies were allowed to call each other mushers.

I didn't actually get to give him another ride, though I saw him around town often enough, until … it'd be 1936. By then I had a Beardmore Mark V; the Paramount Ace it was called, from Beardmore Motors of Paisley up in Scotland. Wonderful machines. They'd be worth their weight in gold now.

I was working lates – 10.00 pm until morning – and cruising

Shaftesbury Avenue, though the theatres had long since chucked out. Still, there were plenty of punters floating up and down the streets.

I spotted Lord Peter in full theatre rig: top hat, dinner jacket, the lot. He was standing with another bloke on the corner of Rupert Street, like they'd just come out of a stage door. The bloke with him was a younger chap, dead good looking, wearing a tweedie cap and an overcoat with the collar turned up almost like he didn't want to be recognised.

Lord Peter waves his cane in the air and I cuts across to pick 'em up. As he opened the door, I heard him say to the younger chap:

'Don't be such an almighty ass. This faithful Butterboy will see you home.'

I knew straight off it was 'is Lordship, but I couldn't place the other fella. Not then.

Lord Peter gives me an address off Lisson Grove and then, as I drives off with both of them in the back, he proceeds to give the young fella a right good talking to. All very polite, mind you, 'cos his Lordship always did speak proper and never resorted to effin' and blindin', however much he was provoked. Nevertheless, this was some serious GBH of the lugholes. I mean he was giving the young bloke some rotten stick.

I only caught parts of it, through the screen, and naturally I wouldn't listen in if it was a really private conversation, but he was going on and on about some letters; letters from a woman of course.

'No, I will not return them, you young idiot,' Lord Peter was saying. 'Children really shouldn't play with matches. Do you realise just how close to a major scandal you have come?'

The young chap went wild at that and ranted about he didn't care what society thought. It was his life, wasn't it?

'Not exclusively, my dear chap,' Lord P said – I remember that. 'Your dalliance must rate as the second-worst-kept secret in England this year, and you are in line to cause the second-biggest scandal if we are not all very careful. You are equally destined for greatness, but you will not be allowed to abdicate your responsibilities with a shred, however small, of honour. You will be expelled and shunned: socially, professionally and artistically.'

Then the other bloke starts really shouting: 'What gives you the right? How dare you play God?'

'That is a role I am not qualified for and have no intention of even auditioning,' Lord Peter told him. 'It is not a question of anyone playing God. Look on me only as a safe-deposit box for your conscience and the reputation you will certainly make in the years ahead. It is a task I take on reluctantly, but certain influential people who recognise your genius just as much as you do have asked me to act as honest broker in this, quite frankly, squalid little affair. Consequently I appoint myself the guardian of the knowledge of this particular segment of your past; but past is the operative word. The affair is now history.'

Well, the younger chap came out with some ripe language then and even started jumping up and down, almost trying to get up and walk around in the back of the cab. He was flinging his arms about and yelling, but Lord Peter keeps his head and stays cool.

'No, no and thrice no. I have explained. Your letters to her and her letters to you will remain in my charge, and should anything happen to me I have left instructions for them to be destroyed unread. In the meantime, they are a safeguard. You will no longer moon sorrowfully after her and she, in turn, will not be tempted to risk her marriage and her position by approaching you when your fame increases, as it surely will. The matter is ended; the case is not altered, but closed.'

It was then the younger bloke snapped, and he went for Lord Peter like a real street brawler. I could feel the cab swaying as they crashed about, but all I could see in the mirror was the chap on top of Lord Peter, pummelling away for all he was worth.

Naturally, I couldn't have any of this, so I pulls over onto the pavement. We were cutting through Portman Square at the time, and it was quite quiet, fortunately for all concerned.

So I'm out and round the side just as their door pops open and they fall out at my feet, at it like tigers. I grabs the young bloke by the scruff of his overcoat and yanks him to his feet. He's like an eel, and strong with it. He whips round, kicks me in the shins and elbows me in the face.

I go down, slumped against the cab, me 'ead spinning.

Lord Peter's standing up by this time, his hat missing and his shirtfront all torn. Dead calm, he slips off his cloak and throws it in the back of the cab; then he pulls his gloves tight and gently dusts down his jacket.

The younger bloke's turned on him by now, but Lord P just stands there and takes up a boxer's stance, fists up on guard. Doesn't say a word. The young bloke gives a big grin, pulls off his coat and puts up his mitts, and then they go at it, right there on the pavement in Portman Square. If it hadn't been after midnight, I could've sold tickets.

But it didn't last long. The younger chap has some very fancy footwork, I'll admit that. Moves like a ballet dancer and tries to nip in under with a few jabs, but I don't think one of them connected. No killer instinct, you see.

Lord Peter picks his shots, two jabs to the face then a one-two-one combination to the stomach and jaw, and young Lochinvar is out for the count.

First thing Lord P does, of course, is come over to help me up, telling me how awfully sorry he is about it all. Then I helps him pick up the young geezer and we put him back in the cab, where his Lordship gives him a handkerchief to put on his nose and murmurs 'No lasting damage, thank Goodness'. Then he says something else, about the chap's 'face will be his fortune', which I don't understand – not then, anyway.

Eventually we get to Lisson Grove and we stop, and by now the young tearaway's cooled off a bit and is seeing sense.

He shakes Lord Peter's hand and his Lordship says something like 'You really should take up that Hollywood offer, you know. Out of sight, out of mind and all that. It might even be a good career move. You have the looks and you certainly have the voice.'

The young chap shrugs his shoulders and slinks off, and then Lord Peter turns to me and slips me two tenners – twenty quid, no word of a lie, which was a load of money in them days – and says he fancies a long walk home to take his blood off the boil.

There was no need for him to tell me to keep my mouth shut, you'll note. That was taken as read. After all, I was one of his faithful Butterboys.


'And do you know sumfink?'

Was the old man still rabbiting on?

'You're gonna tell me, aren't you,' I sighed.

'That young bloke went on to become a household name, and people recognised him the world over. Some would say he became more famous than Lord Peter hisself.'

'Really,' I said, deadpan, throwing the jack into Armstrong's boot, then peeling off my sodden gloves. They were leather and would never dry properly; and now I was running late.

'And another thing,' he said.

'I thought there might be.'

'The next day, I'm cleaning out the cab, as you do, and I finds this on the floor in the back.'

He held up something small and shiny between the forefinger and thumb of his left hand.

'What is it?' I asked wearily, squinting through the rain.

'A cufflink, one of his. See the design? Three mice and a cat ready to pounce. I don't think he'd mind me hanging on to it for a souvenir, do you?'

'Probably not,' I agreed, reaching for the driver's door handle and safety.

The old man shuffled up to my window and I lowered it a fraction.

'My granddaughter's always on at me,' he shouted as if I was deaf. 'She says I should write up the whole story.'

'I think you'll find somebody has,' I said, starting the engine.

But a couple of weeks later, while waiting in Marylebone Library for Lorraine (the big blonde one in the music section) to knock off work, I did a bit of snooping and found nobody had.

I've been trying to find that boring old bugger ever since.

# Calling Cards

There was fresh blood on the black guy's hand as he took it away from his nose. This was probably because I'd just hit him with a fire-extinguisher.

Well, it wasn't my fault. I'd meant to let it off and blind him with some disgusting ozone-hostile spray, but could I find the knob you were supposed to strike on a hard surface? Could I find a hard surface? Give me a break, I was on a tube train rattling into Baker Street and I was well past the pint of no return after an early evening lash-up in Swiss Cottage (what else is there to do there?). All I could see was this tall, thin black guy hassling this young schoolgirl. I asked him to desist – well, something like that – and he told me to mind my own fucking business, although he wasn't quite that polite.

So, believing that it's better to get your retaliation in first (Rule of Life No. 59), I wandered off to the end of the compartment and made like I was going to throw up in sheer fright. I thought I did a fair job of trying to pull the window down on the door you're not supposed to open that links the carriages. (Think about it – if you're going to throw up, where else do you do it on a tube?) And, as usual, the window wouldn't open. So I staggered about a bit, not causing anyone else any grief, as this was late evening and the train was almost empty. And while swaying about, which didn't take much acting the state I was in, I loosened the little red fire-extinguisher they thoughtfully tie into a corner by the door.

You can tell someone's put some thought into this, because it always strikes you that it says 'water extinguisher' when you know that the tube runs on this great big electric line ...

Whatever. I got the thing free from its little leather strap and staggered backwards, trying to read the instructions.

After two seconds I gave up and strode down the carriage to

where the black guy was sitting and just, well, sort of rammed it in his face, end on.

He couldn't believe it for a minute or two, and neither could I, but I was ready to hit him again. Then he took his hand away from his nose and there was blood all over it. Then his eyes crossed – swear to God, they met in the middle – and then he fell sideways onto the floor of the carriage.

The train hissed into Baker Street station, and suddenly there seemed to be lights everywhere. I had a full-time job trying to keep my balance and decide what to do with an unused fire-extinguisher.

The doors of the carriage sighed open and I felt the schoolgirl tugging at my sleeve.

'Come on! Let's blow!' she was yelling. 'He'll be coming at you hair on fire and fangs out once he comes round.'

It seemed a logical argument, the sort you couldn't afford to refuse. So I followed her, dropping the extinguisher on the back of the black guy's head, solving two problems in one.

It made an oddly satisfying noise.


Now, to get this straight; she did look like a schoolgirl.

Okay, so I'd had a few. More than a few. That's why I'd left my trusty wheels, Armstrong (a black London cab, an Austin FX4S, delicensed but still ready to roll at the drop of an unsuspecting punter), back in Hackney. I had been invited up to Swiss Cottage to a party to launch a rap single by a friend of a friend called Beeby. So you heard it here first; but then again, don't hold your breath.

It had been my idea of lunch – long and free, though I think there was food there too. And round about half-past eight someone had decided we should all go home and had pointed us toward the Underground station.

Unfortunately, a rather large pub had somehow been dropped from a spacecraft right into our path, and an hour later I found myself on autopilot thinking it was time I got myself home.

So I caught the tube and there I was, in a carriage on one of the side seats (not the bits in the middle where your knees independently cause offences under the Sex Discrimination Act with whoever is opposite) with no-one else there except this tall, thin black guy and a schoolgirl, on the opposite row of seats.

At first the guy seemed a regular sort of dude: leather jacket a bit like mine, but probably Marks and Spencer's, blue Levis and Reeboks and a T-shirt advertising a garage and spray-paint joint in North Carolina. Nothing out of the ordinary there.

But even in my state, I had to do a double-take at the girl he was holding down in the next seat. Not, you note, holding on to or even touching up, but holding down. And when the train hit St John's Wood, she waited for the doors to start to close – just like she'd seen in the movies – and then made a break for it. And, of course, she didn't make the first yard before he grabbed her and sat her down again next to him.

At that point, I lost what remained of my marbles. I interfered.

The thing was, she did look like a schoolgirl. Blue blazer, white shirt straining in all the right places, light blue skirt, knee-length white socks and sensible black shoes. She even had a leather school-satchel-type bag on a shoulder strap and – I kid you not – a pearl-grey hat hanging down her back from its chinstrap.

And this black guy was holding her down. So I asked him to let the young lady go. And he told me where to go. So I got a fire-extinguisher and hit him.

Did I hit him because he was black and somehow defiling a white schoolgirl? Bollocks. Did I step in to protect the fair name of young English maidenhood? Well, it would have been a first.

I did it because I was pissed, but it seemed the right thing to do at the time.

We live and learn.


'Move!' she yelled again as she pulled me down the station toward platform five.

Goodness knows what people thought, though I was in little state to care, as this schoolgirl dragged me down the steps to the

Circle Line platform and bustled me into a crowded carriage, all the time looking behind her to see if the black guy was there and only relaxing when the doors closed and the tube shuttled off.

She breathed a deep sigh of relief. I could tell. We were close and the carriage was full. She noticed me noticing.

'I wasn't really in trouble back there,' she said, looking up from under at me in that up-from-under way they do.

'Nah, 'course not.' I grabbed for the strap handle to keep my balance.

'It was just that Elmore wanted to deliver me – well, had to, really – to somewhere I didn't fancy.'

'That a fact?' I said, which doesn't sound like much but which I regarded as an achievement in my condition.

'You wouldn't understand,' she said quietly, biting her bottom lip.

'You could try explaining. I'm a good shoulder to cry on and I had nothing planned for the rest of the evening.'

Now, in many circumstances, that line works a treat. On a crowded Circle Line tube when everybody else has gone quiet and is looking at this suave, if not necessarily upright, young chap chatting up what appears to be the flower of English public school girlhood, it goes down like a lead balloon.

She saved my blushes. In a very loud voice above the rattle of the train she said: 'Then you can take me home.' And then, even louder: 'All the way.'

After that, what could I say?


All the way home turned out to be Underground as far as Liverpool Street station, then a mad dash up the escalator and an ungainly climb over the ticket barrier to get to the mainline station just in time to grab two seats on a late commuter bone-shaker heading east.

Trixie lived in one of those north-eastern suburbs that if it had an Underground station would call itself London, but as it didn't preferred to be known as Essex, but wasn't fooling anyone. There was nobody on duty at the station, so we got out without a ticket again and she led me across the virtually deserted pay-and-display car-park to a gap in the surrounding fence. That led on to a side street and just went to prove that for early morning commuters the shortest distance between two points is a straight line. I wondered when British Rail would catch on.

Her house was one of a row of two-down, three-ups that backed onto the railway line. The front door had been green once, but the paint had flaked badly and under the streetlights looked like mould. The frame of the bay window onto the street was in a similar state, but through a gap in the curtains I could see a TV flickering.

'Who's home?' I asked, not slurring as much as I had been.

'Josie, my sister. I told you,' she said.

She had too, on the train. Told me of 14-year-old Josie who was doing really well at school and had only Trixie to look out for her now that their mum had died. There had never actually been a dad, well not about the house and not for as long as Trixie could remember. And yes, Trixie was her real name, though God knows why, and she was thinking of changing it to something downmarket like Kylie.

She opened the front door and stepped into the hallway, calling out: 'It's me.'

I stepped around a girl's bicycle propped against the wall. It had a wicker carrying-basket on the front in which were a pile of books and one of those orange fluorescent cycling-poncho things that are supposed to tell motorists you are coming.

The door to the front room opened and Josie appeared. She was taller than her sister and she wore a white blouse with slight shoulder pads, a thin double bow tie, knee-length skirt, black stockings and sensible black patent shoes with half-inch heels. She had a mane of auburn hair held back from a clean, well-scrubbed face by a pair of huge round glasses balanced on her head. She held a pencil in one hand and a paperback in the other. I read the title: *The Vision of Elena Silves* by Nicholas Shakespeare. I was impressed.

'You're early,' she said to Trixie, ignoring me.

'This is Roy,' said Trixie.

Josie frowned. 'You know our deal. I'm the only one in this house who does homework. '

'It's not like that, honey. Roy's a friend, that's all. He helped me out tonight, saw me home.'

Josie gave me the once-over. It didn't take long.

'Well, at least you'll be able to press my uniform before school tomorrow,' she said to Trixie.

'Of course, honey, now you get back to your studying and I'll make Roy a cup of tea in the kitchen.'

In the kitchen, she said: 'Don't mind Josie, she doesn't really approve. Put the kettle on while I go and slip into something less comfortable. '

While she was gone, I plugged in the kettle and found teabags and sugar. Then I ran some water into the kitchen sink and doused my face, then ran the cold tap, found a mug and drank a couple of pints as a hedge against the dehydration I knew the morning's hangover would bring.

Trixie returned wearing jeans and a sweatshirt, no shoes. She busied herself taking an ironing-board out of a cupboard and setting it up, then plugging in an iron and turning the steam control up. She began to iron the creases out of Josie's school skirt.

'It was good of you to see me home,' she said conversationally.

'Yeah, it was, wasn't it? Why did I do it?'

'And the way you sorted out Elmore ... I hope he's all right, mind. I've known a lot worse than Elmore. '

Thinking of what I'd done to Elmore made my hands shake.

'You haven't got a cigarette on you?' I asked.

'Sure.' She picked up the school satchel she'd been carrying and slid it across the kitchen table.

I undid the buckles and tipped out the contents: two 12-inch wooden rulers, five packets of condoms of assorted shapes, flavours and sizes, two packets of travel-size Kleenex, cigarettes, book matches and about a hundred rectangular cards.

I fumbled a cigarette and flipped the cards. They were all roughly the same size, about four inches by two, but printed on different coloured card, pink, blue, red, white, yellow and red again. A lot of red in fact. The one thing they had in common was a very large telephone number. Each had a different message and some were accompanied by amateur but enthusiastic line drawings. The messages ranged from 'STRIKING BLONDE' to 'BLACK LOOKS FROM A STRICT MISTRESS'; from 'BUSY DAY? TREAT YOURSELF' to 'TEENAGER NEEDS FIRM HAND'. They all carried the legend 'Open 10 am till late' and 'We Deliver'.

I made a rough guess that we were not talking English lessons for foreign students or New Age religious retreats here.

All the cards had a woman's name on them: Charlotte, Carla, Cherry and so on. I split the pile and did a spray shuffle, then dealt them on to the table like Tarot cards.

'No Trixie,' I said.

'Are you kidding? Who'd believe Trixie? I'm Charlotte and Carla, among others. '

I ran my eye down the cards. Charlotte apparently demanded instant obedience and Carla was an unruly schoolgirl. So much for biographies.

'Working names?' She nodded. 'And tonight was Carla, the one who needs a firm hand?'

'Yeah, but not Mr Butler's.'

'Mr Butler?' I asked, pouring the tea.

'That's where Elmore was taking me. But he didn't tell me it was that fat old git Butler – if that's his name – until we were on the tube. I'd swore I wouldn't do him again, not after the last time. He is *molto disgusto*. Really into gross stuff. He waits till everyone's gone home, then he wants it in the boss's office. I know he's not Mr Butler, but that's what it says on the door.'

'Hold on a minute, what's all this about offices – and where does Elmore come in?'

'It's on the card,' she said taking a cigarette from the packet.

'I've seen hundreds of these things stuck in phone boxes. You ring the number and get told to come round to a block of council flats in Islington,' I said. Then hurriedly added, 'So I'm told.'

'Ah, well, read the difference, sunbeam. "We Deliver" it says.'

The penny dropped. Then the other 99 to make the full

pound.

'Elmore delivers you – to the door?'

Trixie blew out smoke.

'To the *doorway* sometimes, but mostly offices, storerooms, hotel rooms. Sometimes car-parks, sometimes cinemas. Once even to a box at Covent Garden.'

'You mean one of the cardboard boxes round the back of the flea-market? Which mean sod was that?'

She caught my eye and laughed.

'No, chucklehead, a box at the opera. You wouldn't believe what was playing either. It was a Czech opera called *King Roger*, would you credit it? I thought that was a male stripper.'

'This wasn't one of Mr Butler's treats, was it?'

'Oh no, he's too mean for that. He likes humiliating women, that's his trouble. And I told Elmore never again, but he was just doing what Mrs Glass told him to do.'

'Mrs Glass?'

'Oh, never mind about that. ' She turned off the iron and held up Josie's school skirt. 'That's better.'

She folded the board away and joined me at the table, indicating the cards I had laid out.

'Anything there you fancy?' she tried softly.

'Would you be offended if I said no?'

'Too right – I need the money. Josie's expecting to take thirty quid to school tomorrow to pay for music lessons, and I'm skint.'

'Elmore handles the money, right?'

She nodded and ground out her cigarette.

'Are you sure you wouldn't ...?'

I held up a hand, stood up and emptied the contents of my pockets onto the table. As I had been at a freebie all day, I hadn't thought to pack credit cards or anything more than a spot of drinking money. I had £2.49 left, which wouldn't even cover the train fare back to town.

'I was thinking of asking you if you could see your way ...' I started.

She slapped a hand to her forehead.

'Just my luck,' she muttered under her breath. Then she

quietly banged her forehead on the table twice.

'Hey, don't do that. I'll get us some dosh. What time does Josie go to school?'

She looked up. There was a red bruise on her forehead.

'8.30.'

'No problem. Do you have any black plastic dustbin liners?'

'Yes,' she answered, dead suspicious.

'And some string?' She nodded, biting her lower lip now. 'And an alarm clock?'

'Yeah.' Slow and even more suspicious.

'Then we should be all systems go.'

She gave me a long, hard look.

'I've heard some pretty weird things in my time ... This had better be good.'

I slept on the couch in the front room and promptly fell off it when the alarm went at six. It took me a couple of minutes to remember where I was and what I was supposed to be doing, and another twenty or so to visit the bathroom as quietly as possible and get it together enough to make some instant coffee.

Then I pulled on my jacket and zipped it up, stuffing the pockets with the dustbin liners and string Trixie had supplied. Over my jacket I attached the fluorescent orange warning strip that I borrowed from Josie's bicycle, then I slung her empty school satchel around my neck to complete the ensemble.

I was ready to go to work.

In the station car-park, I pulled the dustbin liners over the four pay-and-display machines nearest the entrance and secured the open ends with string around the machine posts. It was still dark and I was pretty sure no-one from the station saw me.

The first car arrived at quarter to seven and I was ready for it, leaping out of the shadows and holding the satchel out toward the driver's window as he slowed.

'Morning, sir. Sorry about this, the machines are out of action. That'll be two pounds, please.'

It was as easy as that.

After an hour, I got cocky and embellished it slightly. There had been an outbreak of vandalism and the machines had been superglued, or the mainframe was down (whatever that meant) but we were doing our best to repair things.

Then one smartarse in a company Nissan asked for a ticket, and when I said I didn't have any, he said 'Tough titties then,' and almost drove over my foot.

He looked just the sort to complain once he got inside the station, though I bet he wouldn't say he parked for free. So I decided to quit while I was ahead. Josie's satchel had so many pound coins in it (no notes as everyone had come expecting a machine) that they didn't rattle anymore. It was so heavy, I was leaning to port.

I waited for a gap in the commuter traffic and headed for the hole in the fence. When I got back to Trixie's we counted out £211 on to the kitchen table. I was furious.

At two quid a throw it should have been an even number. One of the early-shift commuters had slipped me an old 5p piece wrapped in two layers of tinfoil.

Somebody should complain to British Rail.


'So what are you going to do now?' I asked, distributing fifty of the coins between two pockets of my jacket and hoping I didn't distress the leather any more.

'Buy some groceries, pay a bill maybe.'

Trixie buttered herself more toast. Josie had taken her music lesson money, satchel, bicycle and uniform, stuck a slice of toast in her mouth and left without a word to me.

'And then?'

'Oh come on, get real,' said Trixie impatiently. 'Then I ring Mrs Glass and go back to work.'

'When?'

'This afternoon, probably.' She glanced at the piles of one - pound coins on the table. 'How long do you think this will last? It'll take a damn sight more to buy me out. This is very useful, but it don't make you my white knight or guardian angel.'

I bit my lower lip. I hadn't told her my full name.

She put down her toast but held on to the butter-knife, so I listened.

'I chose to go on the game, so there's no-one else to blame. I don't like working for somebody else, but I don't have any choice just at the moment, so that's that. Okay?'

I picked my words carefully.

'This Mrs Glass, she has something on you?'

'Not her; she just runs the girls from her off-licence in Denmark Street. That's the number on the cards. It's her husband, Mr Glass, who recruits us. And we don't have a choice.'

'Is this Glass guy violent?'

'Not that I've ever seen.' She went back to buttering.

'Then why stick with him? Why not do a runner?'

'He'd find us. He's our Probation Officer.'


I got back to Hackney by noon, in order to collect Armstrong.

The house on Stuart Street was deserted, most of the oddball bunch of civilians who share it with me not yet having given up the day job. Even Springsteen, the cat I share with, was missing, so I opened another can of cat food for him, showered, changed and left before he could reappear. I couldn't face one of his and-where-do-you-think-you-were-last-night? looks.

Before I'd left Trixie's, she'd leaked the basic details of the operation run by Mr and Mrs Glass. Talk about sleazeballs! But then, he who lives by sleaze can get turned over by sleaze, and Trixie had given me plenty to go on.

I spent the afternoon sussing out the off-licence on Denmark Street. It wasn't difficult to find, there being only a dozen or so businesses left there now that the developers were moving in. There was just so much time even I could hang around a Turkish bookshop without raising suspicion, but there were still a handful of music shops left where the leather-jacket brigade could kill a couple of hours pretending to size up fretless guitars and six-string basses.

There was nothing obviously unusual about the off-licence's

trade, except that on close inspection there did seem to be a high proportion of young females going in, some of them staying inside for a considerable time. And although they went in singly, they came out in pairs. Not surprisingly, Elmore hadn't turned up for work, so the girls were doubling up as their own minders and 'deliverers'. It was time to put in an appearance.

I retrieved Armstrong from around the corner outside St Giles-in-the-Field. As Armstrong is a genuine, albeit delicensed, taxi, there had been no fear of a ticket, even though I had parked illegally as usual. You had to be careful of the privatised wheel clampers, though, as those guys simply didn't care and slapped the old yellow iron boot on anything unattended with wheels.

There wasn't an excess of riches for the shoplifter, that was for sure. Many of the shelves were almost bare or dotted with mass-market brands of wines – the ones with English names to make ordering easy. Only the large upright cold-cabinet seemed well stocked, mostly with cans of strong lager or nine-percent alcohol cider, which were probably sold singly to the browsers in the next-door music shops.

At the back of the shop was a counter piled with cellophane-wrapped sandwiches, cigarettes and sweets. Behind it, standing guard over a big NCR electronic till, was a middle-aged woman who wouldn't have looked out of place serving from a Salvation Army tea-wagon or standing outside Selfridges on a flag day for the blind or similar.

'Need any help, love?' she asked. The accent was Geordie, but maybe not Newcastle. Hartlepool, perhaps, or Sunderland. 'Er ... I'm not sure I'm in the right place,' I said, shuffling from one foot to the other, trying to look like a dork.

To be honest, I suddenly *wasn't* sure. She looked so – normal.

'Pardon?'

'Well ... I was told you might have a spot of work going.'

Mrs Glass drew her head back and fiddled with the fake pearls around her neck.

'Work? What sort of work?'

'Er ... delivering things.' I jerked my head toward the window and Armstrong parked outside. 'I get around quite a bit and a friend said you could always use someone to drop things off.'

'What sort of things?'

'Calling cards.'

She looked me up and down, and then at the till again, just to make sure it was safe.

'Who told you?'

She glanced over my shoulder at Armstrong's comforting black shape. And why not? Policemen, VAT-men, National Insurance inspectors and the Social Security never went anywhere by taxi. Or if they did, they didn't drive it themselves.

'A young lad called Elmore,' I risked.

'When did you see him?'

'Last week sometime.' When he could still speak; before he ate a fire-extinguisher.

She seemed to make a decision. She could have been judging jam at the Mothers' Union.

'It's £20 a throw,' she said, businesslike.

'I thought thirty was the going rate,' I said, knowing that it was at the time.

'You'll be taking the taxi?' I could see her working out the possibilities. Who notices black cabs in London?

'Sure.'

'All right then, thirty. Wait here.'

She fumbled with a key to lock the till, and I saw she wore a bunch of them on an expandable chain from the belt of her skirt. She opened a door behind the counter and stepped half in just as a phone began to ring. Holding the door open with one foot, she took the receiver off a wall mount and said 'Hello' quietly. Further in the back room I could see a pair of female feet half out of high heels begin flexing themselves.

Whoever it was must have arrived when I was fetching Armstrong; I hadn't seen anyone else come in. I hoped it wasn't Trixie.

'Why yes, of course Madame Zul is here,' Mrs Glass was saying softly. 'Yes, she is as cruel as she is beautiful. Yes, she is available this afternoon. When and where? Very good, sir. Madame Zul's services begin at one hundred pounds.'

I was straining my ears now and hoping no real customers

came in. Not that Mrs Glass seemed in the least bit inhibited. Business was business. 'May I ask where you saw our number? Ah, thank you.'

She concluded her deal and replaced the phone, then, to the girl I couldn't see, she said: 'On yer bike, Ingrid my love. You're Madame Zul this afternoon.'

'Oh, bugger,' said the voice above the feet, the feet kicking the high heels out of my line of sight.

'Sorry, my dear, but Karen's tied up as the naughty schoolgirl.'

Somehow I kept a straight face.

Mrs Glass scribbled something on a sheet of paper and handed it over. A red-nailed hand took it.

'The costume's hanging up and the equipment bag's over there.' Mrs Glass was saying. 'You'd better get a move on.'

Then she turned back to me and she had a Harrods carrier-bag in her hand. She placed it on the counter and turned down the neck so I could see four white boxes, each about three inches by four.

'One of each of these four in every phone box, right?'

I nodded, knowing the score.

'British Telecom only, don't bother with the Mercury phones. '

'Wrong class of customer?' I said before I could stop myself.

She looked at me with a patient disdain normally reserved for slow shop assistants.

'The Mercury boxes are too exposed. They only have hoods, not sides and doors. The cards blow away. '

'Do you use the sticky labels? I've seen those around, you know, the adhesive ones.'

Mrs Glass sighed again, but kept her temper. She was good with idiots.

'If you're caught doing them, you get charged with vandalism 'cause you're sticking something to the box – defacing it. Right? With the cards, all you get done for is littering, and they've never prosecuted anyone yet as far as we know. '

'But don't get caught.'

'Right. Now, the cleaners for the Telecom boxes are under

contract to clean first thing in the morning every other day. Your patch is Gloucester Place from Marylebone Road down to Marble Arch, and don't forget to hit the Cumberland Hotel. There's a bank of phone boxes in there and the place is always full of Greeks. Then work your way over the parallel streets in a square, okay?'

'Baker Street, Harley Street, Portland Place?'

'And don't forget the ones in between. There's a good mixture of foreign students, embassy staff and BBC in that area.'

Again, I thought she might be kidding, but she wasn't. She was obviously proud of her market research.

'We do a random check on you to see that the cards are up. If you're thinking of dumping them, then don't come back. If we don't get a call from one of these boxes within 12 hours, we assume you've dumped them.'

She pulled on her key chain again and flipped open the till to remove three £10 notes. She pushed them across the counter along with the boxes of calling cards. Then she added a five-pound note.

'Make sure Madame Zul gets to the Churchill Hotel by four o'clock, while you're at it, will you?' Then, over her shoulder, she yelled: 'Ingrid, this nice young man's going to give you a lift!'


Madame Zul, she who was As Cruel As She Was Beautiful, smoked three cigarettes on the way to her tea-time appointment, and as I drew up outside the hotel, she stuffed two pieces of breath-freshening chewing-gum into her mouth, picked up a sports bag that positively clanked, buttoned her trenchcoat around the black plastic outfit she was wearing and stomped off toward the lobby.

I watched her go through the sliding doors, then gunned Armstrong and headed south-east, away from the West End and my card-drop zone.

She had not proved the greatest conversationalist. I had tried a few pleasantries and one obvious chat-up line. I had even tried the heavy stuff and asked her if, as a woman, she felt exploited.

'The punters need us more than we need them,' she answered curtly. 'And I could always work the check-out down the supermarket.'

I was thinking about that, wondering just why I was doing what I was doing, when I arrived at Peter's in Southwark.

Printer Pete's Place is tucked away in a smelly courtyard off Marshalsea Road, not a spit away from the old Marshalsea Prison site. Somehow I always suspected Peter – he hated 'Pete' but there had been a typographical cock-up on his business stationery – took pride in that. He loved dealing in anything shady. Probably that's why he became a printer.

I showed him the boxes of calling cards. I had been prepared to scour the phone boxes of the West End collecting them, but now I had about a thousand in pristine condition, not one thumbed by a sweaty hand.

'Nice enough job,' said Peter, turning one over in his hand. '150 gsm card, centred up, neatly trimmed. Most of the girls working on their own do real hash jobs. It's like trying to see how many different typefaces you can get into six square inches.'

'Can you do what I want?'

'Sure. These babies'll go through the machine easy enough, but I'll have to put one of my night-shift on it. This is what we in the trade call a hand job.' He roared at his own joke. 'Hand job, geddit?'

'Not often enough,' I countered.

'Got the numbers?'

I handed over a piece of paper with two 081 London phone numbers and he laid out one of each of the four cards on top of a packing case of printer's ink. The four each had a different catch-line, but the same phone number and the words 'Open 10 am till late' and 'We Deliver'. The messages were: 'CARLA, TEENAGER, NEEDS FIRM HAND'; 'CHARLOTTE THE STRIKING BLONDE'; 'RELAX IN SAMANTHA'S FIRM HANDS'; and, of course, 'MADAME ZUL, AS CRUEL AS ...' and so on. You know the rest.

'So you want these 081 numbers above the 071 number?' Peter asked.

'If you can overprint easily.'

He nodded.

'So how much?'

'A ton,' he said immediately.

'Get outa here, ' I responded.

'Seventy-five, then. It's night work. Overtime.'

'Bollocks. Thirty.'

He squinted at me over his wire-frame glasses.

'Any chance of a freebie?' He waved vaguely at the spread of cards.

'Which one?'

He blushed and tapped the MADAME ZUL card with a shaking forefinger. Really, Pete, I had no idea.

'I had that Madame Zul in the back of the cab less than half an hour ago. I can certainly ask for you. '

'Okay then, thirty, and you can pick 'em up tomorrow morning, first thing.'

'Thanks Peter, see yer then. But hey – let me tell you, this lady really can be cruel.'

So cruel, she could easily say no.


The best time to catch a Probation Officer is when the pubs and courts are shut, so I was knocking time spots off a £10 phonecard from a booth in King's Cross station by nine the next morning.

He answered his direct line at the third ring.

'Islington Probation Service. '

'Mr Glass? Mr Colin Glass?'

'Yes. Whom am I speaking to?'

'Nobody if you've got this on tape, for your sake.'

There was a pause.

'There's no recording. State your business.'

The accent was northern, unexceptional and not as sing-song as that of Mrs Glass, your friendly off-licensee.

'I need to talk to you about some of your clients – and before you tell me you don't discuss clients, the ones I'm interested in are Carla, Charlotte, Samantha and Madame Zul, as cruel as …'

'Who is this?'

'Someone who is going to make you an offer you can't ...'

'How did you get this number?'

I was getting annoyed with him. He was cutting off all my best lines.

'Get down to York Way in half an hour. Be on the flyover where it goes over the railway. Just walk up and down, I'll find you.'

I hung up and retrieved my phonecard, slotting it back into my wallet along with the white business card from Islington Probation Service that I had lifted from Trixie's handbag.

Very usefully it gave me Mr Glass's direct line at the office, as well as his home phone number.

I noticed an old, half-scraped-off adhesive card on the side of the phone. In handwritten lettering it advertised 'BLACK AND BLUE, THE STRICT TWINS'. The number it gave seemed to follow the series of the phone box I was in, and for curiosity's sake I checked. It turned out to be four booths away, a distance of maybe 12 feet.

Some people had no imagination.


I cruised up and down York Way, which is just around the corner from King's Cross, until I saw him hop off a bus and begin to look around. He was alone.

I parked Armstrong on the waste-ground that leads to the Waterside pub and Battle Bridge Basin, where the longboats attract the groupies in summer (as most are owned by rock musicians), and locked him. I had two pocketfuls of cards, which I had collected from Peter the printer at 8.00 am.

Being out on the road at that time was almost a first for me. Wearing a suit was another one. I hoped the cards didn't spoil the cut of the double-breasted.

I put on a pair of Ray-bans (fakes, but good fakes) and marched up the road to meet him.

Colin Glass was a worried man. He was about fifty, short and thin and thinning on top. He wore a Man at C & A suit, and as it flapped open I could see where a pen had leaked in his inside pocket. I pegged him as a civil servant who had changed to the Probation Service rather than be made redundant from some other department.

'Mr Glass, we need to ...'

'Just what is going on?' he blustered. 'How dare you ring my office?'

'You'd prefer me to ring you at home?'

I reached into my jacket pocket and he flinched away from me. My hand came out holding a selection of calling cards. I fanned them like a magician.

'Go on, pick a card, any card. '

He picked a blue one: Charlotte, the Striking Blonde. One of Trixie's.

'So what the hell is this? What are you trying to say?'

'Ever seen one of those before?' I asked, dead polite.

'Of course not. '

'Check out the phone numbers.'

'Jesus Christ!'

'I doubt it,' I said.

Below us, an Inter-City train picked up speed and headed north. Colin Glass looked as if he wished he were on it. Or under it.

'Try another,' I offered, showing him the full wedge of cards from my pocket. Then I reached for my other pocket. 'Or how about teenagers in need of a firm hand, or Madame ...'

'Who ... did ... this?' he spluttered.

'I have no idea, but unless certain things happen, about a thousand of these things will hit the phone boxes this afternoon, and there could be a specially targeted drop in certain areas of Islington. Not to mention a few through the post to various people. '

He was ashen now, but still holding the cards at arm's length as if they would bite.

'There's ... Can we ...?'

'How many girls have you working for you, Colin? And do tell the truth. You know it makes sense.'

'Six in all.'

'All clients of yours?' He nodded. 'All on probation?'

'They are … or they were.'

'That's naughty, isn't it, Colin. Abusing your position and all that. What a story for the newspapers, eh?'

'Look, they were on the game anyway. If anything, we made it safer for them, made them pool their efforts.' He was trying out arguments he'd rehearsed but hoped never to have to use. He wouldn't look me in the face.

'And I bet Mrs Glass made them cups of tea and saw to it that they had condoms on tap, and probably did a bit of counselling on the side.'

He looked up, and there was a faint spark of hope in his dead-fish eyes. I blew it out.

'Tell it to the judge. And the papers. And the Civil Service Commission. '

He bit his lower lip.

'What is it you want?'

'You out of business, that's what. This afternoon. Close up the Denmark Street shop – man, that's so obvious a front I'm surprised you haven't been raided by the drugs squad. Rip the phone out and pay off all the girls. Give them a grand each, cash. Call it their redundancy money.'

'Six thousand? I can't ...'

'You will. Where's all the profit gone, eh?'

'You don't understand ... The pension they give is pathetic.'

'Stay lucky and you might get one. If you don't come across by four o'clock this afternoon, these things go out.' I waved some more cards at him. 'By breakfast tomorrow, you'll be giving press conferences – and so will your bosses. Mind you, look on the bright side. Your wife could pick up a bit of business overnight once this number here …'

'All right, all right, I'll do it.'

'Remember, a thousand to each girl. Got anyone else working for you?'

'No.'

I dropped a couple of the cards on the pavement and he scuttled after them before they blew into the gutter, moaning 'No, please ...'

'How about a dude called Elmore?'

'Only him. He sub-contracts jobs when he has to.'

'Then a grand for him too, and tell him to retire. If any of them ask, just say it was a present from a guardian angel, got that?'

He stood up again, the knees of his trousers filthy from where he'd scrabbled on the pavement.

'Why are you doing this to me?' he asked nervously. 'What's in it for you?'

I looked up and down York Way. There was no-one else in sight and traffic was light. I slipped my left hand into my jacket pocket.

'There's nothing in it for me,' I grinned. 'And I'm doing it because I don't like your attitude. You're supposed to be one of the good guys.'

It was the only answer I could think of, and I didn't want to debate it, so I threw a fistful of his calling cards into the air and left him on his knees again, frantically trying to pick up every last one.

I told the story to my old and distinguished friend Bunny in a pub in Hackney about two months later.

Bunny is very interested in all matters female and feminist and for all the wrong reasons. He regards it the same way as opposing generals regard intelligence on troop movements.

'But what did you get out of it, Angel? A quick bonk?'

'Just a good feeling, ' I said, not really knowing myself.

'So you did get to ...'

'Please, curb that one-track mind of yours.'

'I can't help it if I'm over-healthy.'

I spluttered into my beer.

'What's wrong with that, then?'

'Nothing,' I choked.

We had got onto this subject because Bunny had found a red calling card stuck in the doorframe by the pub's public phone. I hadn't read it properly until now.

'Well, I think it shows great initiative,' he was saying. 'A working girl's got to work, so why not employ the latest technology?'

He was referring to the card, which listed an 0860 number – a mobile phone.

I read the legend: 'CARLA, TEENAGER, NEEDS A FIRM HAND.'

I suddenly knew how Trixie had spent her redundancy money.

# Brotherly Love

'Who's an ageing hippy?'

'You are. I thought they'd died out in the last century.'

'Say that again,' I snarled, 'and I'll defenestrate you, if that's the correct term for someone who carries their teeth in their top pocket.'

'Okay, okay, calm down. Watch the blood pressure, Angel.'

'Then you watch your lip. Just remember, I don't have to be doing this.'

'I know. And we appreciate it.'

At last the royal 'we' had appeared. I'd wondered how long it would be.


Technically, he was right about the last century. It was the first year of the new millennium, that no-man's-land between 1999 (year of religious fanatics and mega-huge newspaper supplements on who had done what and who was going to do what) and – at last – Stanley Kubrick's 2001. The newspapers were getting ready for that one, too, offering prizes to anyone who could name another film with Keir Dullea.

People had gone ape-shit over the New Year, as you might expect, and I can't say I'd had a quiet time myself.

The 'in' Christmas gift had been a chequebook, even for people who hadn't written a cheque for ages, because the date lines had all been reprinted '20–'. The Jazz Warriors were top of the charts all over Europe, and the newest house release had an electronic drumbeat of 190 beats per minute. All this (except the chequebooks) made my New Year's resolution an early retirement from the music scene. The old B-flat trumpet was upended for the last time on New Year's Eve. That was it, no more jazz for me, I said. 'No heart in it anymore?' asked the few friends who noticed. No, too bloody difficult; though I never said it.

I was even sticking to my job (well, four nights a week) as meeter and greeter at the Ben Fuji's Whisky and Sushi Bar in Threadneedle Street. I had done it originally just for a weekend as a favour to Keiko, the daughter of the owner, who was called neither Ben nor Fuji, who had got me out of a tight spot in a night club in Chancery Lane (now there was a sign of the times!) one evening by proving to three argumentative out-of-towners that she really did have a black belt in karate.

To be honest, I quite liked the job. I knew enough about sushi, without actually eating any, to blag my way through, and with a copy of Sir Michael Jackson's *Guide to Whisky* (twenty-ninth edition) under my desk in the entrance hall at Ben Fuji's, I could always come up with a nugget about the 350+ whiskies the place stocked.

And business was booming, especially now we were starting the Golf World Cup, hosted in England for the first time. Since the anti-Japanese measures passed by the US Senate in the mid-'90s and the subsequent boycott of anything involving the Japanese, the Americans were not taking part. Consequently, England were joint favourites with the Japanese, although we had Scotland in our qualifying group, which meant the odds were still generous. The World Cup, said to draw the largest television audience in the world, meant a large screen in the bar, showing golf (edited highlights in a window to the top right of the screen showing live action) 12 hours a day with video back-up facility if an act of God stopped play. The sponsors had ensured nothing else would.

It also meant lots of package-tour golfers, many of them Japanese, flocking into and through London, and Ben Fuji's was well and truly on their 'must visit' lists. Knowing that the big prize money was put up by the Japanese these days, we also had a regular clientele of British and European golfers, many of them including a visit as part of their preparation for entering the Japanese Open. Keiko would teach them Japanese food and manners, and I would tell them about Japanese drinking habits, then take their photographs on my Nikon Instanto and get their autographs. (To sell later if they made it.)

It was mostly a load of bull, as Ben Fuji's was hardly a traditional Japanese restaurant. The basement had originally been a 'Japanese Room' with paper walls and floor mats. That had given way to a Nintendo virtual-reality golf driving range, which was far more profitable. In any case, European labour laws now prevented waitresses from serving men on their knees.

Basically, my job was vetting – and being nice to – the non-Japanese clientele. No rough stuff was required. Keiko and a couple of the waiters were more than capable of handling that, and one of the sushi chefs could pin a fly to the wall at thirty feet if the mood took him. The official job description was a sort of junior maître d'. The subtext was more subtle. After their experience in America, every Japanese business preferred a domestic front man, however limited his powers.

So there I was, the acceptable face of sushi in Threadneedle Street.

Not that what happened had anything to do with Ben Fuji's being a sushi and Scotch bar. It was just that I was working there the night Sam 'Sinister' Dexter decided to call in and get drunk.


I had actually met Sam Dexter once before, though he wouldn't remember.

It had been at a press party to mark the engagement of rock 'n' roll legend Rory D to that season's hot starlet from the Royal Shakespeare Company (sponsored, that year, by Brahma beer from Brazil – 'Where the nuts come from'). Rory D, or Rory Dee to be more accurate but less commercial, had played in a heavy metal band I knew called Astral Reich a few years before, and so I claimed lifelong friendship in order to get at the free booze and canapés. To be honest, I was going through a bad patch at the time, and I would have adopted Rory if it had got me into a free lunch.

I was standing at one of the buffet bars, balancing two plates and two glasses (all mine, though it looked like I was waiting for someone) and talking to a couple of Rory's roadies, when Dexter swayed across the room and aimed at a waitress clutching a tray of drinks.

I recognised him from the picture above his byline in the newspapers and also the two or three times I'd caught him on a late-night TV show. With 26 channels now, *anyone* can get on, but Dexter – 'Sinister' to the media world – was usually good for some choice titbits of scandal. Ironically, he could get away with hints and innuendos on TV that he would never dare print, even as 'alleged' rumours, in his newspaper columns, since the latest tightening up of the Privacy Charter Act (1993).

'C'mon, darling,' he boomed as he reached the waitress. 'Stop resting your tits on that tray and bung me some booze. I'm Sam Dexter and famous with it, and I don't intend paying for my drink.'

'Why change the habits of a lunchtime?' I muttered, and the roadies sniggered in agreement.

Dexter made no sign that he'd heard me, and our paths didn't cross for the rest of the party. But three days later he used the line in one of his columns as if he'd said it about Rory D.

Isn't it amazing how long you can hold a grudge?

When Dexter came into Ben Fuji's that night, he didn't notice me. He staggered up to my desk and breathed second-hand alcohol at me and spoke to me, but he didn't *notice* me. I was not there to be noticed. I was there to serve.

'Table for one, my son. At the sushi bar'll do if you've nothing else, but don't cram me in like a fuckin' sardine. Give me two seats and some elbow room, the most disgusting thing on your menu, four portions – four, mind you – of that horseradish sauce shit you serve and let me work my way through the whisky list. Is that clear? Like me to run any of it by you again?'

He rocked back a little too confidently on his heels and

produced a packet of cigarettes and a disposable lighter. The cigarettes were American and a brand I hadn't seen since they banned advertising cigarettes altogether.

He lit up and ignored me, pretending to examine some of the prints on the wall. I wondered if he was expecting me to ask 'Smoking or non-smoking?,' but I assumed he knew that no Japanese restaurant was non-smoking. As just about everywhere else in London was, it was actually good for business.

'Table for one, sir, right this way,' I said, turning my back on him and leading him into the restaurant.

I held a menu to my chest, and as I caught Keiko's eye, I upended it, showing her three fingers of my right hand. That was our agreed warning sign for *Potentially difficult customer.*

As I was doing it, Dexter breathed in my ear: 'Do the *geishas* come in the service charge, or do I have to negotiate privately?'

I added the fourth finger to the hand code: *We've got a right bastard here.*


Keiko, all neat in a black two-piece suit, skirt one inch below the knee as was proper and, as it happens, fashionable, made her own code sign to me (two specks of imaginary dust flicked off her sleeve), which meant she wanted me in the kitchen, pronto.

Actually, she wanted to talk to me in the kitchen, and no matter how many times I'd deliberately misunderstood her that way, she never laughed. This, after all, was business.

'Okay, Tenshi, who's your friend?' she opened as soon as the curtain hissed to behind us. She called me 'Angel' in Japanese because it is my name.

'No friend of mine, though beings lower down the food chain might claim an affinity with him,' I said, keeping a watchful eye on Mr Iishi, the sushi chef, who was sharpening his eighth knife of the evening.

'Speak English,' snapped Keiko. 'That's what we pay you

for.'

'He's a shit, Grade A.'

'Then why didn't you bump him?'

'He's also a journalist, a notorious one, and your standing orders say I have to be nice to journalists. It's part of your public relations policy. You know, Rule One: Keep smiling, but don't turn your back.'

Keiko looked at me over the top of her glasses and shook her head slowly. I don't know why she blamed me for her headaches, though I've noticed other people do too.

'Keep an eye on him, eh, Tenshi. Let me know if the boys have to deal with him.'

She straightened her skirt to go back into the restaurant, then remembered the monitor. Ben Fuji's had video cameras hidden in four strategic points, with two monitors, one in the kitchen and one in the manager's office, which for all intents and purposes was Keiko's, where there was a VCR. You'd never guess where the equipment was made.

The kitchen monitor showed Dexter sitting at his table, two glasses of whisky and one of iced water in front of him. He was scanning the other diners and leering at the waitresses, all dressed in kimonos and clogs, making them easy, slow-moving targets. Dexter wasn't quite ready to start groping yet, though. He kept looking at the menu and narrowing his eyes. He'd obviously had a long day, and I didn't think he'd spent it at the opticians.

He also did something else. Every few seconds his left hand would swoop near, sometimes onto, the brown envelope jutting out of his jacket pocket. It was the action of a man who thinks he's left his wallet in another coat and needs reassuring.

There wasn't time to watch him further. Above the monitor a green light flashed on, which meant someone had trodden on the sensors under the doormat outside the entrance. More customers, so I had to get back to my desk. (I'm sure they only have the sensor there to check up on me.)

'Try and get the boys to serve him,' I told Keiko, 'and get

the chef to hurry it up. Tell the girls to keep clear and not to be cheeky. And don't refuse him any alcohol.'

'If you say so, but I hope you know what you're doing,' she said primly.

I thought I did, up to that point.

Three of them were lurking in the entrance as I made it back behind my desk, and the first thing that struck me was how young they were. One was early twenties, but the other two must have been teenagers, especially the one hanging behind at the back with his jacket collar turned up.

The one who looked old enough to vote (though few people did that these days) approached me, his right hand in his pocket, his left tweaking his nose. Interesting body language. He was a policeman – and wouldn't you know it, they *are* getting younger.

'Do you have a bar?' he asked in a London accent, but a posh one.

'Certainly, sir, but it's for diners only. Will that be a table for three?' I could behave myself when it was called for.

'Er … the bar is in the restaurant?' he fumbled.

'Yes, quite correct.'

'There isn't a separate bar?'

'No, only in the restaurant. We have a restaurant licence. People eat here. Occasionally.'

He stopped tweaking his nose at that and wanted to say something, but held himself back. One of the younger lads behind him whispered something I couldn't catch.

'Do you mind if I just have a quick look around the restaurant before we decide ...?'

I'd had enough of this.

'Is there a problem, officer?'

That stopped him for a second, then basic instinct took over.

'How did you …?'

'The Doc Martens,' I said smugly. 'Nobody else wears them these days.'

He looked down at his shoes, then mentally kicked himself for doing so. They always do, though; it never fails. I could have added that the Marks & Spencer's suit one size too big, so as to cover the gun in the belt holster, was also a dead giveaway, but you can go too far.

He recovered well. He held up a finger and said, ''Ang on a minute,' then turned to his two young companions, and they went into a huddle.

Then he came back to me, and he had a warrant card in his hand.

'Is there anywhere we could have a word?'

'Downstairs.' I pointed to the stairs, knowing that the virtual-reality driving range was unoccupied. 'I'll get cover and join you in one minute.'

He looked relieved and said 'Thanks' almost as if he meant it.

I stuck my head into the restaurant and made eye contact with Keiko, then jerked my head toward the entrance. She acted like she hadn't seen me, but I knew she had.

Without making it obvious, I clocked Dexter, who now had four whisky glasses in front of him and was perusing the whisky list for more.

When Keiko joined me, I explained that we had some more out-of-the-ordinary customers, one of whom was a senior policeman, and I would happily put myself on the line dealing with them to avoid any confrontation with the management. That usually worked, and it did again. Keiko said she would get Hiroshi, who had good English (in fact, better than mine when he wanted to), to man the desk, and I could sort out the police downstairs, which she was sure would take all my charm, diplomacy and skill, *and no more than ten minutes.*

'You'd better call me Tom,' said the policeman.

'Oh yeah? And they're Dick and Harry?'

I nodded toward the two lads who were examining the virtual-reality gear like it was Christmas.

The young copper was staring at me.

'That's Gordon and Henry,' he said, as if reading it off a card.

'I'm looking after them.'

I couldn't keep a straight face.

'Come off it, Tom. I've read *Thomas the Tank Engine.*'

Then I stopped. I suddenly realised he hadn't.

'You know, Gordon the stuck-up Blue Engine and Henry the wimpy Green Engine with the sad expression ... Thomas – Tom – Gordon and ...'

He blushed then, and turned a killer look on the two teenagers he was 'looking after.'

'They thought up the names, didn't they?' I asked softly.

'Yes, but that's not important. Look, I need – we need – to know about the movements of somebody upstairs in the restaurant. We need to keep an eye on him without being seen. Can you help?'

'Is this official?'

'Semi-official,' he said carefully.

'Then glad to help, officer. Detective Sergeant, wasn't it? Sorry, but I didn't get a chance to examine your warrant card very closely.'

'It's real, that's all you need to know.'

'Fine by me, Tom. Can you tell me what this is about?'

'No.'

'I have my employers to think about.'

'No.'

'Very well, we at Ben Fuji's are always anxious to cooperate with the law and will do so respectfully and diplomatically. Oi! Harry!'

The younger of the two youths looked up from the VR helmet he was examining like a rabbit caught in headlights.

'What's your father do these days?' I shouted as if doing a stand-up routine.

'He's still King,' he answered.

Then he bit his tongue.


'Gordon – that really is his name – is a friend from school, one of the few I can trust,' he told me. 'Thomas is actually Sergeant Dave

Thomas.'

'Your bodyguard.'

'Yes, and I don't want to get him into trouble. I'm not really supposed to be out with just one. I'm afraid Gordon and I rather conned him into accompanying us into the Forbidden Zone.'

'London?'

'Yes. We're almost out-of-towners now.'

'So why the expedition?'

He gave me another once-over (the fifth by my reckoning) before answering.

'My brother, my elder brother,' he started, as if he had lots to choose from, 'does not pick his friends as well as I do. One of them has talked to the press about a party that brother-dear attended last month where there was some silliness involving a swimming pool and various naked ladies in compromising positions.'

'Nobody invited me,' I said before I could stop myself. 'Sorry. Go on.'

'Worse still, someone had a video camera and recorded some of the ... er ...'

'Juicy bits?'

'Yes. Juicy bits. God, that sounds disgusting.'

He was young.

'Anyway, this so-called friend has sold the tape to an absolute shit.'

'Sam Dexter.'

'Why, yes. How did you know?'

'I recognised him from your description.'

He smiled at that, something he rarely did, if the newspapers were to be believed.

'Does your brother know?' I prompted.

'No, and he wouldn't know what to do if he did. Anyway, he's on tour at the moment.'

He said it as if he were talking about a second-rate rock band doing one-night stands around the Midlands.

'So what did you have in mind?'

'Well, Plan A was to stop my brother's dippy friend from

selling the tape. God knows, he doesn't need the money; just doing it for the mischief. But we were too late. He'd done the dirty deed by the time we got there. Fortunately, Dexter had gone straight to the local pub to celebrate.'

'Does he know what's on the tape?'

'Yes. He insisted on a viewing before buying.'

'Can I ask how much?'

'Thirty thousand quid, the friend said, and he felt pretty shitty when I called it thirty thousand pieces of silver,' he said proudly.

I'll bet. I could feel lower than toenail dirt for that sort of money.

'So you followed Dexter?'

'Well, Thomas – Dave – did, at least into the first three pubs. Then he took a cab here. Dexter has the tape in his pocket. I saw it.'

So did I, in a brown envelope.

'And just how were you going to relieve him of it?' I asked gently.

'We never actually got down to detail on Plan B,' he said seriously. 'Gordon thought we should borrow Dave's gun and mug him, but I don't think Dave will go along with that. So, really, we haven't got a plan. We just need to keep an eye on Dexter and wait our chance. Would you help us do that?'

How could I refuse?

'I tell you what; you stay here and I'll check out Dexter. There's no way you can show your face in the restaurant without him seeing you, and if he thinks you're after him, it'll just convince him he's on to something big.'

'Good plan. Thanks. How can I repay you?'

'I'll think of something.'


I didn't have to go far to get a situation report on Sinister Dexter. Keiko was waiting by my desk.

'He is a pig, that man. He is griping everyone. Not only my girls, but customers, too!'

'I think you mean "groping,"' I said calmly.

'Whatever. Get rid of him, while he can still stand.'

Now I only usually listen to about forty percent of what Keiko says, but as she once bested me in a nine-hour saké drinking session, I do respect her views on male alcohol consumption.

'How pissed is he?' I asked seriously.

'Weaving in the wind. Another three or four scotches and he'll start griping the men.'

'Keiko, you've just given me one of my brilliant ideas. I want you to keep him here and keep the table next to him free.'

'No problem. I wouldn't put anyone there.'

'Good thinking. Now tell one of the waiters to drop something or spill something on Dexter's table. Then we want lots of profuse apologies and take him the bottle – the bottle, mind you – of the Tobermory Malt, the 12-year-old.'

Well, that's what it said on the bottle, but I knew it to be a single malt that had gone over-proof and now clocked in at nearer sixty percent than forty percent alcohol.

'Give him the bottle …?' Keiko started, but she was talking to my back as I headed for the office.


'Glenda?'

'Perhaps. Who wants to know?'

'Angel.'

'Darling! Long time no … well, no anything, really. Whadderyerwant?'

'I want you to seduce somebody in a Japanese restaurant and pick his pocket, and within the next hour.'

'Seems reasonable. Have I time to put my face on?'


'Got any money on you?'

'Not a cent, but Sergeant Dave has.' Henry smiled.

'Has he £250?' I asked, swapping my dinner jacket (Keiko had insisted) for my leather bomber.

'I'll ask.'

Henry and Sergeant Dave went into conference. Gordon was

fully plugged into the VR machine, whapping balls down a fairway somewhere.

'He wants to know what you want it for,' Henry came back.

'I'm hiring somebody to pick Dexter's pocket and get that tape for you.'

'In that case, I'll get the cash.'

No questions, no arguments. Who says breeding doesn't tell?

'You didn't have to come,' I told them for the tenth time.

'Listen, Angel, if that's your name, I'm going to have enough trouble accounting for £250 without receipts as it is. If you just drove off into the night with it, I'd be back on traffic duty.'

'You have a point, Sergeant.'

'Plus' – Thomas put his face up to the open glass partition – 'I'm not supposed to be more than five feet from his nibs even when he's peeing. Where the hell are we, anyway?'

'The Barbican.'

'Do people still live here?'

Now if 'Henry' had said that, it would have made headlines. Instead he chimed up with: 'This is a taxi, isn't it?'

'It was,' I said over my shoulder. 'A Fairway.'

'Do they still make them?'

'No.'

'Is it old?'

'About 12 years. You still see them around.'

Ordinary mortals do, anyway.

'It's not a real one, though. I mean a licensed Hackney Carriage?'

'No, it's delicensed,' I answered patiently. After all, the kid still probably went train spotting.

'He's called Armstrong Two,' I said.

There was a half minute of silence from the back.

'Why Armstrong *Two*? What happened to *One*?'

Bright lad.

'That's a long story.'

The one advantage Armstrong Two had over Armstrong One – apart from being in one piece – was the mobile phone fitted in a dashboard mounting. I used it to call Glenda when we were close.

'Be outside and ready to jump in exactly two minutes,' I told her when we were five minutes away.

'You've got to be kidding, Angel. I'm nowhere near *dressed* even.'

'Good, that'll speed things up.'

'Oooh, you smooth-talking fucker, you.'

I hung up and pulled Armstrong over to the kerb, got out and walked to the boot, where I keep various emergency-only items.

I moved round to the nearside passenger door and opened it.

'Take off your jacket,' I said to Henry. 'And put these on.'

I handed him a sweatshirt three sizes too big for him advertising a now bankrupt chilli-to-go and carwash in Bangor, Maine, and a baseball cap (adjustable – one size fits all) plugging the Romford Spartacists, which was a gridiron football team, not a political movement.

Henry complied with enthusiasm.

'This is so Glenda won't recognise me, isn't it?' he chirped, crumpling a suit jacket that probably cost half an Armstrong.

'That's right, and just hope she doesn't.'

He looked at me quizzically.

'Trust me on this one,' I said.


'Do you *know* who you've got in here?' Glenda hissed out of the side of her mouth. As she was sitting in the rumble seat behind mine, I could hear her perfectly well without her spitting in my ear.

'Shut up and forget it,' I hissed back.

In my mirror I saw Sergeant Dave Thomas reach for his wallet.

'Payment on results,' I said loudly. 'That's the usual way, isn't it Glenda?'

She straightened up in her seat and made a futile effort to

drag her short skirt down an inch. If she'd succeeded that would have made it only seven inches above the knee.

'Haven't had any complaints so far, Angel,' said Glenda.


Henry, Thomas, Gordon and I were in the manager's office looking at the restaurant on the video monitor. Glenda was out there doing her stuff, and it was Academy Award-winning stuff.

Keiko had done her bit, organising a minor accident, grovelling apology, and then a free (or at least to-be-paid-for-later) bottle of the Tobermory head-banger. And Dexter had gone along like he'd read the script. If his pupils hadn't been so dilated, there would have been a glint in them saying he was going to finish the bottle just to show them. Whoever 'they' were.

Glenda had tick-tocked her buttocks into a chair at the table next to him, fluffed up her auburn curls, smoothed her skirt and picked up a menu. Dexter was at her like a shark coming out of Lent.

He persuaded her to try a whisky as an aperitif. Then as an alternative to saké. Then just for the hell of it. Then to finish the bottle.

Glenda, who could drink me under the table and carry me home (and, indeed, has), matched him drink for drink and then – master stroke – ordered champagne. Even without sound, we could feel Dexter say, 'And why not?'

When I lip-read Glenda describing the basement room with its virtual-reality golf range (about which I'd briefed her) and then pantomime that she needed to use the toilet, I knew he was hooked. Glenda stood, played with the hem of her skirt and the string of large (fake) amber beads balanced on her bosom, fell back a pace, and allowed herself to be steadied by Dexter's outstretched, sweaty hand.

'Nice touch, that,' I said, admiring a professional when I saw one.

I realised no-one was listening; they were all looking at the monitor as if they'd never seen anything like this before. Then Henry looked at me, dead serious.

'You're getting a kick out of this,' he said, deadpan. 'And I've been wondering why, because there's nothing in it for you. In fact, you haven't even asked for anything. You're helping us just for the hell of it, just to stir things up. You don't really care one way or the other, do you? You don't have problems like this, do you? You're like one of the old hippies who just drift through life in your battered old delicensed taxicab, just to be a rebel, thinking it all a bit of a bad joke.'

The kid was getting too close for comfort.

'Who's an ageing hippy?' I snapped.


It got triple X-rated (as they say now on TV) pretty quickly once Glenda and Sinister made it to the virtual-reality room.

The VR driving ranges had semi-circular control panels raised on small platforms like a conductor's rostrum. They contained all the electronic gizmos needed to run the ranges, and to protect them from the helmeted VR golfers they were leather padded.

Glenda realised the erotic potential of the podia immediately, and as Dexter bent over to examine the virtual-reality helmet, Glenda goosed him something rotten.

'I say!' said Gordon, glued to the screen.

'Ignore him,' whispered Henry. 'He's very young in many ways.'

'I'd forgotten he was here,' I said, fiddling with the VCR controls.

Dexter couldn't quite believe it either. He swung round and walked into Glenda's open arms. Glenda backed him up against a podium and planted a smacker on his lips, her hands disappearing inside his jacket. Without unplugging her lips, she slipped his jacket off and held it with her left hand while her right went to his groin.

Sergeant Thomas and the Green and Blue Engines were watching her right hand, as was Dexter. I was watching her left as she freed him from the jacket and then hitched it round until she was near the pocket with the envelope. Dexter's hands and mind were fully occupied in trying to push up her skirt. That short leather skirt, which had flown up like a Venetian blind in the restaurant, now seemed to be glued to her long, high-heeled legs.

Just as Glenda's red fingernails closed around the envelope, Dexter decided the skirt problem needed a better perspective, and so he took an unsteady step backwards.

The problem was that he kept going, the back of his thighs hitting the edge of the podium and tipping him backwards. Glenda, probably thinking he had realised she was doing a lift, dropped the jacket and removed her support from his back. He toppled over, hit the floorboards and bounced slightly before coming to rest. I hoped the alcohol had acted as enough of a muscle relaxant to prevent serious damage.

Glenda looked down at him in amazement from the control panel. She stamped one of her high heels so effectively that the four of us jerked back from the monitor, as if we'd heard it. Then she pulled off the curly auburn wig and flung it over Dexter's face.

'Bloody hell,' said an aristocratic voice. 'She's a man!'

'Welcome to the world, Harry.'


I had to introduce him to Keiko and the staff; that became part of the deal, though they were sworn to secrecy. We did it in the kitchen so the punters couldn't see, and it went down well all round. He said he knew their emperor and what a jolly nice bloke he was. They said they didn't but, of course, they'd take his word for it.

Then we paid off Glenda, and I offered to drive her home, but she said she had never finished her dinner and sushi was *so* erotic … On Henry's instruction, Sergeant Thomas put enough cash behind the bar to ensure she wouldn't go hungry.

It was my idea to pile Dexter into the back of Armstrong. Sergeant Thomas (and Henry) knew he lived in Finchley, and a Euro driving licence in his wallet confirmed the address and that he had enough cash to pay even my exorbitant rates. (I also took the trouble to remove £90 for his meal, and one of these days I must remember to pay it into Ben Fuji's.)

'If he wakes up,' I said, pulling on my leather bomber jacket and smoothing my hair flat with hair gel (hair gel was back in a big way), 'I'll just play the aggrieved musher.'

'Pardon?' asked Gordon politely.

'Cabbie. Ferryman. Hackney Carriage operative. Hatless chauffeur.'

'Oh,' he said vaguely. It was way past his bedtime.

I took Henry to one side as I closed Armstrong's boot. The street was deserted, but he had turned up the collar of his jacket, and he still wore the sweatshirt and hat I had given him.

'You want these back,' he said, starting to peel off his jacket.

'No, no. Keep them. I'll add them to the bill.'

He fixed me with his eyes. I'd read somewhere they'd been trained to do that.

'There will be a bill?'

Sergeant Thomas hovered close behind him, so I dropped my voice.

'We ageing hippies aren't into money, man. Can you dig that?'

He smiled, and for once the newspapers were right, he didn't smile enough.

'You've got the tape?' I asked.

He patted the inside pocket of his coat.

'And you'll turn it over to your brother?'

He waited five careful seconds before answering.

'I'll bring it to his attention.'

They were taught not to tell lies as well.

'Are there any copies?'

'No.' He was confident. 'There wasn't time.'

'Good. Then this is the one we put in the envelope in Sinister's pocket.'

'What's that?' He stared open-eyed at the cassette I offered him.

'I taped the scene in the basement, right up to Glenda revealing her … er … credentials.'

'Christ, he'll have a heart attack,' he said gleefully, grabbing it. 'I hope he doesn't watch it before he gives it to his editor.'

Then he flashed a look at me.

'Are there any copies?'

Good thinking, kid, you're coming on.

'No. But Dexter doesn't know that.'

Henry's face bisected.

'Way to go, Angel. You used to say things like that, didn't you?'

He put the new cassette into Dexter's brown envelope. 'May I do the honours?' He indicated the slumped figure of Dexter, snoring loudly, stretched across Armstrong's back seat.

'Be my guest.'

He turned, then stopped and offered his hand. I wasn't sure whether I should bow or not. So I didn't.

'Thank you, Angel, if that's your name. I still don't understand why you've helped us, but I'm grateful, and if there is ever anything I can –'

'Don't worry, I'll call.'

He looked puzzled.

'I know where you live,' I explained.

He smiled again and pulled me closer as we shook.

'You know, I was going to ask you for Glenda's phone number for my uncle,' he whispered. Then he squeezed my hand. 'I still might.'

It was my turn to grin.

Sergeant Thomas hadn't finished with me, though. As Henry put the new tape onto Dexter's comatose person, Thomas took me to one side as only policemen can.

'I don't have to remind you, sir, that –'

'No you don't; it's okay.'

'And I hope you'll give me your address so that –'

'No way, Mr Tank Engine. You'll just have to trust me.'

He sized me up.

'Well, we have to trust somebody, I suppose.'

'That's the spirit, Sergeant. And should I ever have my collar felt, you won't mind if I mention your name, will you? Of course, I won't say how we met.'

Mr Nice Policeman was in danger of giving way to Mr Nasty.

There's a Jekyll and Hyde gene in all of them.

'So that's your price, is it?'

'Partly, Dave, partly. And I may never call it in. I may not have to, seeing as how you've already noted my registration number and will no doubt put it through the police computer tomorrow.'

Even in the streetlight he blushed.

'Don't worry, Dave, always CYA – cover your arse. That's all I'm doing.'

'So what else do you get out of it? Come on, I want to know.'

'Well, Sergeant, look at it this way. You like young Henry, don't you?' He nodded. 'And he's going to go far, isn't he?'

'I … er …'

'Put it this way: if you were a betting man, would you put money on *his* being the face we see on our stamps in a few years' time?'

'Possibly.'

'So would I. And I'll be able to say I had him in the back of the cab once.'

# Angel Eyes

Because I just *knew* he would give me trouble, I recorded the phone call on our answerphone and typed it up later to put on file so that Estelle could read it. Not that she spends much time going through the filing cabinet, because of her nails. Perhaps I'll e-mail it to her.

VB: Hello? Is that Angel?
ANGEL: *(In a silly voice.) Pronto! Pronto!*
VB: Angel? That is the right number, isn't it?
A: *Que?*
VH: I know this is the right number. Can I speak to Angel please?
A: *Ich bin ein Auslander, ich spreche keine Englisch ...*
VB: That *is* you, Angel, stop messing about. This is Veronica. Veronica Blugden.
A: *(Unintelligible – possibly Japanese.)*
VB: Hello, Angel What's that noise? *(Beeping sound.)*
A: ... or you can send a fax right now.
VB: Angel, *will* you behave? This is Veronica from Rudgard and Blugden Investigations.
A: ... at the third stroke it will be 10.53 precisely. Bip! Bip! Bip! 10.53. Wow! Time travel!
VB: I'm not going to let you put me off, Angel. I know you, you know.
A: *(Funny voice)* Earth to Major Tom, Earth to Major Tom ...
VB: Are you drunk, Angel? Or just messing about? You've no right to mess me about. I'm ringing to offer you a job.
A: *(In a very bad Scottish accent.)* Ah, to be sure, darlin', yer man will be off for a wet of his morning pint o' stout and you'll not be wantin' to make him late for Mass, will yer?

VB: It's an undercover job and you'll get paid.

A: *(Persisting with his stupid Scottish character.)* Ah, whisht, woman, yer know yer man doesn't agree with work. He'll work like the vurry divil to avoid it.

VB: It involves working in a bar. A girlie revue bar, I think they call them.

*(12 seconds silence.)*

A: Give me that phone! Get back to the attic! Sorry about that, Veronica. My mad cousin Dorian *(Check spelling?)* got to the phone before me. What was that about a revue bar?

VB: So, suddenly I have your attention, do I?

A: Absolutely, hanging on your every.

VB: I thought I might. You know, this hard-to-get act you put on really is rather tiring. The one thing they stress on my Interpersonal Communication Skills course is that you never –

A: Get to the point. Can we do that? Preferably while I'm still in my thirties?

VB: There's no need to take that tone. It might be better if you came to the office for a briefing with the client. When are you free?

A: Hang on, I'll consult my diary. *(Sound of faint whistling.)* Now's free.

VB: Pardon?

A: I'm free now. Today. All day, actually.

VB: I think I can get the client to come in at about 2.30 this afternoon.

A: Sounds good, see you then. Oh, Veronica?

VB: What?

A: Will Stella be around?

VB: No, Estelle is giving a talk at Hendon Police College today. *(Silence.)* Hello? Angel, are you still there? Is that you laughing?

I've never been too sure exactly what Angel's relationship with Estelle is, other than that he insists on calling her 'Stella' like the so-called friends she goes drinking with do. But since we started up the agency he has always checked to make sure she is out if he ever comes to the office.

Estelle, of course, comes from a good family. Her father is Sir Drummond Rudgard, who used to run a classic car museum out at Sandpit Lodge, the family home in the country. There was some sort of incident there and a lot of the cars got damaged and had to be sold off, though the auction was in all the papers. I always suspected that Angel had something to do with the trouble there, but neither he nor Estelle has ever talked about it. I suppose I was responsible for introducing them in the first place, though I've heard Angel say it was he who brought me and Estelle together – the very idea!

I was actually 'tailing' (as we say) Estelle for Albert Block, my old boss who used to run the agency. It was, I suppose, my first 'case', and Estelle had run away from her father and was living with a religious cult down near Sloane Square. I had to get her out of their clutches and organise her 'deprogramming'. It's something we've been consulted on quite a few times since we started the agency together, and it's involved some sons and daughters of really quite well-known people, although Estelle prefers to handle that side of the business herself.

All Angel had to do with it was that he just happened to be there in that taxi of his, pretending to be a taxi-driver like he always does. I thought it was a genuine cab. A lot of people do. He relies on it.

But at least through him I got to meet Lisabeth and Fenella (he sub-lets a room in their house in Hackney) and they helped me a lot with that first case. I don't think Angel ever really liked that. And I just know he resented the way his cat used to make a beeline for me, looking for affection.

After Estelle and I started the business, R & B Investigations (which Angel always thought funny for some reason), we did try to put the odd bit of work his way whenever we needed someone to go in the places where women on their own ought to be able to go but don't feel comfortable doing so.

When we heard he'd got involved with that Amy May woman who designs the clothes – they're in all the shops now – I thought he'd have other things on his mind. Estelle (who had laughed a lot when she'd heard the news) said that we ought to 'give him six months' and then he would 'be up for it' – whatever that means.

Mrs Delacourt had taken the initial call from the brewery telling us how worried they were about their new girlie bar down near Piccadilly Circus, and she was the one who arranged for me to see their District Manager.

Even as she gave me the message, she couldn't help smirking, 'This is one for your friend Angel; sounds right up his street.'

One of these days I'm going to have to remind Mrs Delacourt that despite her age and all those certificates she has now for computing, not to mention the law degree she's studying for, she is in fact the junior of the office.


I was, naturally, delighted to see that the brewery's District Manager was a woman, but I certainly hadn't expected one so young.

Her name was Deborah Tracy Rex according to her business card, but she told me straight away to call her Debbie, so I did. I had never heard of the company she worked for, and while we were waiting for Angel to be late (as usual), I got Mrs Delacourt to make her a coffee and tried to put her at her ease, because visiting a detective can be rather stressful.

'I suppose you have to drink a lot of beer in your job?' I said.

'Christ, no,' she said rather abruptly. 'I can't afford to lose my office, and anyway it would go straight on my hips and they're like Zeppelins as it is.'

Quite honestly I don't know what she was complaining about as she had a perfectly trim figure, verging on the skinny. She wore a blue blazer with a gold salamander brooch on the lapel, black trousers that used to be called flares but are now bootlegs for some reason and, of all things, a white TALtop – the blouse that made Amy May's name as a designer. (Though before she met Angel.)

'Lose your office?' I asked her.

The card she had given me had just phone numbers on it –

four of them – but no address. I hadn't noticed before. I mean, it's not the sort of thing you do notice.

'My car is my office,' she said. 'I have a mobile, a car phone and voice mail, and I hot desk it when I have to do paperwork. Car-parks cost less than office space in London – and you can have a cigarette when you want one.'

'Interesting,' I said. 'I suppose that means you can get round your pubs more easily.'

'That's the theory,' she said, 'but it's an impossible task. I'm responsible for over three hundred RLOs within the M25. Take out holidays, sales conferences and marketing presentations, not to mention licensing appeals, new product launches and staff recruitment, I'm lucky if I get round half of them once a year.'

'What exactly is an RLO?' I asked.

'Retail Leisure Outlet. We don't call them pubs anymore.'

'Don't you? I didn't know that.' It was true, I didn't. 'But it must be fun mixing with all those customers. You must get to meet all sorts.'

'Customers? Sh–!' she said, just like that, out loud. Then, without asking, she lit up a cigarette and used her saucer as an ashtray. 'Don't get time to talk to them. We have to *count* them of course. The success of an RLO depends on its RVFBs.'

I wondered if I should be taking notes, and she saw my concern.

'Repeat Visits for Food and/or Beverage,' she said, 'but don't worry about it. The punters aren't the problem this time; I'm pretty sure it's an inside job.'

For once I was rather glad to see Angel arrive, even though Mrs Delacourt buzzed him straight up without asking him to identify himself and there was a lot of silly banter in the outer office about who was 'looking well handsome' and 'tasty yourself', all of which we could hear quite clearly.

'Do come in and join us when you have a minute, Angel,' I said as loudly as I could. Giving an impression of the command structure in an organisation is very important, and one of the modules on my Interpersonal Communication Skills course.

'Yo, boss,' he said as he sauntered in, not hurrying himself.

'My, Vonnie, but you're looking good. You've lost weight, and you've been pumping iron, I see.'

I knew it was just his way of trying to disarm me, but I took it as his best attempt at an apology for being late.

'Can I introduce Deborah Rex, from the brewery,' I said, but Angel was already grasping her hand.

He seemed very interested in the TALtop she was wearing, and its plunging V-shaped neckline. No doubt he would be reporting back to Amy May on another successful sale, as I had seen him do this before and he had called it 'market research'.

Ms Rex handed him one of her cards when she managed to break his grip.

'Great T-shirt,' she said to him as he read it.

I didn't see what was so great about it. It was just a white T-shirt with some printing on that read: 'MY OTHER T-SHIRT'S A PAUL SMITH.' Though I might have known he wouldn't bother to wear a tie or anything, just his leather jacket, a pair of black jeans and some Reebok trainers that, frankly, had seen better days. With all Amy May's money you'd have thought he could have afforded a suit.

'Thanks,' he said, smiling, showing his teeth. 'You must be 27, and your father was a Marc Bolan fan.'

'Spot on,' she laughed, showing *her* teeth. It was like they were snarling at each other. 'You're quite a detective.'

'You don't have to be Sherlock,' he said, laying it on a bit thick. 'Deborah like the song, Tracy gives you the initials for T Rex. I was guessing at the date of birth. Bit of a glam rocker, was he?'

'Still is. Sad case.'

'I know a few.'

'Could we get on?' I said, re-establishing control of the situation. 'Ms Rex is very busy and her time is valuable.'

'Sorry, I forgot the meter was running,' he said, pulling up a chair and placing it very close to Ms Rex's knees.

I really wanted to tell her not to encourage him, but he seemed to have put her at her ease and that's always important with first-time clients.

While she spoke he at least pretended to be attentive, sitting there and hanging on every word almost, leaning forward with his forearms on his knees and his head on one side. I had never really noticed his profile before, but it is quite impressive if you like that sort of thing. The short, curly hair makes him look a lot younger than he is, or course, but even so he does have the air of a young Roman emperor like you would see on a coin. Estelle once said she thought he had the touch of the gypsy or a Heathcliff about him, but I think that's going too far. He's softer than that and he does have a nice smile – everybody says that. In fact, Mrs Delacourt says that his smile 'starts in his eyes and works its way down'.

'The pub was originally called the Disraeli,' Ms Rex was saying, 'but the name was changed to the Greasy Pole about ten years ago.'

'Fair enough,' Angel said, as if that made sense.

'So it seemed the ideal place to introduce our new TLC – sorry, Themed Leisure Concept – especially as the site is so central, just off Piccadilly.'

'I know it,' he said. 'I went the week it opened.'

'Like it?' she asked with an odd smile and, I think, a hint of colour in her cheeks.

'It's well done and will be popular with a certain clientele. It's not that far from the House of Commons, is it? Not for me, though. Don't like the house rule.'

'You mean, "Look but don't touch"?'

'That's the one.'

They grinned stupidly at each other and I began to wonder just how Ms Rex had got on in her job.

'So what happens in this Greasy Pole pub?' I asked, my notebook open and my pencil poised.

'Pole-dancing,' they both said together, looking at me as if I was slow or something.


Estelle staggered back to the office at about six o clock, claiming that her speaking engagement at Hendon had turned into a 'late lunch' and she had been driven back in a police car.

'You missed your old friend Angel,' Mrs Delacourt told her as they both slumped into the chairs in my office.

'How was he?' Estelle asked her, perking up.

'Fit as a butcher's dog!' said Mrs Delacourt coarsely. 'He had this Ungaro jacket that was soft as a baby's bottom ... and talking of bottoms, that guy has buns you could take bites out of. If only he was 20 years more desperate.'

'What was he doing here?'

'Your partner here has him working undercover in that new girlie bar near Piccadilly – you know, the one with the pole-dancing at the tables.'

'What, the Greasy Pole? You've got Angel a job there?'

'Must've thought it was his birthday,' said Mrs Delacourt, breaking into a fit of giggles, which Estelle soon joined in.

When I finally managed to get a word in, I explained the situation.

The Greasy Pole did indeed have scantily-clad young girls (mostly American, I was assured) dancing suggestively around poles that ran through the middle of tables. It was an American idea, and the brewery was hoping it would catch on so they could franchise the formula to other Retail Leisure Outlets.

They employed six girls to do the dancing, and all had been thoroughly vetted, so Deborah Rex had said. (At this point, Estelle made rather a crude remark about Angel 'going to the vet' if he had to work there.) But the dancing girls as such were not the problem. ('They will be,' Mrs Delacourt interrupted.) The brewery had received complaints from a sister company that installed AWPs in the pub. (I thought at first that Deborah had said 'OAPs', but then she'd explained that she was talking about Amusement-With-Prizes machines, the slot machine things that used to be called one-armed bandits.) Apparently, the pub had twenty of these machines and all were losing money at the rate of twenty to thirty pounds a week, and the machine company couldn't work out how it was being done.

Apart from the money being lost, the brewery was concerned, because the Greasy Pole 'concept', as they called it, was being investigated by the licensing authorities, and if it didn't get a full bill of health they would have trouble franchising the idea elsewhere. So they wanted this business cleared up ASAP, and they were convinced it was an inside job.

'How do they empty the machines?' Estelle asked.

I was ready for her, with my notes.

'One electronic key opens the back of all the machines. It's just a little thing like an earring on a chain, but the machine company keeps them for when they have to empty the machines. The pub doesn't have one.'

'That they know of,' said Mrs Delacourt.

'But the machine company reps do,' Estelle observed rather airily, 'and I'll bet the guys who come to empty them could be sorely tempted by half-a-dozen pole-dancing bits of totty.'

'That was my initial observation,' I said, stretching the truth a little, 'but Ms Rex assures me that the licensee, who's a woman, keeps the girls well away from the customers. She's very strict; that's why she got the job. So it must be one of the bar staff who has got hold of one of these keys somehow. That's why Angel starts tonight as a relief barman, to keep an eye on things.'

'Does the landlady know who he is?' Mrs Delacourt had a lot of questions considering she wouldn't actually be involved in any executive decisions.

'No, she doesn't. She asked the brewery for a stand-in while one of the staff goes back to Ireland for a funeral.'

'And what do we know about her?' Estelle asked me, just as Angel had asked Deborah Rex, funnily enough.

'She's called Opal Smith and sounds a bit brassy. She's been a licensee for ten years, divorced twice, has a good track record with the brewery, but is rather – eccentric – with a private business in aromatherapy massage.'

'Why does that make her "brassy"?' Estelle asked in a sarcastic tone she really shouldn't use in front of the staff.

'She wears a lot of jewellery it seems, a bit like a trademark. All opals, because of her name. Earrings, necklaces, rings. Ms Rex said she never goes abroad on holiday because she'd set off all the metal detectors at the airport.'

Estelle and Mrs Delacourt looked at each other and then started giggling again.

'So,' said Estelle, 'you've put Angel in a pub with six pole-dancers and a tarty landlady with a sideline in unguents and massage for – how long?'

'Five nights.' I said. 'The pub only does the pole-dancing in the evening.'

'Boy'll be able to sleep during the day,' burst out Mrs Delacourt. 'Get his strength back!'

'Bit like Dracula with the keys to the blood bank!' shrieked Estelle, and that set them off again.

I call it childish.

In fact, Angel needed only three nights, and then there was a fax waiting for me as I got to the office. From the top of the first of the two sheets I could see it had been sent at 04.32 that morning and it was handwritten. It said:

TO: VERONICA BLUGDEN AT R & B

Opal Smith DOES have a spare key to the AWP machines. Don't know how she got it but suggest that Debbie checks back on recent employees of the machine suppliers who might have taken up an interest in aromatherapy.

She keeps it attached to her pierced navel ring, something not as rare as you might think in women of her age. This is not obvious, except on close examination.

Tell Debbie to arrange a visit to the pub TODAY with someone from the AWP company. Get them to empty the machine nearest to the door to the Ladies lavatory, the one called '5 Card Stud'.

You'll find one of Opal's opal rings in the cashbox inside at the back. That should be proof enough.

Opal is offering a £25 reward for anyone finding her lost ring. It's mine.

Expenses to follow.

Going to sleep for two days.

Angel.

I rang Deborah, getting her on her mobile, and told her what Angel had written, and she said that was great and she would act on it; and, sure enough, she rang me back after lunch to say that Opal Smith, once confronted with her ring where it most certainly should not have been, had admitted everything.

Deborah said she was pleased with our work and I offered to pass on her thanks to our operative, but she mumbled something about doing that herself and all I had to do was send her the bill, including Angel's expenses.

I was glad she raised that point, as I was a bit dubious about the expenses he had listed on the second sheet of the fax.

That afternoon I told Estelle and Mrs Delacourt about the successful outcome of the case, but quite honestly, they did not seem able to take it seriously.

'How'd he slip her ring?' Mrs Delacourt asked, wiping a tear from her eye.

'And how did he get the key?' Estelle shrieked as if she was in a playground.

'How did he find it?'

They looked at each other and then collapsed into each other's arms, their shoulders heaving with laughter.

I thought showing them Angel's expenses claim would bring them down to earth.

Instead, it just made them roar even louder.

'Well, I don't think it funny,' I said. 'How do we explain to the client this claim for a £147.50 bar bill? I mean, there aren't even any receipts!'

Estelle took the fax I had thrust at her, and Mrs Delacourt read it over her shoulder. 'That's how!' they blurted out together, and collapsed in hysterics.

'What do you mean?' I think I was shouting now. I was angry enough.

'Not the drinks,' gasped Estelle, trying to draw breath. 'The other items.'

I looked at the fax again.

Expenses:

| Bar bill | £147.50 |
| Bottle of Johnson & Johnson Baby Oil | £1.35 |
| Use of microwave oven (estimate) | £0.10 |

'Oh, I see,' I said. But I didn't.

# Ealing Comedy

'You don't look much like a private detective,' said Mrs Romose.

'Surely that's to my advantage,' I answered politely.

'And I assumed …' she said as the thought hit her '… that when I contracted an all-female enquiry agency, they would send a female detective. You are not female.'

'Well spotted. Perhaps *you* are the detective in the room,' I admitted with my best smile. 'I am, as it happens, the only male operative employed by Rudgard & Blugden Investigations –' out of habit I bit my tongue at the word 'employed' '– and I wasn't aware you had specified a female investigator.'

Good luck getting one from R & B if she had. Veronica Blugden, my erstwhile boss (or 'line manager' as she insisted), didn't do house calls, and everyone involved in R & B thought it better for business if she didn't get out much. All the younger, female operatives – both of them – had discovered they had heavy caseloads as soon as the words 'old people's home' were mentioned. I just didn't react quickly enough; so I got the job.

'Not,' she went on haughtily, 'that I know what a private detective *should* look like.'

'Most people have a stereotype based on the books of Chandler, or Hammett, or Ross MacDonald.'

She furrowed her brow. The effort seemed to exhaust her.

'Books? Oh, I'm afraid I don't have time to read books. Who does these days? This place keeps me so busy and so … stressed.'

'It must be very stressful,' I lied sympathetically.

In fact I hadn't experienced a quieter, more restful workplace atmosphere than that converted Victorian mansion on Broughton Road, Ealing, since I had waited all day to catch a notorious pick-pocket (aged 12) red-handed in the dimly-lit Hadrian Exhibition at the British Museum.

'How many patients do you have here at Curtains?'

'We have five permanent guests at the moment. We call them guests, not patients, Mr Angel.'

I took the rebuke on the chin, relieved that I hadn't said 'inmates'.

'And one of them has, you think, committed a crime? That was the gist of your e-mail, wasn't it?'

For the first time since I had arrived and sat, as instructed, in an uncomfortable metal chair across from her over a rather severe white wood desk straight out of the Ikea catalogue, she seemed unsure of why she had called me in.

'It's a question of money,' she said at last.

'It usually is,' I agreed. 'Somebody stealing from the Christmas club? Or is it that one of your guests can't afford the fees?' I hated to think what the fees might be, but I knew I couldn't afford them. 'I hope you saw in our terms and conditions that we don't do bailiff work, debt-collecting or evictions?'

She held up a forefinger, its nail manicured to a stiletto.

'It's not what you think.'

It rarely was, but I didn't say it. Instead I was trying to place her accent, and had got as far as north European, though that didn't exactly narrow it down, when she continued.

'There is no money missing from, or owed to, this establishment, Mr Angel. My concern – the concern of the management – is that one of our guests, a certain Mr Geoffrey Spruce, seems to have far too much money.'

'One hears these things, Mrs Romose, about people who have more money than they need,' I said straight-faced, 'and it is quite tragic, but I'm not aware that it's a crime as such, unless of course they've robbed a bank or something.'

'But that's my point, Mr Angel. You see, Mr Spruce seems to be banking between two and three thousand pounds a month on a regular basis. Now where does an 82-year-old gentleman, confined to a wheelchair in a residential care home, who goes out only twice a week, get that sort of money?'

'Stocks, shares, dividends, investments, interest on savings?'

'No, Mr Angel, you are misunderstanding me. Mr Spruce has

an *income*. He is paying cash and cheques into his bank each month. How is he *earning* such amounts without doing any work?'

'I have no idea,' I told her with absolute honesty, 'but I'd love to find out.'

I was given the official guided tour of Curtains by one of Mrs Romose's minions, a middle-aged, pleasant-enough Italian called Verbena who seemed to be something of a cross between nurse and housekeeper. My cover, should the need to explain my presence arise, was that I was checking the place out with a view to depositing an elderly parent there.

As residential care facilities went – I was learning that I had stop calling them maximum security twilight homes – the place seemed to tick all the boxes. Broughton Road was a quiet enough street, one half modern flats, the other the original Victorian villas, though most of them converted from their original use. Traffic in the road outside was calmed by ranks of sleeping policemen, double yellow lines and residents'-only parking spaces, whilst pedestrians were sheltered by well-trimmed hedges and the occasional ornamental palm planted in timber boxes by Ealing Council.

The residential rooms of Curtains were in sharp contrast to Mrs Romose's Ikea-themed office. I was shown a 'reading room' that had leather arm-chairs and all the books Mrs Romose had not the time to read, a 'television room' that boasted a wall-mounted plasma screen offering more channels than I knew existed, and a 'music room' that contained a dusty upright piano and a CD player flanked by towers of disc holders. I flicked an eye over some of the discs in the collection and took heart from the fact that this generation of pensioners were not going quietly into the night after singing 'Roll out the Barrel' or 'There'll Be Bluebirds Over the White Cliffs of Dover' around the piano, but rather to the remastered strains of the Beatles, the Stones and Cream. Good for them.

'And this is the communal living room,' said Verbena, my

guide, showing me into a space larger than my rented flat in Hackney. There were French windows at one end, looking out into a rectangular garden that had not a leaf out of place. That was bigger than my flat too.

This room did not break the Trades Descriptions Act: it had living people in it, and by the looks of things they were drinking their coffee communally.

'Good morning, ladies and gentlemen,' Verbena announced us, and a voice responded with 'Bear in the room', which I thought distinctly odd, but Verbena didn't seem to notice. Perhaps it was her nickname. What was the Italian for teddy bear? *Orsachiotto*, that was it; though God knows why my brain had filed that away.

'Allow me to introduce you to some of our guests, Mr Angel. This is Mr Spruce, our senior resident.'

She indicated an elderly gentleman in a wheelchair with a blanket over his knees who did a handbrake-turn toward me. He had a few strands of hair splayed across a wrinkled, liver-spotted pate, but nature had compensated by giving him a very full, almost excessive, and luxuriant white beard. With a fatter, redder face he could have advertised fish fingers or played Santa in any department store. Perhaps he did, and that was where all the money came from. He held up a hand for me to shake.

'It's Geoffrey, Geoffrey Spruce,' he said, watching my face. 'And I'm senior only in age, not status. We all get equal billing here. Did she say "Angel"? No connection to Angels and Bermans?'

I shook my head as he pumped my hand. ''Fraid not.'

Verbena swept a generous arm swiftly over the other residents.

'That's Mr Simper and that's Mr Hoyle, and over there are Mrs Hayter and Miss Pope.'

The supporting cast seemed friendly enough, raising eyebrows and coffee cups in greeting, but it was clear that Spruce was the leading light.

'I presume you're prospecting, Mr ... er ...?' he prompted.

'Angel, Roy Angel,' I said, though he'd heard my name clearly enough when Verbena had said it. 'I'm not sure what you mean by prospecting.'

'Well, as you are far too young to be thinking of joining our happy company yourself, I'm presuming you are prospecting for a suitable retirement home for some aged relative who has outlived their usefulness.'

'Now, now, Geoffrey, tone it down a notch, darling,' chided the woman who had been introduced as Miss Pope. 'None of us here is old and bitter.'

'No, that's my mother-in-law!' said the man called Simper, and the others laughed politely, probably through familiarity.

Spruce angled his wheelchair toward Miss Pope, who smiled at him from behind large round spectacles.

'I sit corrected, Dorinda. You are quite right. We are a happy breed here at Curtains, and we should at least offer Mr Angel some coffee. There's still some in the pot, but can we get another cup, please, Verbena?'

'Of course. I won't be a moment.'

As she left the room, Spruce said, almost to himself, 'Exit bear,' and I spotted one of the other men mouthing the same words in chorus. Then Spruce turned his expanse of white beard in my direction.

'We are not formal here, you know. I'm Geoffrey, Geoffrey Spruce. These two ugly sisters are Colin Simper and Angus Doyle.' He paused between each name, almost as if making sure they had registered with someone as obviously slow as me. 'And the two beautiful ladies are Emma Hayter and Dorinda Pope, and we all get on famously together.'

'I'm delighted to meet you all,' I said, leaving out a sarcastic 'again'. 'This seems a very nice ... place … home.'

'It is a home,' volunteered the frail Mrs Hayter, who looked as if she would blow over in stiff breeze. 'We have everything we need and it's so convenient for the West End.'

'Where we like to go shopping,' said Dorinda Pope quickly. 'Even if it's only window-shopping these days.'

The others all laughed politely.

'You probably have lots of questions about the place, Mr

Angel, if you're thinking of parking an elderly relative here. Well, fire away. If we can help, we will. Anything you need to know about the food, the medical facilities, the fees? Just ask away.'

'I was wondering why you referred to the staff here as bears,' I asked.

'Do they get out much?' I asked Mrs Ramose, back in her static-free office.

'Often. They're always out.' She sighed loudly. 'Missing meals, forgetting they have visitors coming. Sometimes I think they do it deliberately. It shows they are fit and active, and of course I cannot stop them. I would not want to. In Denmark, where I come from, we encourage independence among the seniors.'

'Is there any pattern to it?'

'Well, at least two of them go out every day, and always the women. I think the women encourage the men to spend their money on them.'

'I thought the problem was money being earned, not spent.'

She shrugged that off.

'All I can tell you is that Emma and Dorinda are always involved, taking the men up the West End. Mr Spruce always goes with Dorinda Wednesdays and Thursdays. Tomorrow is Wednesday.'

'And what do you expect to happen?'

'A mini-cab collects them here at nine o'clock and takes them to Ealing Broadway tube station for the Central Line. They come back by taxi when they feel like it. We have no curfew here at Curtains.'

'Can I ask why this place is called Curtains? It seems a rather odd name for an old people's … a residential care home.'

Mrs Romose twitched her shoulders slightly, indicating she was in a state of high emotion.

'It was called that when the company Carestream bought it from the previous owners. I always thought it referred to those large bay windows on the front.'

'Has the company owned it long?'

'About a year-and-a-half.'

'And you came with the new company?'

'Yes, I did. All the staff here are new. They came from other facilities in the company.'

'Are they mostly foreign?' I asked carefully.

'They are all EU citizens,' she bridled, 'mostly from Portugal and Italy, but they are all properly qualified. Is that at all important?'

'Probably not,' I said.


I briefly – very briefly – considered doing the job with Armstrong Two, my trusty delicensed black cab, but although he was still running sweet as a nut, he was a Fairway, a design that was rapidly becoming extinct thanks to the ubiquitous TX4 model and, lately, Metrocabs and even – heaven forfend – electric cabs or emission-free hybrids. The thing was that, these days, if a black Austin Fairway was seen tootling around the streets of London, most people would assume there was a movie being shot or there was a rally of vintage vehicles on somewhere, and tourists would take selfies with them on their phones. The old-style black cabs, once totally anonymous thanks to familiarity breeding contempt, were now just too damned distinctive, although Armstrong Two still earned his keep thanks to my arrangement with Duncan the Drunken ('Probably the best car mechanic in the world' as his advertising campaign would say, if he ever bothered to advertise). In exchange for free garaging over in Barking, Duncan would hire out Armstrong Two for weddings and funerals, mostly in darkest Essex, and, ironically, to TV and film crews doing 'period pieces' – a phrase that made me feel very old, but relieved that Armstrong One (an even older, FX4 design) wasn't around to see the state of the world. He'd blown up in a freak agricultural accident over ten years ago, and I like to think it was the way he'd have wanted to go.

So there I was, that first day on the case, waiting at Ealing Broadway from 8.30 to 11.00 am, hopping from foot to foot, trying and failing to blend in with the crowd (I felt very obvious, as I was the only person in the postal district without wires coming out of their ears), on the look-out for an elderly white-bearded gent in a wheelchair being pushed by a frail, bespectacled old lady. Nobody showed, but by then The North Star was open and offering a wide range of cask ales for the weary private detective in search of refreshments and VAT receipts.

The next day I was clever. I arranged for Mrs Romose to call my mobile the moment Geoffrey and Dorinda left Curtains and to give me two pieces of information: what make and colour of car the mini-cab firm had sent and what Dorinda Pope was wearing.

She obviously thought I was crazy but did as I had asked. The mini-cab would be the same as always – a blue Renault people carrier – and Dorinda was wearing her Barbour Derby raincoat.

About 15 minutes after I hung up on Mrs Romose, a blue Renault mini cab did indeed draw up outside the tube station. Lurking behind a set of large municipal wheelie bins, I got a perfect view of the passengers climbing out of the back seats, and I realised how useless Mrs Romose was as a detective's assistant.

Dorinda Pope was wearing a bright elderberry raincoat (Mrs Romose had forgotten to mention the Barbour was reversible) and had exchanged her large round tortoiseshell-framed spectacles for very fashionable small, square metal-frames.

Mrs Romose had also forgotten to mention that Geoffrey Spruce was wearing a brown fedora at a rakish angle, was totally clean-shaven and had miraculously recovered the use of his legs.

The pair of them skipped by within ten feet of me, gazing into each other's eyes and giggling like schoolchildren, and disappeared into the station. I pulled out my trusty Oyster card and went to work.


I strung it out for a week, but by then Mrs Romose and Carestream were demanding results or their money back. So I told her the story, trying not to laugh.

I had followed Geoffrey and Dorinda – and then on other occasions Dorinda and Colin Simple and then Emma Hayter and Angus Hoyle – on the tube as far as Marble Arch and then through the backstreets to Portman Mews South, where they appeared to turn smartly into a pub called The Three Tuns.

On closer inspection, they hadn't popped into the pub, but into a doorway next to one of the two doors to the pub. The door had a sturdy brass handle and matching letter box and a small brass plaque bearing the legend Golightly Investigations.

I found myself a spot further down the mews, where I could hide in the entrance to an underground garage and observe any comings and goings. Black cabs – ghastly, modern real ones – would draw up and passengers would get out and approach the door next to the pub. All the visitors were elderly, some so frail that the cabbie would pile out to help them the few steps across the pavement. Most cabs waited with their meters running, collected their passengers and drove off. About one o'clock, Geoffrey and Dorinda stepped out, locked the door and entered the The Three Tuns. By the time they left to go back to whatever they were doing next door, my stomach was rumbling, so I decided to risk a pub lunch as well.

I was chewing on steak pie and sipping beer when a small crowd of smartly-dressed young guys entered and gathered at one end of the bar. Given the time of day and the proximity of Seymour Street police station, it didn't take a detective to realise this was some of the morning shift coming off duty. It was true the policemen were getting younger, but luckily I recognised two of them as nodding acquaintances, and the nods turned into my buying a round.

It was someone else's money well spent. Of course they knew about Golightly Investigations next door: a couple of their IT lads had helped the old guy set up their computers and wi-fi. Cops would do anything for Old George, who was a Top Man.

George? Didn't they mean Geoffrey?

Well of course his name was Geoffrey Spruce, they said, but he would always be Superintendent George Golightly to them.

He would?

Course he would. He was a legend, was George Golightly, a straight-up London copper of the old school, though it must be 35 years – certainly before my new best friends were born – since *Golightly* was on the telly. All the shows were on DVD now though, and they had the full set over at the station house. It was good to see the old boy keeping himself busy, and he often called in the pub and always bought his round. Even got a girlfriend – and him at his age – used to work on the show with him, he says, and some of his mates are always using the place next door. There was that Colin Simper – the one who used to play the camp vicar in *Heaven Below* – and that Angus something-or-other who was the pompous bank manager in *No Overdrafts*.

I observed that today's coppers seemed to watch a lot of old TV shows.

No, they said, they just did a lot of pub quizzes. Apart from *Golightly*, of course – that was a favourite. And naturally *The Sweeney* – that was required viewing, if not compulsory.

'You didn't really need to call me in at all,' I told Mrs Romose when I handed her my bill for services rendered. 'You had a firm of private detectives operating more or less right under your nose all the time, or at least actors playing the part.'

She appeared totally confused. It was a look that suited her.

'I should have guessed at the start they were all thespians. Your residents refer to the staff as "bears" and Geoffrey Spruce told me it was because when they were chased off to bed at night, someone had coined the phrase "Exit pursued by a bear", which is the famous stage direction from Shakespeare's *Winter's Tale*. He also asked me if I was anything to do with Angels and Bermans, the famous theatrical costumiers who now do fancy dress hire.

'A bit of research on my part turned up the fact that Curtains, with a suitable touch of black humour, had been founded by a retired actor as a home for retired actors. Either your company Carestream didn't check or didn't care when they took over. As most of the incoming new management were foreign, they were not watching British television thirty years ago and so didn't recognise the names or faces of the guests.

'Mind you, neither did I, and Geoffrey made a point of repeating their names and watching me to see if any of them rang a bell with me. Well, they didn't, but I had a look on the Internet Movie Data-Base and I found Geoffrey and Colin Simper and Angus Hoyle, who all had their moment in the sun, or at least on television. Dorinda Hope and Mrs Hayter were a tad tricky to find, because they weren't actors, but both were listed as make-up artists on just about every major TV show in the 1970s.

'Then I called round to the mini-cab firm you always use: Carmichael's Cars. They were very helpful, in fact quite proud to be taxiing Superintendent Golightly around. It turns out that the Mr Carmichael who started the company was a former BBC driver until he got laid off, and he knew all the stars. He liked the thought of having them in the back of one of his cabs.

'Which is where they got their make-overs. They would get in the car here and get out at Ealing Broadway in different clothes and in theatrical make-up that made them look ten years younger and put a spring in their step. Geoffrey had to go the extra mile, though, maybe because he's the biggest ham. He wears make-up and a false beard while he's here, but they come off once he's in the mini-cab, and he doesn't need that wheelchair at all. I think he pinched that idea from an Agatha Christie.'

'And you say they run a detective agency?'

'Named after Geoffrey's most famous starring role. I even picked up one of their visiting cards in the pub next door: Golightly Investigations, 5A Portman Mews South, W1. They've got a website and they seem to specialise in the more mature end of the client spectrum, doing a lot of work for old thespians trying to track down missing managers or repeat fees or children who've dumped them in … residential care facilities. It's all useful work and fairly safe. They seem to enjoy it.'

'They are all involved?' Now she was confused and surprised.

'I think so, and they might even draw in other old actors. If an investigation called for a vicar, they'd give it to Colin Simper; if they needed a bank manager or a retired army type, it might be Angus Hoyle. Mrs Hayter and Dorinda would be in charge of make-up and wardrobe. A nice little set up. Very versatile, and it earns them a few quid as well as keeping them off the streets.'

And probably keeping them alive, I said to myself.

'That's the most outrageous thing I've ever heard,' blurted Mrs Romose.

If it was, I thought, then she couldn't be as old as she looked.

'Isn't it a crime?'

'The only crime I'm aware of is you going through Geoffrey Spruce's bank statements. I reckon that's a bit naughty. But I must go. He's invited me to have coffee with him.'

'Are you're going to tell him about me?' She was definitely worried, and I liked that look on her.

I pushed back my chair and stood up.

'No, I was going to ask him for a job.'

# OTHERS

# The Body Of The Beer

'In those days,' said the official guide, 'it was not unusual to have two breweries next door to each other.'

Well, at least he was right about that.

'The museum we are about to enter was the brewhouse of the old Wellbeloved & Barnard brewery, established in 1867 and registered as a company in 1896. Over there' – he pointed to the wet tarmac of a National Car-park – 'was the brewery of P & A Appledore. That was originally a vinegar brewery and switched to beer production in 1892 under the brothers Peter and Arthur Appledore. Of course the locals joked that they hadn't really changed trades.'

Polite laughter from the shivering visitors.

'But they were proved wrong, for in the decade before the First World War, Appledore's ales took major prizes at every national beer competition, winning the *Brewers' Guardian* trophy for draught beer three times, something no brewer has done since. Now we'll go inside. No high heels, ladies? Good. We've got a lot of steps to climb. Brewing begins at the top.'

Never a truer word. Arthur Appledore recognised in 1901 that if he wanted to improve the name of his beer, a top brewer was what was needed. And while other managing directors visited the Brewers' Exhibition in Islington looking for new plant and equipment, Appledore went hunting for a brewer.

'Right at the top of the brewery would be the malt store. When we get there, you'll see that brewing in those days was literally an up-and-down process,' said the guide. 'Please be careful – these steps can be rather dangerous.'


Othniel Saggers knew his trade.

Pupilaged at the last of the big London porter breweries, he learned the craft of brown beers and stouts before moving to Burton to unlock the secrets of pale ales. An early member of the Laboratory Club, he spanned both the art and science of brewing, and at the 1901 Exhibition, three of his beers took major prizes. Arthur Appledore offered him total control of his brewhouse and he jumped at the chance.


'This is the milling machine,' said the guide. 'Malt, which has been hauled up a pulley, is finely crushed to form a grist for mashing. It's where we get the expression "grist to the mill".'


Success was the incentive for Othniel Saggers; the grist to his mill: to be the best. Within a year he had launched a new portfolio of Appledore Ales. Sales rose, prizes were won. *Ale to Adore* read the posters on the sides of trams; *I Adore Appledore* said the advertisements in the local *Gazette*.


'In this vessel, the malt grist in mashed with hot water. It's a bit like mashing tea – people still say that, don't they? This is the first stage of any good brew.'


By the time Sir Robert Barnard became chairman of Wellbeloved & Barnard in 1912, the company was undoubtedly the second brewer in the town.

Sir Robert recruited new brewers, invested in the most modern equipment, insisted on a spotlessly clean brewhouse. Still Appledore Ales won the prizes and sold the most. Even though no Wellbeloveds had actually entered the brewery for twenty years (except for annual general meetings or to draw their directors' allocation of spent hops for their rose gardens), their name was used mercilessly. *I'd Love A Wellbeloved* read the signs on the horse-drawn buses; *Wellbeloved … For Taste* said the hoarding at the railway station.

But try as he might, Sir Robert could not dent Appledore's growing reputation. Then the Kaiser came to his aid.

'This is one of the two coppers – think of them as large kettles, ladies –where hops were added to the wort. No, we don't call it beer yet. These were installed in 1915, no mean feat with a war on, after the brewery was hit during a Zeppelin raid. The locals reckoned that Mr Appledore next door must have had the Germans on his side!'

It was a fluke of course. A homeward-bound Zeppelin lightening its load of bombs. One landed in Wellbeloved's main yard, killing two under-brewers and a cooper and taking out the wall of the brewhouse.

Sir Robert responded with furious activity. Beer from stock was blended and reblended to keep the pubs supplied. More beer was bought in from a friendly brewer in the next town (even though Appledore was just down the street) and a new slogan appeared everywhere: *Wellbeloved by King, Not Kaiser*. Public sympathy turned into increased sales; but Sir Robert's masterstroke was to appeal to the patriotism of Appledore's quiet genius, Othniel Saggers.

In a move that made the front page of the *Gazette*, Mr O A Saggers was appointed head brewer and director of Wellbeloved & Barnard, with *carte blanche* to rebuild the brewery. What was not reported was the private arrangement with Sir Robert that Saggers would become full partner and the name of the company changed to Wellbeloved, Barnard & Saggers on the winning of a major brewing prize, as soon as national competitions resumed in peacetime.

Patriotism is all very well but sometimes needs a hand.

Down these steps and then up those over there and we go into the fermentation room. That's where the serious business starts and we get al-co-hol.' The guide rolled his eyes and paused for audience reaction.

'Hopped wort from the coppers would be cooled and run into these fermentation tanks and then the yeast, a living organism, is pitched in. Yes, this is where things really happen.'

In anticipation of the 1920 Brewers' Exhibition, Saggers had put aside the smallest of his fermentation vessels for what was to be his first Wellbeloved competition brew. He had the ten-barrel circular vessel, made of best pine from New Zealand, scrubbed spotless and a wrought iron catwalk and stairs erected over it so he could examine the yeast head and crust from above and aerate the brew from the centre by hand. (All brewers have their idiosyncrasies!)

The only thing known about the brew was that it would have a ten-day fermentation followed by two weeks' conditioning in cask in a roped-off area in the brewery cellar. The original gravity was known only to Saggers and the local Excise, but it was rumoured to be high. The raw materials were drawn from store and handled by Saggers alone.

It was to be his finest brew. It was to be his last.

'Fermentation produces alcohol and carbon dioxide,' said the guide, 'and that can be dangerous. Why, the head brewer at Wellbeloved's was overcome by $CO_2$ fumes and died right here, in 1920. And he should have known better.'

The early shift boilermen found Othniel Saggers at 5.00 am, on the floor of the fermentation room.

The local doctor said he had been overcome by carbon dioxide, missed his footing, toppled off the catwalk and smashed his head in on the stone floor. Quite likely he had been drinking. A succinct if not terribly scientific diagnosis from a Temperance member of the medical profession.

Sir Robert ransacked the brewery until he unearthed Saggers' Brewing Room Book, then gave orders that Saggers' instructions were to be followed to the letter. The brew was racked into cask, nurtured and nursed and packed off to the Brewers' Exhibition.

The result was humiliation. 'Mawkish, thin and sour' were some of the kinder comments of the judges in private. In public, the beer was labelled 'Unfit for Competition' and returned to Wellbeloved & Barnard.

'But of course,' said the guide, beaming, 'this fermentation room is famous not for its beer but for the murder that took place here in 1936.'

Every four years, Sir Robert tried to recreate a competition brew from Saggers' notes. Good management and sound investment helped Wellbeloved & Barnard through the recession years – in fact they prospered while Appledore's fortunes declined. But this brought him no cheer. Between the companies was a wall of silence, and nothing would persuade Sir Robert to ask the ageing and increasingly embittered Arthur Appledore what the secret of the 'lost' brew could have been.

In three successive competitions, Wellbeloved's beer was rebuffed and (politely) ridiculed, but Sir Robert persisted.

In one last attempt in 1936 (the year of his retirement at a lively 75), Sir Robert determined to supervise the brew personally. He even went to the extent of carrying out a personal examination of the first setting of a 'rocky' yeast head, as Saggers had done on the day of his death. That was how, at 4.00 am, he found Arthur Appledore mounting the catwalk above the competition brew.

Appledore, himself 85 at this time, climbed slowly and carefully, and did not even falter when Sir Robert spoke to him for the first time in over 20 years.

'What in God's name are you doing in my brewery, Appledore?'

The older man mounted the last step on the catwalk before he turned and looked down.

'Your brewery, Barnard, but my beer! Saggers created this for me!'

Appledore's left hand pointed accusingly at the open fermenter below him. His right hand remained deep in his overcoat pocket.

'We'll see about that! ' shouted Sir Robert as he started up the iron steps.

'If you don't mind the crush,' said the guide, 'we can all fit on the catwalk, which is where the bodies were found. Be careful, though. It can be very slippery.'

Appledore was struggling to free his right hand from his pocket as Sir Robert reached him –struggling to pull something free.

Sir Robert assumed it was a weapon and hesitated a yard from his quarry. Below them, through the slatted iron catwalk, the competition brew foamed quietly.

'Get back!' shouted Appledore, freeing his hand at last.

He held not a gun but a conical flask with a cork stopper, which he reached for with his left hand. Sir Robert lunged for his arms. As they struggled, the cork came out, and straw-coloured liquid splashed over their clothes. Sir Robert inhaled the fumes it gave off.

'Vinegar! You swine!'

'Acetic acid culture, you ignorant upstart,' gasped Appledore as they struggled. 'You never even suspected, but my culture is what has turned your thieving brew bad.'

They were swaying wildly now, locked together. The liquid from the flask was spilling onto the catwalk but missing the yawning fermentation vessel below.

'You've poisoned my brews,' wheezed Sir Robert.

'Saggers created them for *me!*' shrieked Appledore. 'The culture works when the beer goes into condition in the cask. The stronger the brew, the more alcohol gets turned to acid. Your so-called tasters don't notice a thing, but by the time it gets to the competition, your beer is rank and foul, and I'm damn glad of it!'

'Well not this one!'

With a huge effort, Sir Robert pulled Appledore off his feet and to one side. The flask spun away, shattering on the catwalk but missing the precious brew.

Appledore's eyes ignited.

'If I can't kill your beer, I'll kill you!' He lunged for Sir Robert's throat. 'Just like I had to get rid of that turncoat Saggers.'

Frightened now, Sir Robert backed away, looking to escape. But the exertion of the tussle had been too much.

Perhaps he felt a stunning pain down his left arm, perhaps he heard the pressure explode in his brain. He could say nothing, for his jaw had gone slack.

Sir Robert crumpled into a seated position on the catwalk and expired.

Appledore swayed back on his heels stunned – then jubilant.

'I'll show you what an old vinegar brewer can do,' he muttered as he bent over to scoop up the remains of the flask, determined to sweep the culture into the beer with his bare hands if necessary.

His fingers closed around the broken neck of the flask. A few drops had remained clinging viscously to the glass, but in his haste to shake them into the fermenting vessel he slipped.

A younger man would not have noticed, but Arthur Appledore was not young. He pitched forward, sprawling over the edge of the catwalk.

Still clutching the broken neck of the flask, Arthur Appledore's arm and hand had been bent under him, jammed by the edge of the ironwork. The jagged glass entered his throat as he fell, slicing the jugular. He rolled over onto his back and bled to death, his blood making quiet plopping sounds as it dripped into the yeasty crust below.

'The local *Gazette* called it a "tragic occurrence",' said the guide. 'Sir Robert had obviously killed Arthur Appledore and then has a heart attack when he realised what he had done. Insane jealousy, they put it down to. What may surprise you is that the special brew was racked and sent to the Brewers' Exhibition as if nothing had happened. A lot of people thought that was in bad taste – and it certainly did not win any prizes that year!'

But there again the guide was wrong.

Tasted 'blind', Wellbeloved & Barnard's competition brew was unanimously voted champion beer by the judges, without recourse to a second-round 'taste-off'. It was the only time, before or since, that a beer achieved such an outright win. It was only when its identity was revealed that the Exhibition organisers awarded premier place to the runner-up, out of deference to the memory of Arthur Appledore.

In conclave, the judges all remarked on the distinctive flavour of the beer, and all agreed that it was 'an exceptionally full-bodied brew'.

# Gold Sword

'I knew your father for over forty years,' said old man Potts as soon as we were a decent distance from the grave, 'and only once did he do something totally surprising.'

'You mean selling the family firm, I suppose?' I tried to sound polite, but I had heard this opening gambit many times before.

'That was anything but surprising,' blustered Dr Crumley ungraciously. 'Think of all those takeovers in the '60s.'

There had been takeovers, of course, but my father – like many others – had sold up rather than be bought up.

'No, no,' said Potts irritably, 'I meant when he sent back his OBE. Returned his "gong" as he called it. Damn funny thing to do, if you ask me.'

No-one had, but that was unlikely to deter the venerable editor of the *Seagrave Packet*, our noble, moral, crusading, and only local newspaper.

Nor our venerable local doctor.

'Wasn't it because of the Beatles?' Dr Crumley shouted. I had forgotten the deafness in his left ear and his assumption – odd for a medical man – that the affliction was contagious. 'Didn't everybody send back their gongs in protest when the Beatles got the MBE?'

'I'd be surprised if Sydney knew who the Beatles are,' said Potts.

Were, I thought; but I said nothing.

'The one thing Sydney did that shocked me,' Crumley pressed on, 'was when he stopped brewing Gold Sword. It wasn't long before he sold the brewery, come to think of it. That was the best barley wine I've ever drunk. Before or since.'

The doctor closed his eyes to help conjure up a long-lost flavour. 'In summer, we'd drink it half-and-half with mild ale. My God, if we did that today, old Potts here would call us "lager louts" in that paper of his. '

'I was a bitter man myself,' said Potts dreamily. 'I even remember the old adverts we put in the paper: "Seton's Seaside Ales". But you're right for once, Crumley. Sydney's Gold Sword was a cracking beer. '

Potts turned on me as we reached the churchyard gate. 'Haven't you ever felt cheated of your heritage, young Pip? If Sydney hadn't sold up, you'd have been – what? – the fifth generation of Setons to run the firm?'

'Wouldn't have to work for a living, like you do now, eh?' cackled Crumley.

'Seriously, Philip,' Potts persisted, 'don't you resent your father selling up back in the '60s?'


The fact that he was totally unsuitable for service in any of the armed forces on the outbreak of war in 1939 greatly depressed my father. Poor eyesight from birth and a permanent limp (acquired after a clash of wills with an unruly Percheron in 1937) ruled out his chances for the commission that so many of his brewer contemporaries proudly boasted.

He had been appointed managing director of the family brewery in early 1939 when my grandfather had inherited the chairmanship from my great-grandfather, and he had been left to 'get on with it'. (Grandad saw the chairmanship as a chance for early retirement to indulge his passion for bird watching; a trait, happily, not genetic.)

Newly married, in his early thirties, and mentally supremely fit, he set to with a will, pulling the brewery out of the tail-end of the Depression, which had hit even our sleepy South Coast home town of Seagrave. The war served only to increase his energy supply. His own experiments with pressurised metal casks were halted and he organised the Spitfire for Seagrave drive to collect aluminium. He recruited local women as drivers and sales representatives to replace called-up brewery workers. (They had been confined to the bottling sheds in World War I.) He rationed raw materials, and then beer itself; reduced his gravities as requested; and promoted draught rather than bottled beer to save on glass, rubber and petrol. He also found time to organise Seagrave's Air Raid Precautions and then the local Home Guard, and sat on dozens of committees for fundraising or the adoption of evacuated children.

Still it was not enough.

His chance to do more – much more – came in 1942.

For the first two-and-a-half years of the war, brewers had supplied troop canteens with beer through their local NAAFI organisation; Seton's brewery being ideally placed to supply the army's Southern Command. Yet relations were far from smooth. Local brewers resented using their meagre petrol ration to deliver to army bases when the army seemed to have petrol to burn. The 24-hour-a-day army couldn't understand why brewers could not brew any quantity desired whenever needed (immediately), or why they made such a fuss about not getting their casks back. In fact, both parties seriously wondered if the other knew there was a war on.

If civilian evacuation, the drive for munitions, conscription of brewery workers and drinking customers and air-raids had not disrupted life enough, to cap it all, the Yanks were suddenly Over Here.

By mid-1942, with the influx of Allied troops, brewers faced an extra demand for at least 600,000 barrels of beer a year, and there were already acute shortages in country pubs. But unlike in the First World War, beer was seen – by a very different prime minister – as a morale-booster rather than the Germans' secret weapon. Something had to be done, and the Ministry of Food called on the Brewers' Society to establish a Beer For Troops committee to bring order to the growing confusion.

My father, already the company's representative at the Society, was delighted to be asked to serve. He would have been mortified not to be.

Until the war finished, he spent at least three days a month in London working for the Beer for Troops committee, each problem that came before it being examined in minute detail. Where could extra coal for malting be found? How quickly could

10,000 gross screw-stoppers be produced? What was the most economical specification for badly-needed casks and crates? Which British regiments preferred dark mild to light ale? Should the brewers concentrate on producing one uniform 'Army Ale'? (An overwhelming 'No'.) How could 200 tons of Oregon hops be kept fresh on the convoy across the Atlantic? (By lining the sacks with old newspapers!)

And not only was there the NAAFI to deal with, but a new and very demanding customer in the form of the Headquarters of Services of Supply, US Army, European Theater of Operations.

For convenience, the American supply office became known as the 'Selfridge Annex', after its allocated offices between Wigmore and Oxford Streets, and my father took it upon himself to liaise directly with the commanding officer, Colonel Garrett M Ayres QM. They became close friends, keeping in touch after the war. My father had often told the after-dinner story of how the Americans were not given stationery to use, as paper was in short supply, and had to conduct their correspondence on the back of pre-printed forms headed 'Meat and Livestock Control – Record of Inedible Offal'. Either through good manners or blissful ignorance, none of the Americans ever asked what 'inedible offal' was (and much of the correspondence is still on the files).

As became his custom on his Beer for Troops days in London, my father would meet Colonel Ayres for dinner. He got into the habit of telephoning the Selfridge Annex at about 5.00 pm and then walking from Society headquarters in Upper Belgrave Street, arriving in time for what the US Army called the 'cocktail hour'.

On one such occasion, in January 1944, he had telephoned to Ayres and was pulling on his overcoat when one of the Society secretaries informed him there was a telephone call for him.

'Mr Seton? Mr Sydney Seton?'

'Yes.'

'Mr Seton, you don't know me, b-b-but I would l-l-like to talk to you. My name is Russell, and it is, as they s-s-say, a matter of national sec-sec-security.'

'Well, this is … er … not usual, er …' My father, unconsciously copying the caller's stutter, would have blushed at himself.

'It is irregular, Mr Seton, I g-g-grant you that, but I am in – shall we say – the irregular part of the war effort. Could you spare me a few minutes at Baker Street this evening, before you meet Colonel Ayres?'

'If it's important, of course. Whereabouts?'

'The bottom end of Baker Street, at Portman Square. As soon as you can, if that's all right.'

Intrigued – how had Russell known about Colonel Ayres? – my father set out, skirting Hyde Park. As the Blitz was over and the V-bombs had not yet replaced the Luftwaffe, the main hazard in the blackout was London's black, almost invisible, cabs.

Harold Russell, as he introduced himself, was a handsome, dark-haired man in his early thirties. He showed my father a pass that identified him as an operative of SOE – Special Operations Executive – based on Baker Street – the organisation that Churchill said 'would set Europe ablaze' – and he suggested a stroll around the damp and dark Portman Square.

'This must be quite a pleasant area to work in,' said my father for the sake of something to say.

'I suspect it will be after the war,' said Russell. 'I really don't n-n-notice such things. I wanted to serve abroad, you see, but although I speak the lingo, I s-s-stammer in English.'

My father would have smiled at that, thought of his own disabilities that had excluded him from a more active role, and felt an instant affinity with the man from SOE.

Russell lost no time in getting down to business. It was no secret, he said, that the Allies would be invading northern Europe that year. What was essential was to fool the Germans as to when and, more importantly, where the landings would come. If the Germans thought the beachheads would be the Pas de Calais (the narrowest part of the Channel), then that's where the Panzer divisions would be stationed; totally useless if the invasion actually took place on, say, the Cherbourg peninsula, hundreds of miles away.

Where Sydney Seton, and the brewers, came in soon became clear.

As Russell rightly described, an invasion force required ships, landing craft, supplies of all sorts, and men. Ships and supplies could be camouflaged or kept on the move, but men were more difficult. They had to be fed and watered during training, assembly and embarkation and they all required beer, even the Free French.

If you were invading at the Pas de Calais, explained Russell smoothly, then your invasion force would be based in East Anglia. If the target was the Cherbourg area, the marshalling zones would be Hampshire and Dorset or Devon. If you could find out where the invasion troops were massing, then you had a very good idea of where they would be landing. How did you discover where the troops were being billeted and trained? You followed the beer supplies.

The logic of it all would have been stunning to an innocent like my father. Most of the paperwork generated by the Beer for Troops committee was not even marked 'Confidential', let alone 'Secret'. His own correspondence with Colonel Ayres, he realised, could have identified the location of two units of US Rangers on exercise in Scotland that month.

'Something must be done about this,' he would have said to Russell.

'No,' Russell had replied, 'exactly the opposite.'

Feed the *wrong* information about beer movements to the Germans, and on invasion day they would be in the wrong place looking in the wrong direction. Russell could do that; that was his job. But, of course, he needed to be given the correct information to begin with – and very secretively, to make sure no-one could suspect a trail of deliberate misinformation. Not even the Americans must know, or they might inadvertently break security.

For the following five months, my father doubled his trips to London, meeting Russell every fortnight and outlining the latest shipments and requirements of beer for troops, particularly the British forces in Southern Command and the massing Americans and Canadians. In fact, seeing my father off at Seagrave station is one of my earliest childhood memories, along with my mother saying he was 'off to his war work'.

Russell would meet my father either at the SOE or in Portman Square, using my father's regular visits to Colonel Ayres as 'cover'. After several months of meetings, Russell expressed delight at the 'intelligence' he was able to pass on. He openly hinted that my father's efforts would not go unrewarded.

It was in May 1944 that Russell, normally cool and businesslike, became openly excited at their regular meeting.

My father had shown him the Brewers' Society circular of 25 May, which advised all brewers that the Government and the Ministry of Food had revoked, with immediate effect, all export licences – which were required for sending beer to troops abroad. Furthermore, the Beer for Troops committee was authorised to advise members that the licences would be reinstated after 'a short duration'.

As if that were not enough to indicate that something big was afoot, the circular asked brewers to supply details of their current stock of export beer (i.e. bottled) and give an estimate of how much they could have ready by 30 June at the latest.

'This is it!' Russell had exclaimed. 'Give me a t-t-tide table for France and I'll pinpoint the landings to the minute.'

Less than two weeks later, on 6 June, the greatest armada in history appeared off the Normandy coast, heralded by airborne troops and backed by an air force of 11,000 planes, to begin the liberation of western Europe.

The Germans were caught napping, fully expecting the invasion to be in the Pas de Calais. In Seagrave, the church bells rang for the first time in nearly five years and closely-guarded stocks of the brewery's barley wine were broken out and distributed to the workforce. My father, leading the celebrations, announced that – as soon as peace came – a new barley wine would be brewed in honour of our valiant forces fighting on the beaches in Normandy. Thus was Gold Sword promised – and my father was as good as his word. The name, he always said, chose itself. Gold and Sword were the two main British invasion beach code names. (Utah and Omaha were American, and Juno mostly Canadian.)

Gold Sword, which became a prize-winning beer, was seen by many brewer friends as a personal tribute to himself 'for something Sydney did in the war', although my father never did breathe a word of his relationship with Harold Russell.

For his part, Russell also seemed to prove as good as his word.

My father was awarded the OBE in the first honours list published by the King after the war.

In fact, my father only saw Russell once after D-Day, and that was in 1949.

I was even introduced to him, as I was home from school for the summer vacation at the time. He had simply turned up at Seagrave station, amidst a crowd of holidaymakers, and telephoned the brewery, and my father had sent a car for him. They lunched together in The Seton Arms hotel and Russell congratulated my father on his honour. He also asked if the Beer for Troops organisation, or rather its successor Export Committee, was involved in supplying Allied forces in West Germany. My father, who had cut down his visits to the Brewers' Society to rebuild the firm's peacetime trade, admitted that he did not know, as he was 'a bit out of touch'. Russell had said no matter, it wasn't important. Russell returned to London the same afternoon, staggering under the weight of a presentation crate of Gold Sword barley wine.

The brewery did well enough in the '50s, and Gold Sword did extremely well, being listed by other brewers who had discontinued their own barley wines. The company remained firmly in family hands, my father owning the majority of shares, which would, in turn, come to me.

Even though I had gone up to Cambridge to read history, rather than Birmingham and the Brewing School, it was always expected that I would have 'great expectations' in the firm – hence I became known as Pip rather than Philip.

It was a stunning blow, although he told me before anyone else, when my father announced that he was halting production of Gold Sword and approaching two large regional brewers with a view to selling the company. Later that year, it was 1963, he returned his OBE, and the following spring, he retired to an isolated farmhouse ten miles inland from Seagrave, where he remained a virtual recluse after the death of my mother in 1966, until his own, lonely death.

His retreat from business, brewing and all forms of public life (the Town Council, the Magistrates' Bench and so on) had been sparked by a chance turning on of the family television set in February 1963.

He rarely watched television, but a documentary caught his eye and he sat and followed it in total silence.

The programme was devoted to the story of a dark-haired, handsome man with a stammer who had disappeared from Beirut and was thought to be seeking asylum in the Soviet Union. It was claimed that he had held a senior position in British Intelligence while in fact he had been spying for Stalin since the 1930s.

His name was given as Harold Adrian Russell Philby.

Better known as Kim.


'No, I don't feel cheated of my heritage, Mr Potts,' I said, keeping one eye on the road for my car and driver. 'My father did what was best for the family – and himself – in the long run. And I've made a fair career for myself.'

'You're one of these civil servant chappies, aren't you?' said Dr Crumley with a slight sneer.

'Yes. Foreign Office,' I said vaguely, noticing with relief that Sergeant Evans was nosing the Jaguar round the corner of the church. Perhaps when I got back to the office I would have one last look at the file on Sydney Seton before it too was buried.

'Still can't understand about his OBE,' said Potts. 'He was proud of that. Odd thing to do – return it. '

The Jaguar pulled up at the kerb and I said my goodbyes.

'It was because of the Beatles, Mr Potts,' I lied. 'That was all it was.'

# Our Man Marlowe

## ACT 1

'Our man Marlowe,' said the head of Her Majesty's Secret Service, 'was one of the best agents we ever had. He did a particularly good job for us in France. '

'Cambridge man, wasn't he, sir?' asked Smillet, who was not.

'Yes. Recruited him myself.'

'Like the others,' said Smillet, though not softly enough.

'Cambridge has proved very useful,' said the head of the Secret Service ruefully. 'Of course, he gave us problems. You have to expect them from someone like him. Highly intelligent, artistic, an unhealthy fascination with religion and, at the end of the day, he preferred boys to women. It may have had something to do with his death.'

'I thought his killer was known to us, sir. ' Smillet knew he was.

'In more ways than one. There is no doubt that Freiser knifed Marlowe. The lamplighters who found him say it had been made to look like a bar-room brawl. A fist fight followed by one fatal stab wound through the eye. The problem is, Freiser used to work for us too, and that's where it could get tricky. I want you to examine the case and bring me a reason why it happened. Put nothing on paper; just take as long as you need and then report to me in person. You have *carte blanche* to use who you need. The files will be made available to you. That's all.'

Smillet nodded politely and withdrew.

The head of Her Majesty's Secret Service eased himself from behind the wide oak desk and warmed his hands at the open log fire. He spent a moment gazing out of his window at the early morning traffic already clogging the London streets below. Then he took an iron poker from the fire, its four-inch tip red and smoking, and plunged it into the wooden mug of ale his servant had left on the hearth.

A pox on current medical thinking. He had his own remedy for the plague.

## ACT II

'God's blood!'

As he cursed, Smillet hopped to the street corner and steadied himself against the flaking plaster wall of a spice merchant's shop. He removed his right boot and shook it angrily. A dozen pieces of brown shell trickled out into the dust of the street.

'Acorns,' said Smillet to the man with him, pulling the boot back on over holed and threadbare hose. 'They cover the floors of the theatres with them to soak up the piss and the puke of the audience.'

'I thought the theatres were closed, Eminence, because of the plague,' said the man called Chandler meekly.

'They are, as far as the public are concerned, but it's still the place to find the damned players. Why can't the plague take a few actors? No-one would miss them.' Smillet stomped his boot. 'And don't call me Eminence.'

'As your lordship pleases,' wheedled Chandler.

'Now where exactly is this alehouse, man? I have no intention of being in Southwark by the time the Watch comes round.'

'The very next street, my lord.'

Chandler made to take Smillet's arm but drew back when he encountered Smillet's no-nonsense stare, but the officer was grateful for the informer's guidance. He would certainly have walked by the alley that led to the alehouse known as the Angel, an alley reeking of foul smells and seemingly inhabited only by a suspiciously plump black cat.

'This is the unworthy place, my lord,' whined Chandler. 'An alehouse in name only, for the scum of a landlord has to brew his own liquor as his credit is too poor even for the lowest of common brewers. And he brews beer using hops, which he buys from Dutchmen, not honest ale, and has brawled in the street with the ale-conner twice already this month …'

Smillet cut him off with a wave of a gloved hand. His one good ring, a ruby, showed off well against the fading green glove and caught the informer's eye.

'My lord would be advised to hide such precious stones,' he whispered. 'This hovel is a den of Catholic cutthroats.'

'Catholics?' hissed Smillet, tugging at his gloved fingers.

'My lord, that is why they call it the Angel. In the days before the Queen's noble father broke with Rome, this was a papist house, owned by the Church and named for the Virgin Mary. They still meet here even though the good and great King Hal …'

'Yes, yes, enough. You are sure that this is where you saw the man Freiser?'

'Yes, my lord. I name Ingram Freiser as God is my ….'

'We are not in court yet. You are sure you know Freiser by sight?'

'I have seen him before many times when performing a service – a very small service – for my Lord Walsingham, but the other man I know not.'

'This other man, the man you call the Poet, he is here today?'

Chandler nodded enthusiastically.

'Today and every day, my lord. He sits and drinks and eats and writes. Writes poetry; long, long poetry.'

'Then we go in and we have a drink and you point him out to me, but say nothing.'

'Very well, my lord, but …'

'But nothing. Just do as I say and you will be paid. And if you keep your tongue still, you will be paid the amount agreed once more, at the end of thirty days. '

'After you, your Eminence …'

The alehouse was as unappetising and the ale as undrinkable as Chandler had warned. But in the dim light from the few open shutters, Smillet got a good look at the man Chandler called the Poet.

He had taken a corner table and provided his own candles. Three quills, a flask of ink and a length of parchment occupied the parts of the table not covered in apple cores, lumps of bread and empty tankards. The Poet constantly tugged at a wispy beard, and when he looked up from the parchment it was only to gaze out of the window. The only sound came from the scratching of his quill.

That's him, my lord,' whispered Chandler. 'That's the man who gave Freiser the money. '

## ACT III

'Well, Smillet, ' asked the head of Her Majesty's Secret Service, 'what have you found?'

It was September and the nights had drawn in. Smillet waited until a servant had finished lighting the tallow lamps and left before he cleared his throat and began his report.

'With your leave, sir, we know that our man Christopher Marlowe died on the thirtieth day of May. The hand that killed him was that of Ingram Freiser, and it happened at the end of a bout of drinking and gambling in a house of ill-repute run by one Eleanor Bull of Deptford. So much is known about the where and how and who, but little is speculated on the why.'

Receiving a generous nod from his superior, Smillet continued. 'There are four obvious possibilities, sir – perhaps five.'

'Proceed, Smillet.'

'First, it was genuinely a tavern brawl. Marlowe was said to be drunk, as was everyone in the Bull house that day. He had already a conviction for street fighting, and only last year was again bound over to keep the peace.'

'But you do not think it was so simple?'

'I report, sir, I make no conclusion.'

'Second?'

'That it was a quarrel between depraved lovers. Freiser had the same unnatural desires as Marlowe, though of course he came from an even lower station in life. Perhaps some betrayal, some sleight. Men like that can be unpredictable, and they and their sort are naturally secretive.'

'Hence their use as agents. Unlikely. Continue.'

'The fact that Marlowe was a spy. Perhaps Marlow's death was paid for by enemies of the State. The French King? Perhaps the long-suffering King of Spain? '

The head of the Secret Service allowed himself a smile at that.

'Vengeance among spies? No, theirs is an honourable profession, such as it is. Kill, yes, but only if there is an immediate advantage. Revenge as a motive? I don't think so. Not our – their – style. The fourth possibility?'

'A plot within this country, sir. ' And now the older man sat up and took interest. 'Marlowe never actually took holy orders, though he had strong views on religion, sir. Radical views. Views that led to a formal accusation of atheism being made against him by one Richard Baines two days after his death. There is gossip that a plot against our Church – and therefore our Queen – was being formed and involved some of the highest in the land. '

'You mean Sir Walter Raleigh, I suppose?'

Smillet's jaw dropped. While he did not believe a word of the rumour himself, he had thought it at least *fresh* gossip.

'Discount that one,' said the head of the Secret Service. 'Sir Walter gets blamed for most things these days. You said a fifth possibility?'

Smillet recovered himself.

'The most incredible of all, sir. Marlowe was thought of as our leading dramatic writer, but there are more knives looking for shoulder blades in that business than there are in ours. I have proof that Freiser met with and was paid gold by another of these theatre scribes, a rival to Marlowe, anxious to establish himself if and when the theatres reopen. He already has some following, and with Marlowe out of the way, can command higher prices for his work. I have established that he is the son of a glove-maker from Stratford and his name ...'

'Yes, Smillet, I know his name. You do not go to the theatre, do you?'

'No, sir. I consider the players to be coarse, stupid and almost as crude as their audience. ' He realised what he had said. 'Begging your lordship's pardon, that is.'

'Granted. I like this fifth theory, Smillet, I like it very much.'

Smillet recovered his confidence.

'Shall I have the poet brought in for questioning?'

'No, I think not,' said the head of the Secret Service. 'Well, not in the usual sense. I will have him brought to me, but discreetly so that we may talk. I have a few suggestions for him.'

'Suggestions, sir?'

'Yes, Smillet. You may not think much of the theatre, but others do, and some would have us believe it to be quite a powerful weapon when it comes to keeping the people happy. That great unkempt, crude audience of yours – they like to be reassured from time to time. For example, they like to be reminded of past glories of battles and heroic deeds by kings and noblemen of the past. Especially if they happen to be the forebears of our beloved Queen, whose popularity has slipped somewhat since the Armada. I'm sure our poet friend – our ambitious poet friend – will understand we have the same interests at heart.'

Smillet realised his jaw had dropped again.

'Well done, Smillet, ' said the head of the Secret Service. 'You have helped me make an important decision that might prove to be very beneficial to all of us. That will be all.'

London
St Michael's Day
Year of Our Lord 1593

*Warning to Scholars*:

With apologies to John le Carré, Caryl Brahms and S J Simon, this story is fundamentally unsound.

# The Trouble With Trains

'I have always been lucky with trains,' said the dapper little Belgian.

'They're useful,' said the Inspector, 'for getting up to the opera, or establishing alibis.'

'Try not to use them, meself,' said the Aristocrat, adjusting his monocle.

The Inspector looked at the Aristocrat and wearily curled a lip. 'Do you know how close that came to a Bertie Wooster?'

'Yes, I do,' nodded the Aristocrat. 'It's a thin red line we tread in this game, isn't it?'

*But that's the trouble with trains. They encourage you to play games because while you are on them you are cut off from reality; caught in a funnel of time and space beyond your control. And if the train is stopped – stuck in an unseasonably heavy snowfall in the deserted Lincolnshire countryside – and you're only on it in the first place because you are playing a game …*

'How did we get into this?' the Inspector asked, but he was staring out of the window, the squares of the carriages' lights reflected in the piled snowdrifts alongside the track.

'You know that very well, old boy,' said the Belgian. 'We have to keep the writers happy, as well as the fans.'

'Watch it, your accent's slipping,' snarled the Inspector.

'Well just be thankful you do not 'ave to talk like zis.'

The Inspector nodded. 'Yes, I suppose that's something.'

'Oh come on, you two,' said the Aristocrat. 'The conference was fun and we didn't have to sit through all three days. We had some decent meals – and breakfast in the hotel wasn't half bad. I put away enough this morning to feed half the Royal

Shakespeare Company in a lean patch. Look on it as a free holiday.'

'In Leeds?' challenged the Inspector.

'Well, yes, there was that. But they've laid on this special train, and you don't often get to travel in authentic 1930s Pullmans these days, do you? And at least we have some privacy and the champagne keeps arriving every time we press that little buzzer thing ...'

'And even British Rail should be able to chill it properly, with all this snow and ice about,' observed the Belgian.

'But what about *them*?'

'Oh, I suppose we'll have to go and mingle with Second Class sooner or later,' conceded the Aristocrat, 'and sing for our supper. It's the crime writers who keep us going, you know.'

'True,' said the Belgian, 'though *en masse* they can be quite daunting.'

*Trapped on a British Rail special train in an unseasonably heavy snowfall. One Pullman car of sanity where the guests of honour dined and rested in private before rejoining the two hundred crime writers busily stripping the buffet bar at the other end of the train. Keeping their spirits up until the track was cleared, all of them delighted that the delay would give them longer to rub shoulders with the embodiment of their imaginations. Some of them posted as guards along the train to catch the first glimpse of their heroes, who sat in their reserved compartment. A locked room within a much longer, brightly lit, immobile, locked tube.*

'Was everything satisfactory, gentlemen?' asked the white-coated steward from the compartment doorway.

'Simply splendid,' said the Aristocrat.

'We don't get many chances to push the boat out on the catering side,' said the steward chattily. 'That's why we like these special trains. The Royals have travelled in this carriage, you know. That was a trip, I can tell you.'

'Perhaps zat one was – how you say – on time?' the little Belgian asked softly.

'Well, no, actually … Can I get you anything else, gentlemen? We may be here for some time. May I be so bold as to suggest a *tisane*, a bottle of Tokay and a pint of bitter?' He grinned inanely.

'Three brandies – big jobs,' said the Inspector curtly.

'Certainly, sir'. The steward took his leave.

'I suppose we could do a question-and-answer session to entertain our hosts,' said the Aristocrat thoughtfully.

'Again?' sighed the Belgian.

'How about bloody charades?'

'Don't be so depressed, old boy.'

'I thought I was supposed to be.'

'Well, we'll have to do something for them. Only manners, after all.'

The dapper Belgian stabbed at his last piece of cheese with a knife. 'I think this cheese came with the Pullman car,' he said to himself. Then, to his fellows: 'How about getting them to exercise –'

'If he says "little grey cells" I'll hit him,' the Inspector whispered.

'– their imaginations. Let us give them a scenario for a murder. And let us begin with a train stranded in an unseasonably heavy snowfall.'

And that was when the shot rang out.


*Of course, it might have sounded like a shot, though many would have described it as a muffled pop. That's the trouble with trains: they distort things. But there was no doubt about the scream or the noise of a compartment door slamming open that followed.*


The three heroes stared at each other.

'It's a set-up,' said the Inspector.

'One of their stupid games, no doubt,' said the Aristocrat.

'But did you not just say,' the Belgian said cuttingly, 'that it was only good manners to join in their games?'

The Aristocrat flipped his eyes up to the ancient light fittings and the net luggage racks. 'I suppose we have to go through with it, however embarrassing. Come on, then.'

The Belgian slid open the compartment door and poked his balding, not-quite-egg-shaped head out into the corridor. He turned back to his companions and shrugged.

As the Inspector and the Aristocrat joined him, the steward appeared to their right, bearing a tray of drinks.

'Sorry for the delay, gents. Had to take an order to the kitchen for Compartment B.'

The heroes looked at each other knowingly. The Belgian held up the forefinger of his right hand, indicating for the steward to wait. He wished he had remembered the pearl-grey gloves.

The Aristocrat raised a finger also and pointed to the second compartment to their left, the door of which lay open.

'Let's get on with it,' said the Inspector, squeezing between his colleagues.

There was a table laid out for dinner in Compartment B exactly as their own had been, but dinner had yet to be served. Apart from two glasses, an open bottle of champagne in an ice bucket and the cutlery, there was nothing on the table except the slumped form of a well-dressed middle-aged man.

'*Voilà*,' said the Belgian.

'The body,' said the Inspector.

'I wonder how long we've got?' said the Aristocrat.

'Bloody hell,' said the steward.

The Inspector stepped into the compartment.

'Touch nothing!' snapped the small Belgian.

'Oh, give us a break.'

'What's going on?' whispered the steward.

'Did you pass anyone in the corridor when you brought the drinks?' asked the Aristocrat casually, helping himself to one of the brandy glasses.

'No, not a soul. Is he dead?' The steward stretched his neck to see over the Belgian's shoulder, the remaining brandies dipping dangerously.

'And what is back there?'

'Just the old-fashioned guard's van, then the real guard's van and mail coach.'

'Then unless our criminal is a member of British Rail staff, our case is almost solved,' agreed the Belgian.

The Inspector put a hand to the slumped man's neck, then recoiled. He turned to his fellow travellers, his face white and his eyes wide.

'What's the matter, old boy? Don't agree?' The Aristocrat sipped his brandy. 'Want to spin it out a bit? Establish motive and all that? No-one went by our compartment, so they must have gone to the rear of ...'

'No ... no ...' The Inspector rubbed his hand down his jacket. The hand that had touched the body. 'He really is dead. It's a real stiff.'

'*Mon Dieu*,' breathed the Belgian, forgetting himself for a moment.

'Nice try, old boy. Well, we'll go along with it, won't we? Play the game and all that?'

'Hang on.' The little Belgian stooped over the corpse. 'He's right. This guy's not breathing and look – there's blood!'

'Hell's teeth.'

'Quick, pull the communication cord,' said the steward.

'We're not moving, you idiot.' The Inspector relieved him of another glass and downed the contents. 'Go and find the guard, or the Fat Controller, or whoever can take charge. Move it!'

The steward scurried off to the rear of the train.

The three heroes stood and stared at the body, then at each other.

'No-one could have laid this on,' said the Inspector.

'It would be fun to try and solve it before the guard comes,' said the Aristocrat.

'Then let us try,' said the Belgian. 'Why not?'

The Inspector turned and gently hit his forehead on the edge of the compartment door. 'Are you out of your mind? Who do you think we are?'

'My point – *précisément*!'

*Does the train leave the platform or the platform leave the train? Isolated and self-contained, reality can blur in trains. That's the trouble with them.*

'But even if this were real – the body is, I know – but if we really were who we are ...'

'The victim was called Cooper,' said the Aristocrat languidly.

The others followed the line of his eyes to the luggage rack and the expensive suitcase complete with matching leather address fob.

'Mr A D Cooper, of Redhill in Surrey,' the Aristocrat read.

'Then who was the woman? Do we *cherchez la femme*? It is traditional,'

'Woman?'

'*Bien sûr*. This is a smoking compartment and look, in the ashtray – a filter tip with lipstick.'

'Not to mention her coat on the other rack,' said the Inspector reluctantly. 'What about the wound?'

The three heroes formed a semicircle around the man slumped over the table and, in unison, bent their knees until three pairs of heroic eyes were level with the head.

'It's difficult to see without moving the head,' said the Aristocrat.

'We must touch nothing,' said the Belgian.

'It looks like he's been shot between the eyes,' said the Inspector. 'There's a round mark, like a coin. And ... blood.'

'But not much,' said the Belgian.

'How much should there be?' asked the Aristocrat. 'That was a serious question. I've never actually seen ...'

'Neither have I,' said the other two as they stood up.

Somewhere down the train a door slammed.

'So what do the little ... *Pardon*. What can we deduce? He was a rich man?'

'Comfortable enough to hire this compartment and lay on a dinner for the missing lady,' said the Aristocrat. 'What's our betting? Stockbroker?'

'Advertising man, judging by the suit,' said the Inspector.

'Was it his wife, or a bit on the side?'

'Someone he knew very well,' said the Belgian. 'We heard no raised voices, there is no sign of a struggle. He was not expecting to be attacked.'

'Looks more like a celebration, with the champagne,' the Inspector observed. 'But the glasses are clean, so they never got that far.'

'Perhaps they argued over the menu,' suggested the Aristocrat facetiously.

'The British Rail do not provide sufficient choice for an argument,' said the Belgian dismissively. 'Yet if this was planned, how could the woman – wife or mistress – know that the train would stop here? This was not planned.'

'So it was an impulse killing.'

'A crime of passion? The end of an affair, perhaps?'

'You mean he told her he was dumping her so she whipped out a gun and shot him?'

'*Un petit* ... conventional. We should expect the unexpected.'

'You mean she dumped him, so he shot himself out of remorse?'

'Stranger things have happened, old boy.'

'In fiction, maybe.'

'Then where's the bloody gun?'

'Removed by some devilishly ingenious automatic device, no doubt. Or carried by the woman's real husband, who shoots his rival, grabs the fair lady and leaps off the train into a snow drift, leaving two sets of prints in the snow ...'

'*Mais* – that is what she wants us to think, for this woman is very clever. Very clever indeed.'

'You mean ... there was no second man?'

'What about a second woman?'

'What about *no woman at all*? After all, there is no handbag here. A woman is likely to leave a coat, but not a handbag, or is that what we were supposed to think? Could a man get away with wearing a fur coat such as the one on the luggage rack?'

'What if …?'

'Excuse me, gentlemen,' said a new voice from the doorway. They turned to see a young man in a railway issue anorak.

'I'm Blunt.'

'I'll bet,' said the Inspector.

'Of British Rail Transport Police. We sometimes get gatecrashers on these special trains, or perhaps over-keen trainspotters.'

'So you disguise yourself as one,' breathed the Aristocrat.

Blunt stepped into the compartment and surveyed the scene. 'Ah yes, I see it now.'

The three heroes looked at each other and then at Blunt.

'How it happened. Poor Mr Cooper there, how tragic. Of course he always knew he suffered from a rare bone disease that meant he had a particularly thin skull, unlike most people. But who would have thought that the champagne cork going off like that and hitting him between the eyes would have killed him? A million-to-one blow. Quite fantastic.' Blunt sighed briefly. 'All in a day's work to you chaps, though, I suppose. I hope that's not as heartless as it sounds.'

The three heroes examined their shoes, or in one case, his spats.

'You must have noticed that the champagne was open and the front of Mr Cooper's shirt was soaked with the stuff. I expect you'd worked it all out, eh? What a pity it should happen on their wedding anniversary. Ah, there's the weapon.'

Blunt crouched and put a hand under the table. He emerged with a champagne cork still surrounded by its metal foil and wire cage.

'I think one of you may have kicked it there,' said Blunt.

'How …?' started three voices.

'Mrs Cooper ran straight to the guard's van and told us all about it. Quite distraught she was, and I found her story a bit much at first, I can tell you. Still, it was so crazy it must be true. She'd hardly make it up, would she? Not with you three in the next compartment!'

*And when even fantasy begins to blur, what then? It is a constant trouble with trains.*

'We'll be moving again in a minute. The line's clear and we've radioed ahead so we can pick up a doctor in Grantham and the police will meet us in London. I would appreciate it if you would help calm the passengers until we get there. I know it will take quite a performance, all those crime writers wanting to know how you found a real live body. Well, you know what I mean. And no doubt the press will be waiting for us in London.'

The three heroes looked at each other.

'Did you say you could radio ahead?' asked the Inspector.

'Yes,' said Blunt, wondering why three pairs of eyes had twinkled and three slow smiles appeared.

'Can I call my agent?' they said together.

*Back in reality the only real trouble with trains emerges. They shake up good champagne cruelly.*

# New Year's Eve

*Deja vu? Doppelganger?* Happenstance? A trick of the light? A ghost?

Even I, so morbidly unimaginative, found the escalators at Holborn Underground station an unlikely place for a haunting, especially at just after eight o'clock in the morning of a normal working day. But I was convinced it was her: Eve. Or her double, her twin or, yes, her ghost. For it could not be Eve, not actually her.

The resemblance was remarkable, though. The same physical colouring, the identical hairstyle, the same bright colours in her dress. Loud colours; blowsy colours; tarty colours, my mother would have called them. The same excess of lipstick drawn to form a bright red heart on her face as a blatant sexual advertisement.

And there she was on the down escalator, oblivious to me and the rest of the world. Or was she? My routine for the last 33 years was well known to those who wished to know. Apart from accidents and delays, I was always at Holborn at this time in the morning.

So was it coincidence that Eve's twin or double was going down to the Central Line as I travelled up from it? Was she there by design, a reconstruction of Eve deliberately sent to provoke me?

She could not be Eve herself, unless she really was a ghost, and that I dismissed immediately. I am neither superstitious nor forgetful. I remember killing Eve quite clearly.

Eve had been a disruptive influence from the day she had joined the Accounts Department and I had told Mr Purvis so.

'Don't judge the girl's work by her manners, Bradbury,' he

had said impishly, 'just because she was rude about you in the canteen yesterday.'

'I don't know what you mean, Mr Purvis.' He knew full well that Thursday was my library day and I never ate in the staff restaurant.

'Well, she observed – rather loudly – that you had obviously been born at the age of 42 and had been striving for a mature look ever since.' Purvis had difficulty keeping his face straight. 'Come on, Bradbury, you are a bit of a starchy-knickers at times. Get with it, swing with the times a little.'

Of course I should never have let it worry me; never have let that right little madam (my mother's words) annoy me.


That night I waited at Holborn for an hour to see if her evening journey paralleled mine, but she never appeared. Not her, nor her bright red mini-skirt, the exact double of the one Eve had worn on her last day alive.

They were, so the Newsbites told me, back in fashion yet again.


On reflection, Eve's campaign against me was certainly not premeditated.

There was no point in her playing office politics; her situation was temporary and very junior. In fact, if memory serves, she replaced one of our junior bookkeepers who was on maternity leave. My firm was very progressive in such matters even in those days.

Perhaps too progressive, as standards slipped and discipline became a farce. My father, proud to be one of the last wearers of winged collars (outside a court of law), would have turned in his grave at the disrespect Eve showed me.

But bodies do not turn in their graves, nor do they rise up and go haunting. Once they are under the ground they stay there.

Unless they are found. And so few are.

I spotted her the next morning at 8.06. The following day at 8.07 and the next at 8.01. On the Friday, having lied brazenly to Personnel in regard to a 'forgotten' dental appointment, I followed her.

She used Holborn as a change-over, taking the Central Line eastbound. I pushed myself into the graffiti-covered carriage behind hers. The sign above the sliding door said this carriage had been given a purple aura and the spray-painting was in the style of the constellation of Leo.

As it pulled away, I stumbled against one of the beret-wearing Guardian Angels, who now travel ten per train under the by-laws of London Transport PLC. I apologised, as one had to, and found a strap to hang on that enabled me to keep an eye on her through the window of the connecting door.

I could see her profile perfectly – the hair, the rouge, the heart of a mouth, just like Eve's. She wore sunphones – sunglasses combined with personal stereos – that cut her off from the rest of the world, just as the rest of the world did.

She stood as the in-carriage Newsbite screen announced that we were one hundred metres from Broadgate. I followed her along the platform and to the up escalator, at times so close I could have called her. She was so close I could tell she was perhaps four to five centimetres shorter than Eve and perhaps two kilos heavier.

At the top of the escalator, she waved a ticket in front of the electronic eye and strode off across the concourse. I fumbled out my season ticket (fortunately good for as far as Broadgate) and by the time I was through the eye she was striding away and I had to hurry to keep her mini-skirt, green today, in sight.

I wheezed in relief as she turned off the concourse into a medical booth. The liquid crystal display above it read: 'Homeopathic, Holistic and Reflexologist MediCentre – Alexander Technique – NHS Credits Accepted.'

Through the glass front I saw her greet co-workers and exchange pleasantries and mantras with the patients waiting not only on the chairs provided, but in an orderly queue already stretching some forty metres from the doors. I saw her disappear behind the herbal counter and through a door marked 'Private', to emerge, moments later, wearing a white coat with deep pockets. Hanging from her neck was a spell pouch in red suede, and she carried an electronic clipboard.

This was not Eve; not even meant to be Eve. She had not been trying to trap me or entice me, and deep down I had known it all along.

A police reconstruction was unthinkable after all this time.


Eve had tormented me mercilessly during that autumn of loud music, small cars and outrageous fashion. Most of her references went over my head, but the tone of them hit home. And there were the blatant sexual come-ons that ended in giant pieces of insubordination or downright rudeness, and always in front of the rest of the office. It seemed to be the norm of behaviour for the younger staff, though I was not that much older than they in those days. It was simply that I had had to take on more responsibility at an early age.

I certainly had a more responsible attitude to work, which was why I was in the office at 6.00 that evening.

That year, Christmas fell on a Saturday, and by tradition staff were allowed to leave at 3.00 pm on the Friday, if their work was up to date. Eve's, naturally, was not, but this had not stopped her leading the juniors round to a local pub at lunchtime and not returning; no doubt having persuaded the landlord to remain open all afternoon in contravention of the licensing laws.

She was probably as surprised to see me still at my desk as I was to see her stagger into the empty office. I heard her ridiculously high, wooden-soled boots clack across the linoleum and looked up. She was heading for a bag of shopping she had left at the side of her desk with a drunken sway that made her short skirt ride up even higher.

She saw me and raised an accusing finger at me, then burst into a roar of loud, vulgar laughter.

She did not say anything as such, but I suppose it was true to say she died laughing.

Had they come, I would have told the police that there had been no question of sexual interference.

But then, they had ways of knowing that. If I had volunteered the information, they would have known I was telling the truth about Eve.

And the others.

Eve was the first one I had actually known, and the dangers of being detected had therefore been that much greater.

I left her body slumped inside the fire exit at the rear of the office and hurried home to collect my car. Late that night I buried her out in the soft tidal marshes near the Southend railway line. I can remember the exact spot for Eve.

Not so for the others. Depending upon the year, they could have been in Rendlesham Forest in Suffolk, or the New Forest, or even as far as the Cambridgeshire Fens. And there was always the Thames (though she was found) and many an unattended building site as the London skyline changed thanks to the high-rise developers.

After Eve, I sat at home alone and made myself a promise.

If the police came by New Year's Eve, then I would confess everything. But as the chimes of midnight introduced a new year, then I would be free. Those new year chimes from Big Ben were my sanctuary.

New Year's Eve became my justification – my talisman, as I have learned to call it.

For the police never did come. So many young girls simply disappear. They still do.

And even though it has been a few years now, I will invoke my New Year's Eve talisman again, and then I will be free for another year.

I will spend Christmas alone again and then settle down in front of my flatscreen and watch the traditional New Year's Eve celebrations of people enjoying themselves all over the world.

This year should be special.

Not every New Year's Eve brings in a new century.

# MacEvoy's Revenge

*'Croydon? This time of night? Ooooh ...' The cab driver sucked in air like a drowning man. 'That 'll be thirty quid, guv.'*
*'But I've only got seventeen,' said MacEvoy.*

It had been a bad night.

It had been a disastrous night.

Wipe out; a slaughter; they had seen him coming and taken him to the cleaners without passing 'Go' and certainly without collecting £200. The Gods of Chance had not only deserted him, they had left the answerphone on and were refusing to pick up.

He had lost the lot; well, everything except the seventeen pounds in change he had reclaimed from the various pockets of his dinner-suit and, in the case of four pound coins, a tip he had left for a waitress who had been too slow to collect it.

Not that he had been drinking anything stronger than tonic water. He never drank when he was working – gambling – except perhaps a large scotch and water to end the evening, to celebrate his cashing in of chips, the counting of his winnings, the end of a hard night's work, while he calculated his percentage spread.

That was the System, and the only system that counted. Number patterns, card counting, red-only spreads; they were systems for the social gambler, the amateur. MacEvoy was a professional. He gambled for a living and he played the only system that mattered: the fifteen percent rule.

Fifteen percent of his allocated evening stake after four hours and he would quit. Fifteen percent down and he would also quit. His end-of-year target was to be fifteen percent up on the previous year. That was enough. Don't be greedy.

Of course it never worked, or at least not perfectly. The best he had done in five years was to be eight percent up. But that was enough for him, even though it had not been for Mary.

Mary was the problem; that was why he had lost so badly, breaking his own golden rule.

For a week now she hadn't let up, giving MacEvoy grievous bodily harm of the earholes, going on and on, nagging, threatening, even taking a swing at him one morning – not with anything as clichéd as a rolling pin or as serious as a bottle of milk, but with a rolled up copy of the *Racing Post*. And then in frustration, she had shredded it to pieces before his eyes before he'd had time to read it.

That was when the rot had set in. Not a sniff since, not a horse better than fourth, not a single number up on five lottery cards, a spate of away wins that had torn up the form on the pools coupon. Even the fruit machine down the pub had eaten twenty pounds without spitting once, and then a spotty oik had jackpotted with a single 20p coin he'd got in change from a pint of lager.

And all because she had found his accounts book.

*'Sorry, guv, it's thirty quid to Croydon this time of night.'*

*'Aw, come on, mate, I've had a nightmare. They've fleeced me in there. I've lost a packet. I'm talking third mortgage here, mate, give us a break.'*

*'Not my fault, guv. Thirty quid.'*

For years he had recorded his progress in one of the little red accounts books that had suddenly proved so popular now that self-assessment of income tax had come in. At the end of each year he had drawn a double line in red ink and worked out how close he had come to his fifteen percent ahead target.

How Mary had found the book, hidden in plain view on a shelf of airport thrillers he knew she despised and ignored, he wasn't quite sure. But find it she had and appalled she had been.

Not, as he would have expected, at the recent poor showing of his system: the fact that he was nowhere near fifteen percent ahead. What Mary had gone spare over – totally ballistic – was the turnover.

'You gambled over twenty thousand pounds, you shit!' she had yelled at him.

So he had, but he hadn't lost twenty thousand. You win, you lose, you play the spread. Didn't she understand anything?

*'So how far can you take me for seventeen?'*

*'Brixton? Somewhere like that?' The cab driver stared straight ahead, refusing to make eye contact.*

*'Give me a break, man, it's three o'clock in the morning and I'm desolate.'*

*'Sorry, guv. Like I told you, this time of night ...'*

Yes, yes, but she'd *known* he was a gambler when she'd married him five years before.

She had accepted the fact that he worked the casinos three nights a week, ringing the changes around nine venues, never too regular a visitor or too big a winner to become a nuisance. Never drunk, always polite, the star of a million feet of security videotape.

So maybe she hadn't realised about the afternoons in the betting shops and the pubs, following his own circuit of pubs where new fruit machines had been installed – his theory being that pay-outs were more generous in the first few days of a new machine to encourage the punters.

What did she think he did all day while she was at work?

Had he ever complained when she'd worked late or even gone on sales trips abroad with her boss, the absobloodylutely perfect Paul Parrish?

Other husbands would have put their foot down, or at the least been suspicious. But MacEvoy had trusted Mary because he knew human nature. He had studied it for years across a green baize table. He had out-bluffed the best card players and dealers in London, but he had also retained control of himself. He knew when to quit; that was his great strength. In the study of human nature he had graduated with honours in himself.

*'That's yer lot,' said the cabbie, reaching for the meter. 'Seventeen quid exactly.'*

*In the back of the cab MacEvoy stared out at the shiny wet streets.*

*'Where are we?'*

*'Upper Norwood. That's it, guv.'*

*MacEvoy leaned into the glass partition and pleaded into the driver's ear.*

*'Oh, go on, mate, take us the rest of the way. I've been hung out to dry tonight. Nothing's gone right. I've lost a packet, the wife's not talking to me ...'*

*'Yeah, yeah. Seventeen quid, squire. I told you. Croydon, this time of night, was thirty quid.'*

*MacEvoy sighed and handed over the coins that had weighed down his pockets and become slippery with sweat as he had counted and recounted them on the journey.*

*He got out of the cab and turned up the collar of his dinner jacket against the rain.*

*'I just hope somebody smiles on you when you're down on your luck,' he said.*

*But the cabbie didn't look at him, just swung the wheel and turned in the road and disappeared into the night.*

*MacEvoy walked home.*

MacEvoy came awake just before noon. He was on the sofa covered by the spare duvet that normally lived in the cupboard under the stairs for just such an occasion. After the first year of marriage he had camped downstairs rather than disturb Mary whenever he returned from a shift at the casino in the small hours.

She would have gone to work hours ago. Gone to work as personal assistant to Mr Paul Perfect Parrish at his perfectly successful management consultancy in the City.

A man less in control would have worried about his wife's devotion to her work. But MacEvoy had looked at the situation and weighed the odds. Parrish was old enough to be Mary's father and had two broken marriages and four kids behind him. Too much emotional baggage there for Mary, despite the trappings of wealth and security: the Jaguar Sovereign, the holidays abroad, the big house in Dulwich.

Why was he even thinking such things now?

The spat with Mary would pass. He would cook something for her for when she came home that night, before he went to work himself.

In the kitchen, he flipped on the kettle and opened the fridge door.

Inside was a carton of orange juice and about half a bottle of milk. Neither were cool, let alone chilled, and there was nothing else.

It must be on the blink, thought MacEvoy. Mary had moved things out until the repairmen came.

The doorbell chimed.

'Come about the fridge, mister,' said the youth at the door. He had a two-wheel trolley with him, and in the road was parked a white Electricity Board van with the back door open.

'That was quick,' said MacEvoy, moving aside so the youth could wheel the trolley into the hall. 'Through there.'

'That's handy,' said the electricity man, 'she's defrosted it. You'd be surprised how many don't. Leave 'em in a right state, some of 'em.'

MacEvoy grunted in agreement and busied himself making a cup of instant as the youth pulled the fridge onto the lip of his trolley and heaved it away from the wall.

'She's unplugged it too. Dead thoughtful. She said there'd be no trouble. There usually is.'

MacEvoy looked at him.

'What are you doing?'

'Repossessing, mister. Sorry you couldn't keep up with the payments.'

MacEvoy found the note and was reading it when the men came for the flatscreen television and the VCR. There were two of them and they were big and expecting the worst. People might let their fridges go without a murmur, but taking the television amounted to a declaration of war.

They had no trouble with MacEvoy. He just sat on the sofa reading a single sheet of typed paper he had found in the centre of Mary's bed.

Brian

I have put up with a lot these last few years, but what has hurt most is that you just don't seem to notice me anymore. Have you even noticed I have gone? Will you be surprised to hear that I am going away with Paul? You were never one to hold a grudge. Revenge doesn't play any percentages, you used to say. I'm cutting my losses, so should you.

Mary

The man carrying the video recorder nodded to him as he left, but MacEvoy remained inert, clutching Mary's note as if trying to focus in an eye test.

The man with the video let himself out but didn't bother to close the door.

The men coming for the washing machine had just arrived.


She was so *sure*. That was what got to MacEvoy.

She was sure he would do nothing, just accept it. Sure he wouldn't waste time and energy on revenge. Sure he wouldn't do anything stupid. Being sure of that meant she could leave with a clear conscience and sleep easy in Paul Parrish's bed.

Her very certainty that he would just go with the flow of things, that was what hurt.

*Don't talk certainties to a gambler, Mary.*

MacEvoy taking revenge would be totally out of character. There was, as Mary had said, no profit in it, no system, no sense. That would show her. He would have his revenge on all of them.

It had started with her finding his accounts book and him trying to explain how sensible his system was, never overreaching, just playing for a decent spread. Their fight over that had seen her turn to Paul Parrish and his luck desert him. He had lost over eight grand the night before, more than he had ever lost at one sitting before.

She had broken his concentration and the casino had taken advantage of that, leaving him short of even the taxi fare home. And the cab driver putting him out like that, making him walk home and leaving him so exhausted he had slept like a log, not hearing a thing as Mary must had packed and loaded her car and left him.

They were all to blame.

MacEvoy knew where Paul Parrish lived, had even been there once with Mary to a party, but he checked the address in the phone book just to be sure.

Then he took the Yellow Pages and let his fingers do the walking through the alphabet until he reached 'Waste Disposal', and reached for the phone.

Upstairs, he took a clean white shirt from the wardrobe in what had been their bedroom. As he did so, he pulled open the wardrobe door on Mary's side and saw a rail full of dresses, slips and blouses.

With the kitchen scissors MacEvoy slit every dress lengthwise, bunched the material of the blouses and cut holes front and back and slashed inverted V-shapes into two silk slips. He left all the clothes on their hangers so that at first sight there was nothing amiss.

Satisfied, he turned to Mary's dressing-table and gathered up an armful of cosmetics, creams and lotions, unscrewing caps and removing bottle stops as he moved to the bathroom.

He was pouring the second bottle of perfume into the toilet

bowl when he saw the note sellotaped to the mirror.

> Chuck all the cosmetics down the loo and give any clothes of mine to the Oxfam shop. There's nothing here I want anymore.

She hadn't even bothered to sign this one.

'Oh, bugger,' said MacEvoy.

By the time his minicab arrived, he was ready. Over his dinner-suit he wore a crumpled raincoat, the right hand pocket weighed down with an ancient one-inch diameter spanner.

He had found the spanner in the tool box under the stairs and it had given him his third plan. He had opened the tool box to retrieve his emergency stash of £300, enough cash to see him through until he could get to one of his various building society accounts in the morning.

He checked his watch and found there was just time, if the cab got a clear run, for a brief diversion.

The minicab driver shrugged his shoulders and nodded. If the punter wanted to go via Dulwich, fair enough, it was his money. But he had no idea where Duffy Street was.

MacEvoy did, though, and he directed the driver to it and told him to slow down as they approached a detached Victorian villa set back from the road.

The minicab had to slow down anyway, to pull around the police car and a Ford Galaxy parked outside the entrance to the drive.

Blocking the drive, MacEvoy saw, was a huge metal skip, one of the biggest, he knew, you could hire, that could take over nine cubic yards of building rubble. Standing in its shadow were two uniformed policemen, hats pushed back, barely able to keep their faces straight. Arguing with them were a young Indian couple, the woman quite strikingly beautiful, a child holding her hand and a baby balanced on her hip.

Above her head, framing the scene, was an estate agent's pole

and board. The words 'FOR SALE' had been covered with a strip
banner saying 'SOLD'.

MacEvoy sank back into his seat.

'Oh, shit.'


She was still in there; the minicab had made it. That was
definitely Mary's blue Escort in the small private car-park shared
by Parrish Management Services Ltd.

MacEvoy knew there were security cameras on the car-park
and knew that Mary could come out of work and round the
corner any moment. He had no intention of confronting her yet.

He unbuttoned his raincoat and pushed the heavy spanner
through the lining of his pocket so the jaws showed through. If
anyone saw him, he was a man in a dinner-suit walking with his
hands in his pockets.

He walked across the car-park, angling toward the Escort. As
his coat brushed the headlight, he stiffened his arm and through
his pocket felt the spanner dig into the paintwork. He dragged it
the length of the car, and only when clear did he risk a look back.

Parallel scratch lines one inch apart ran the length of the car.

MacEvoy smiled to himself and then jumped as two girls –
early twenties, short skirts, chatting to each other – almost
collided with him.

'Sorry,' he muttered, and moved out of their way.

They hardly noticed him, breaking step but not conversation
to avoid him.

'It's really good to be independent, though,' one was saying to
the other. 'And it was such a bargain! I couldn't believe what
Mary said she wanted for it last week. I mean, I know she's got
the Range Rover now, but ... Jesus Bleedin' Christ! Look at that!
Some bastard ...'

MacEvoy hurried around the corner, looking for a bin in
which to drop the spanner.

'Oh, fuck,' he said under his breath.

By nine o'clock, MacEvoy was drunk in a pub off Grosvenor Square. He hadn't eaten all day, he hadn't washed or shaved either. He must look a sight in his dinner jacket and greasy raincoat. He could tell from the way the other customers avoided him that he was beginning to smell.

Perfect.

He was ready for Plan Four.

There are few reliable ways of taking revenge on a casino. In fact, MacEvoy knew, there are only two: break the bank or, failing that, annoy the hell out of their best customer.

By midnight, MacEvoy had his mark.

He had flashed his membership card at Security and the dinner- suit had done the rest. He had bought five £50 chips and spent an hour clicking them in his hand, resisting the temptation to play, just circulating through the rooms watching, occasionally nodding at a blackjack dealer or a croupier he recognised.

He broke the habit of a lifetime and took large scotch and waters from the hostesses. He chain-smoked cigarettes, letting the ash fall down the front of his shirt. He gobbled any snacks and savouries going. Not enough to sober him up, just enough to leave a patina of crumbs on the lapels of his jacket.

By the time he spotted his victim, his swaying was not an act.

The mark was a young Italian, obviously rich and with an entourage of two blondes who giggled and wiggled in all the right places.

MacEvoy watched the Italian lose over a thousand at blackjack before boredom set in. One of the blondes pointed toward the roulette table, as they always did.

MacEvoy made his move so that it would seem as if it was pure coincidence that he and the Italian would sit next to each other. The bump of the chairs, the apology, the leaning in, breathing whisky fumes, lighting a cigarette under his nose.

The realisation that one of the Italian's bimbos might want to sit in. The slapping of the knee, indicating, 'Sit here'. The cold snub.

The Italian bet columns and fours, the blondes went red and black alternately. MacEvoy feinted as if to place a chip, then seemed to think the better of it.

MacEvoy ordered more free drinks, demanded champagne for the blondes. The Italian cut him dead.

MacEvoy flicked cigarette ash onto the Italian's dinner jacket, apologising profusely as he brushed it worse. The Italian gave the croupier a killer look. The croupier asked if MacEvoy was going to place a bet. MacEvoy slapped the Italian on the shoulder and said something stupid about letting his new friend warm the wheel.

The Italian lost steadily, the blondes won alternately, but moved out of reach when one of them felt MacEvoy's hand on her thigh.

The Italian was getting testy, the croupier was asking louder if MacEvoy wanted to play.

In the mirror above the wheel, MacEvoy saw two of the casino's security men advancing toward him. They couldn't – wouldn't – touch him if he was playing; that was a house rule, gambling etiquette, custom and practice through the ages.

MacEvoy flipped a chip onto the table. The croupier said 'No more bets' and the ball clicked and bounced over the wheel.

MacEvoy leaned into the Italian's face and slurred: 'How much for one of the girls, then? Just for an hour, outside, up against the wall?'

The Italian recoiled from MacEvoy's stagnant breath, and either he had not understood or he thought he had misheard, but either way, he had had enough and he snarled and swore quietly and made to stand up.

'Eighteen,' said the croupier. 'Winner.'

MacEvoy snapped his face back to the table and registered his chip full square on number 18. Single-number bet. A crazy way to gamble. Odds of 35 (or 36 depending on the house) to one.

The croupier piled £50 chips and pushed them across the table.

MacEvoy forgot the Italian and snapped his fingers for a hostess, ordering a large orange juice with plenty of ice.

He squared himself up to the table and began to examine the table as if seeing it for the first time.

To hell with Plan Four, he thought. Mary had been right. There was no percentage in revenge.

It was 2.00 am when he quit, and he was £17,000 up on the night. No-one had seen such a run for years. MacEvoy had not been able to put a chip or a card wrong. The casino management had even loaned him an electric razor and use of the executive washroom when he had taken a break to freshen-up. The Italian had gone, but the two blondes had remained. MacEvoy had given them a £100 chip each. It seemed only fair.

MacEvoy cashed in his winnings and stuffed bundles of notes into every pocket. Security asked if he wanted to bank it, but he declined.

The doorman asked if he wanted a cab, but MacEvoy said no, tipped him just the same, and walked toward the rank of black Austin cabs sharing a pitch outside with the hotel next door.

Sober now, and high on the adrenalin of winning, MacEvoy had spotted, third in the rank, the cabbie who had dropped him in Norwood 24 hours before.

Plan Five came together in his head as he walked toward the first cab in the rank and the cabbie lowered his window.

'Can you do me Croydon, please?' asked MacEvoy.

'Croydon, guv? This time of night?' The cabbie tried to look concerned. 'That'll be thirty quid.'

MacEvoy kept his hands in his pockets, convinced that bundles of cash were about to fall from him like leaves in autumn.

'But I've only got seventeen,' he said lamely.

'Sorry, guv, thirty quid, like I said.'

MacEvoy leaned in toward the open window and lowered his voice.

'Take me to Croydon and I'll give you a blow job when we get there.'

The cabbie's voice contorted into fury.

'Fuck off out of it, you pervert!'

'Okay, okay, keep your hair on.'

MacEvoy backed off, took his hands out of his pockets and showed the palms; classic appeasement gesture.

He approached the second cab in the rank, flashing a glance to see if the first cabbie was going to get out and make an issue of it.

The second cabbie had his window down as MacEvoy approached.

'Yes, guv?'

'I want to go to Croydon,' said MacEvoy, all innocence, no trouble.

The second cabbie pursed his lips.

'Croydon? This time of night? That's a thirty quid job, guv.'

'But I've only got seventeen,' said MacEvoy meekly.

'Tough shit, mate. Thirty quid this time of night.'

MacEvoy leaned in to the window and whispered.

'Look, I'll give you the seventeen and do you a blow job on the way, okay?'

The cabbie narrowed his eyes, sized up MacEvoy and hissed: 'Piss off, sicko. Don't even breathe on my fucking cab.'

The window slid up and MacEvoy turned, a look of desperation on his face, toward the third cab.

The driver did not recognise him from the night before. MacEvoy had gambled on that, but it was a safe, percentage, bet.

'Can you do me Croydon?' he asked.

'This time of night, guv?' said the cabbie. 'That'll be thirty quid.'

'That will be perfectly all right,' said MacEvoy, reaching for the door handle.

And as the cab pulled out of the rank to pass by the first two cabs, MacEvoy lowered the window in the passenger door and leaned out so that his head and smiling face were framed by it.

He put his fists to his cheeks and stuck his thumbs up in the universal sign of the winner, grinning wildly into the horrified faces of the first two cabbies.

# Old Soldiers

[NOTE: The narrator of this story is a retired veteran of the XXth Legion of the Roman army, being interviewed about his experiences in Britain during the revolt of Queen Boudica and the Iceni in 60-61 AD. (General) Suetonius Paulinus was the Governor of Britannia at the time of the revolt, and the Manlius Valens referred to was eventually made a Roman Consul in 96 AD. The Silures were a Celtic tribe from what is today South Wales who fiercely opposed the Roman invasion of 43 AD.]

It was Julius Caesar who said that the Celts thought it improper to entrust their history to writing, wasn't it? Don't look at me like that. I might be an old soldier but I've read a bit.

Even without learning, some of them Druids were sharp.

I met one once, you know. To talk to, that is, not just to kill.

I was serving with the XXth; this would be about eight years before I went back there with General Paulinus. It was frontier duty in the west, south of the hills where the gold mines were. Real bandit country that was, because one of the local tribes we were keeping an eye on – they were called the Silures - was probably the best the Brits ever had in terms of a fighting force. Those buggers knew what they were doing, and they'd already taken on a couple of auxiliary units and given them a right seeing to.

The commander of the XXth at the time was Manlius Valens. Yes, *that* Manlius Valens, the one who is still hanging around Rome waiting for his consulship. He's what, 86 or something now? They'll probably make him consul just for staying alive so long. He's already got the record for being the oldest legionary commander there ever was, as he never got promoted after being thumped by the Silures.

Anyway, my unit is camped near a small settlement and we've checked things out and there are no armed warriors for miles, just a few old women and some kids. But there is this Druid; a real ancient one, probably older than old Manlius Valens is now, and he was as blind as a bat.

We didn't rate him as any sort of danger to us, though later it was policy to kill them on sight as it saved time. Truth is, he rather amused us and we took the piss out of him. He had this dog, you see, to help him see. It was a big, fat black-and-white bitch dog so old itself it hardly had any teeth and it drooled a lot, but it never strayed more than a yard or so from his side, and when he walked, it walked by his right knee and it would lean into him to steer him round objects or stop dead if it saw somebody coming up to him.

This Druid was, as I've said, bloody old and blind. He'd gone blind with age; nobody had put his eyes out or anything. He was dressed in black, like most of them are, but his robes – if you could call them that – were like sacking, not proper wool or hide. He had long white hair and a long beard in which were bits of twig and birdshite and who knows what, and by Jove, did he stink. But then most of the Brits do. Even now they're not sure what to do with hot water and a sponge.

He had tried to say something to us as we were building the camp for the night, but we couldn't understand a word he was saying so we ignored him and he just sat down on the ground, his dog next to him, and we almost forgot he was there. Then, when we were getting our mess rations for the evening, one of the lads sort of noticed he was still there and flicked a spoonful of curds from his bowl, right at the old man's face as he walked by him.

Fuck me, but the old man's hand shot up and he caught this gob of curd in mid-air and whipped it into his mouth, licking the palm of his hand to make sure he'd got all of it. And I swear none of us had said a word. He couldn't have seen it coming, could he?

Naturally, some other daft footslogger does the same, and he catches that as well. One-handed, sitting on the ground, without moving, and the dog never moves either. Then somebody chucks a piece of bread and he catches that and eats it. By now he's got an audience and he's singing for his supper. When the lads pitch things short or too high, he just lets them go, doesn't even try for them. But when they come near, his hand shoots out and he nabs them. Both hands too; doesn't seem to make a difference to him. Never misses. And the lads love it, laughing and joking, even starting to bet on which hand he'll use.

I see what's going on and it looks pretty harmless, until the old man gets to his feet and waves the nearest trooper to come closer. One of them does – I can't remember his name, but I've a feeling he was one who copped it years later with Boudica's lot – and he stands in front of the old Druid, who is jabbering away and making no sense at all.

The old man then reaches out and takes the trooper's right hand and guides it to the hilt of his sword.

Now all legionaries are taught that their *gladius* is their best friend and they should take care of it and not let anyone else touch it, so, naturally, the lads go a bit quiet at this. But the old Druid doesn't want the sword, he takes his hand away and mimes the action of a fast draw, then he takes a pace back from the trooper and holds his hands in front of him, a good two feet apart.

You won't find the quick draw in any army manual, but all soldiers do it; sometimes for a bet, sometimes to exercise the sword arm and build up the muscles, and sometimes just because your life could depend on it. When you're carrying a shield into battle on your left arm, you're up tight against the man either side of you, and when the order comes, you've got to get your sword out the same time as all the other guys. Otherwise you might cut off somebody's arm or – worse – be so squashed in that you never can get it out of the scabbard and you've got nothing to stab with.

It's a tricky thing to get the hang of at first. You drop your hand to your hip, turn the wrist, grab the *gladius* handle, whip it out, up and then twist again. Hopefully without taking your own nose off.

Part of the quick draw game was somebody stands in front of you and you have to draw your sword before they can clap their hands. In fact if you're good, they can't clap their hands, because your sword is in there between their hands, you see? Get it wrong and you could lose a finger or two.

This old Druid must have heard about the game – he couldn't have seen it, could he? – and there he was challenging the lads of the XXth Legion to have a go. So they did.

I think five or six tried, maybe more, and a couple I knew were very good at the game, but none of them made it. The old man clapped his hands every time, even widening his hands after the first couple to make it easier for them.

Then I put a stop to it, as tempers were starting to run by this time, ordering the lads to get back to their meal. Of course one of them had to shout out why didn't I have a go, as I was an officer (who had been a ranker) and therefore I must be good at something. Like an idiot, I did.

I squared myself up to the stinky old man and, even though he couldn't understand a word, told his blind eyes that he wouldn't see this one coming. And he didn't. I drew and had my sword up as his hands slapped onto the metal, and his mouth opened in surprise, but he said nothing as the lads cheered.

Ever so slowly, he ran his hands down the blade until the skin broke and a thin trickle of blood appeared where his palms had been. Then he let go, and his right hand started to feel toward me, trying to locate my left hip and the scabbard.

Somebody yelled out then that the old man fancied me, and that broke the spell. I slapped the old Druid's hand away, wiped my blade on the grass underfoot and sheathed the sword. By the time I had done so, the old man was sat back on the ground next to his dog.

In the morning as we broke camp, a sentry reported that the old Druid and his dog had gone during the night without a sound.

We had a small unit of Thracian cavalry with us as scouts. They were from the First Ala, I remember that, a crack unit, veterans of the invasion, good trackers. I took some of them with me and we set out westwards into Silures territory, and we found the old Druid, and his dog, just before midday.

We killed him on some marshy ground near the big estuary that leads to the coast.

Had to, didn't we? The old bugger had found out that officers wear their swords on the left hip, not the right like your ordinary infantryman. It was my cross-draw from the left that had fooled him. You can imagine what he would have told his friends the Silures, can't you? Go for the ones with their swords on the left. Take out the officers first.

I should have seen through the cunning bastard a lot sooner, and if he hadn't done a runner it might never have occurred to me.

We killed his dog as well.

Just to be sure.

# APPENDIX

MIKE RIPLEY

# *ANGELS IN ARMS*
# THE SCRIPT

<u>SCENE 1. EXT. COVENT GARDEN PIAZZA. DAY.</u>

COVENT GARDEN'S PIAZZA FILLED WITH
TOURISTS/SHOPPERS/LUNCHTIME CROWD. FOCUS IS ON
THE AD-HOC STREET TRADERS SELLING FROM STALLS OR
SUITCASES AND PARTICULARLY THE STREET
ENTERTAINERS: MUSICIANS, JUGGLERS, MAGICIANS AND
MIME ARTISTS. IT IS ALMOST A MEDIEVAL SCENE,
COLOURFUL AND FRIENDLY.

WE MOVE IN ON A GANG OF FOUR SINISTER FIGURES IN
A HUDDLE. THEY ARE DRESSED INCONGRUOUSLY IN LONG
COATS (WITH SOMETHING CONCEALED UNDER THEM) LIKE
GANGSTERS OR OUTLAWS AS "THE LONG RIDERS". THE
LEADER OF THE GANG IS ANGEL WHO LOOKS AROUND
FURTIVELY BEFORE SPEAKING.

          ANGEL
  Okay, you know what we've got to do. It's
  not pleasant but this guy has moved in on
  Freddy's territory. We can't allow that,
  can we?

THE OTHER THREE GRUNT AND NOD SERIOUSLY.

          ANGEL
  Right then, he's in range. Lock and load.

FROM BEHIND WE SEE THEM CLICKING OR ASSEMBLING
THINGS INSIDE THEIR COATS. WE ARE EXPECTING
MACHINE GUNS AT THE VERY LEAST.

          ANGEL(OVER HIS SHOULDER)
  On me, to the left, after three.

ANGEL STAMPS HIS FOOT THREE TIMES. ALL FOUR SWING
ROUND TO REVEAL TRUMPETS, A TROMBONE AND A
CLARINET. THEY BURST INTO A FAST AND LOUD
DIXIELAND JAZZ NUMBER.

THEIR 'TARGET' IS A WHITE-FACED MIME ARTIST. THE
BLAST OF MUSIC TOTALLY THROWS HIM IN THE MIDDLE
OF HIS ACT AND HE FREEZES. HIS AUDIENCE TURN AWAY
FROM HIM TO ENJOY THE MUSIC, CLAPPING, DANCING,
JOINING IN. OTHER MUSICIANS DRIFT OVER TO JAM IN.

CLOSE IN ON ANGEL TAKING A SOLO. THE WHITE FACE
MIME APPROACHES HIM THROUGH THE CROWD AND TRIES
TO SPEAK TO HIM WHEN HIS SOLO ENDS.

> WHITE FACE
> Oi, smartarse! What's your problem?

ANGEL MUGS (JUST LIKE A MIME ARTIST) THAT HE
CAN'T HEAR ABOVE THE MUSIC. WHITE FACE MOTIONS
HIM OUT OF THE LINE UP BUT HE STILL HAS TO SHOUT.

> WHITE FACE
> I said what's your bleedin' problem?

> ANGEL
> You're trespassing.

> WHITE FACE
> STRAINING TO HEAR) What?

> ANGEL
> (MIMICKING HIM) I said you're trespassing.
> You've nicked Freddy's pitch. (HE POINTS WITH
> HIS TRUMPET) Freddy plays this spot until two
> o'clock.

WE SEE A BLONDE GIRL PUSHING A YOUNG GUY IN A
WHEELCHAIR TOWARD THE MAKESHIFT BAND. FREDDY IN
THE WHEELCHAIR PRODUCES A MOUTH ORGAN AND JOINS
IN, CENTRE STAGE. THE OTHER MUSICIANS PULL OUT
GRADUALLY AND LEAVE HIM TO IT.

ANGEL HELPS THE BLONDE SETTLE FREDDY'S CHAIR AND
PUT OUT THE HAT FOR MONEY FROM THE CROWD. WHITE
FACE DOES A BIG 'OH FUCK IT' GESTURE AND STOMPS
OFF. ANGEL AND HIS GANG COPY HIM AS THEY PACK UP
THEIR INSTRUMENTS.

THE BLONDE APPROACHES ANGEL AND THEY HUG.

> BLONDE
> Thanks, Angel, that was a really sweet thing
> to do.

> ANGEL
> (FALSE MODESTY) Nah, it was nothing.

> BLONDE
> Come on, it was a seriously good deed. You knew
> Freddy wouldn't push himself forward. It shows
> you care.

ANGEL
No. It shows I can't stand white-faced clowns.
Never could. Not since (PAUSE) that incident in
the circus.

BLONDE
(TAKEN IN) What incident? What happened? Do you
want to share it?

ANGEL
(SLIPPING AN ARM AROUND HER) It's not
something I normally tell people. I don't
think it's fair to burden others with ...
Just a minute, you're a Pisces, aren't you?

ANGEL IS LOOKING AT HER GLARINGLY OBVIOUS FISH
EARRINGS.

BLONDE
Why, yes. How did you ...?

ANGEL
It's a gift I have. Helps me to know who to
trust, who to confide in, who to ...

FENELLA APPEARS, HURRYING ACROSS THE PIAZZA,
FLUSTERED AND UNCOORDINATED. SHE IS DRESSED LIKE
A SCHOOLGIRL.

FENELLA: (WAVING)
Yoo-hoo! Angel!

ANGEL GROANS AND RELEASES HIS GRIP ON THE BLONDE,
THE MOMENT LOST.

ANGEL
... who to have as a friend, someone ...

FENELLA
Angel! I've got messages for you!

BLONDE:
(POINTING)Isn't that ... that girl calling
you?

ANGEL
Ignore her.

BLONDE
But she seems to know you.

ANGEL
No, she's confused. It's a trick of the
light ...

FENELLA
(PUTTING A HAND ON ANGEL'S CHEST) Got you.
Now listen, the phone's hardly stopped since
you left. You were up early, that's not like
you. Who's this? She's nice. Better than the
last one. Anyway, first off there
was ...

BLONDE
(DISENGAGING)I'll leave you to it. You've
obviously got a lot on your plate.

ANGEL
No, look, hang on. This is Fenella. Fenella
is my ... my ...

BLONDE
Sounds like she's your answering service. Get
a mobile phone, they're cheaper to run.

ANGEL
(TO HER DEPARTING BACK) And you can turn them
off.

FENELLA
(INNOCENT) Was I interrupting something?

ANGEL LEVELS HIS TRUMPET AT HER LIKE A RIFLE.

ANGEL
Fenella, this being the most powerful B-flat
trumpet in the land, you've got to ask: 'Did
he play six notes or was it only five? Do you
feel lucky?'

FENELLA
Angel, you're weird. Do you want these
messages or not?

ANGEL WALKS ACROSS THE PIAZZA, SHE FOLLOWS.

ANGEL
Are they from women?

FENELLA
(THINKING) No -

ANGEL
Do any involve huge windfalls of cash?

FENELLA
They don't mention money.

                    ANGEL
Then they can wait. I'm going for a drink.
Coming?

ANGEL REACHES A PILE OF SAXOPHONE AND GUITAR
CASES ETC AND SELECTS A BATTERED TRUMPET CASE,
MAKING FENELLA HOLD IT AS HE PACKS AWAY HIS
TRUMPET.

                    FENELLA
But they're important messages.

                    ANGEL
Says who?

                    FENELLA
Says them ... The people who rang you.

                    ANGEL
(PATRONISING) Well, they would, wouldn't
they?

                    FENELLA
You're confusing me, you always do.

                    ANGEL
(SMILING) It's my mission in life, Fenella.
I'm thinking of getting a grant for it.

                    FENELLA
(POUTING) Well, for your information, Mr
Smarty Pants, that nice Mr Tomlin says he's
going to call round if you don't ring him
back. And that Wilf person sounded quite
cross too.

ANGEL STARTS WALKING TOWARD THE NEAREST PUB OR
BAR, FENELLA TAGGING ALONG.

                    ANGEL
Who's this Mister Tomlin?

                    FENELLA
That nice man from Number 23 down the road.
He breeds Siamese cats, you know. He's rung
you five times now.

                    ANGEL
Why does he want me?  I've already got a cat.

                    FENELLA
(SHUDDERING, FEARFUL) Don't we know it.
Anyway, he said he'd pop round if you
wouldn't call him back.

                    ANGEL
Did he say what he wanted?

                    FENELLA
No.

                    ANGEL
Then I'm not in. Ever. What do you want to
drink?

                    FENELLA
We don't have time.

                    ANGEL
'Course we have. They've only just opened.

                    FENELLA
No, I meant we have to get back for when Wilf
rings again.

                    ANGEL
Wilf? Who's Wilf?

                    FENELLA
The other message. Wilf. Wilf Gurney. He said
he would ring back at 12. Every hour on the
hour.

                    ANGEL
(PITYINGLY) Fenella, do I look like the sort
of person who knows a Wilf?

                    FENELLA
Yes, you do.

                    ANGEL
Well I don't. I don't know anybody called
Gurney and certainly no Wilfs.


                    FENELLA
(PETULANT) Yes *you* do. Big Irish friend of
yours, used to play in a band with you. He's
been to the house. He was very loud, from
what I remember.

                    ANGEL
You mean *Werewolf*?

                    FENELLA
That's it! The werewolf. And he's going to
ring back at 12.

                    ANGEL
His name's not Gurney, though, Sweetlumps.

                    FENELLA
(BLUSHING) You're not allowed to call me that.
And anyway, it's not Gurney. Werewolf's on
*Guernsey*, that's it. You know, in the Channel
Islands.

                    ANGEL
(CHECKING HIS WATCH) Then you'll have to buy me
a drink some other time. I'd better get back.

                    FENELLA
Does this mean the Werewolf is in trouble?

                    ANGEL
No, it probably means Guernsey is.


SCENE 2. EXT. SIDE STREET. DAY.

ANGEL AND FENELLA HURRYING DOWN A SIDE STREET.
CARS ARE PARKED, SO IS A BLACK LONDON TAXI –
AUTHENTIC EXCEPT IT HAS NO 'FOR HIRE' SIGN.

AS THEY APPROACH THE TAXI, ANGEL PRODUCES A SET
OF KEYS. FENELLA CATCHES HIS ARM AND STOPS HIM.

                    FENELLA
Wait. I just love doing this.

SHE RUNS TO THE FRONT OF THE TAXI, STOPS AT THE
KERB AND RAISES A HAND.

                    FENELLA
(SHE WHISTLES LOUDLY) Hey! Taxi!

ANGEL, ABOUT A YARD AWAY, GIVES HER A KILLER
LOOK, THEN PATS THE TAXI ON THE ROOF.

                    ANGEL
Just ignore her, Armstrong. She's very sad,
very sheltered and shouldn't really be out in
the community. (TO FENELLA, AS HE UNLOCKS THE
DOOR) Get in. (HE HANDS HER HIS TRUMPET CASE)

SHE WAITS FOR ANGEL TO OPEN THE DOOR FOR HER, BUT
HE GETS IN AND STARTS THE ENGINE. SHE REALISES HE
IS NOT GOING TO, AND DIVES IN AS THE TAXI PULLS
AWAY.

SCENE 3. EXT. TABLE OUTSIDE A BAR/PUB, HARBOURFRONT. ST PETER PORT. GUERNSEY.

CLOSE SHOT OF WEREWOLF. A YOUNG, BEARDED IRISHMAN LIP-SMACKING HIS WAY THROUGH A PINT OF GUINNESS. WE ARE AWARE OF THREE OTHER FIGURES AT THE TABLE - GUENNOC, SUMO AND COWBOY - BECOMING IMPATIENT.

GUENNOC LOOKS AT HIS WATCH AS WEREWOLF FINISHES HIS PINT WITH A FLOURISH AND A SIGH.

                    GUENNOC
     (STANDING SUDDENLY) It is time.

                    WEREWOLF
     (HOPEFULLY) For another?

THE TABLE IS REVEALED AND WE SEE AT LEAST FOUR OTHER EMPTY PINTS.

                    GUENNOC
     To telephone your friend again.

THE OTHER TWO STAND, BUT NOT WEREWOLF.

                    WEREWOLF
     Ah, yes, my Guardian Angel. My old and distinguished friend.

COWBOY MOVES BEHIND WEREWOLF'S HEAD AND OPENS HIS COAT SO THAT A GUN IS VISIBLE IN HIS BELT. HE PUSHES IT TOWARD WEREWOLF'S FACE.

                    WEREWOLF
     My, my, that really is a pistol in your pocket. And here's me thinking you were just pleased to be in my company. Very well, then, you little tinker - (HE MAKES A 'GEE UP' SOUND) - walk on!

COWBOY PULLS ON THE HANDLES OF THE PREVIOUSLY UNSEEN WHEELCHAIR IN WHICH WEREWOLF SITS, HIS BROKEN LEG IN PLASTER. THEY MOVE OFF TOWARD AN ISOLATED PUBLIC TELEPHONE BOX.


SCENE 4. INTERIOR OF ANGEL'S TAXI. DAY.

FENELLA IS KNEELING UP ON A RUMBLE SEAT, TALKING TO ANGEL THROUGH THE CAB DRIVER'S PARTITION.

                    FENELLA
     Who exactly is the Werewolf?

ANGEL
(DRIVING) He's just Werewolf. His real name's Francis Dromey and he's an old and distinguished friend. We go back a long way.

FENELLA
Why do you call him Werewolf?

ANGEL
You ever seen his eyes, close-up, after dark, when there's a full moon?

FENELLA
No, of course not.

ANGEL
Then it's because he's hairy.

FENELLA
What does he do, this Werewolf?

ANGEL
He's with a band.

FENELLA
How exciting! Is he a pop star?

ANGEL
(WEARILY, PATTING THE DASHBOARD OF THE CAB) I keep telling you, Armstrong, you just can't get the staff these days.

FENELLA
Why do you talk to your taxi, Angel?

ANGEL
Because I like intelligent conversation.

FENELLA
Why do you call it Armstrong?

ANGEL
After one of my heroes - Louis Armstrong.

FENELLA
Who's he? Oh, hang on, wasn't he an astronaut?

ANGEL
That's right, the first man to play a trumpet on the moon. (LEANING IN TO THE DASHBOARD AGAIN) (QUIETLY) See what I mean?

# ANGELS IN ARMS: THE SCRIPT

<u>SCENE 5. EXT. STREET. DAY.</u>

ANGEL'S TAXI IN TRAFFIC. IT TURNS INTO A
RESIDENTIAL STREET, DOWNMARKET BUT NOT A SLUM.
STREET SIGN C/V SAYING 'STUART STREET, BOROUGH OF
HACKNEY, E8'. ANGEL SLOWS OUTSIDE NUMBER 9, WHERE
A MAN (MR TOMLIN) STANDS HOLDING A LARGE
CARDBOARD BOX. ANGEL ACCELERATES, GOES BEYOND THE
HOUSE AND PARKS, WATCHING THE MAN IN THE WING
MIRROR.

<u>SCENE 6. INT. ANGEL'S TAXI. DAY.</u>

          ANGEL
(OVER HIS SHOULDER) Did you order a pizza?

          FENELLA
(KNEELING UP TO LOOK OUT OF REAR WINDOW) No I
didn't, what - Oh, its that nice Mister
Tomlin from Number 23.

          ANGEL
What does he want?

          FENELLA
How should I know? You're the one he was
trying to ring. It's okay, Lisabeth is
dealing with him.

          ANGEL
(INTO THE MIRROR) Poor sod.

<u>SCENE 7. EXT. DOORSTEP OF ANGEL'S HOUSE. DAY.</u>

MR TOMLIN IS ARGUING WITH LISABETH, EVENTUALLY
PUSHING THE LARGE BOX AT HER AND MARCHING OFF
DOWN THE STREET, PASSING ANGEL'S TAXI, WHICH
APPEARS EMPTY.

<u>SCENE 8. INT. ANGEL'S TAXI/EXT. STREET. DAY.</u>

ANGEL AND FENELLA SIT UP FROM CROUCHED POSITIONS.

          ANGEL
He's gone.

          FENELLA
Why were we hiding?

                    ANGEL
Just to be sure. Let's go find out what he
wanted.

                    FENELLA
Lisabeth won't be pleased, you know.
Answering the door to a strange man will have
put her in a complete snit.

                    ANGEL
That's why you can go in first.

THEY GET OUT.

                    FENELLA
You know, that Mr Tomlin, he walked right by
us but he didn't see us. It was like we
weren't there.

                    ANGEL
Nobody notices a black cab in London.

                    FENELLA
Don't they?

                    ANGEL
(TO THE TAXI) I hope not. It's never a good
idea to be too conspicuous.


SCENE 9. EXT. GUERNSEY STREET/HARBOUR. DAY.

GUENNOC AND HIS TWO HENCHMEN ARE TRYING TO WEDGE
WEREWOLF AND HIS WHEELCHAIR IN A PUBLIC PHONE
BOX. THEY ARE ANYTHING BUT INCONSPICUOUS, AND THE
SITUATION DETERIORIATES INTO FARCE AND CURSING IN
FRENCH.


SCENE 10. INT. HALLWAY. ANGEL'S HOUSE. DAY.

AS ANGEL AND FENELLA LET THEMSELVES INTO THE
HOUSE, THEY ARE GRABBED BY LISABETH AND PINNED
AGAINST THE WALL.

                    LISABETH
What are you up to, Angel? I saw you drive
past.

                    ANGEL
Just trying to find somewhere to park,
Lisabeth, that's all.

> LISABETH
(IN HIS FACE) No wonder you didn't want to meet Mr Tomlin.

> ANGEL
(PULLING FENELLA IN FRONT OF HIM FOR PROTECTION): Why shouldn't I? I've never done anything to him.

> LISABETH
*You* might not have. (DRAMATIC) But *he* has.

LISABETH TURNS HER HEAD SLOWLY TO LOOK UP THE STAIRS AND THE OTHER TWO FOLLOW HER GAZE. AT THE TOP OF THE STAIRS (AS IF AUDITIONING FOR 'PSYCHO') IS A FIERCE BLACK CAT.

> FENELLA
(NERVOUSLY) Hello, Springsteen!

> ANGEL
(GRIPPING HER) Don't upset him! (TO LISBETH) So what's he done to Mr Whatsisname down the road?

> LISABETH
(SMUG) Do you know what Mr Tomlin does for a hobby?

> ANGEL
No idea. Why should I? I've never -

> FENELLA
I told you. He keeps pedigree Siamese cats.

> LISABETH
Not any more. Pedigree, that is.

SHE MOVES ASIDE AND WE SEE THE CARDBOARD BOX MR TOMLIN HAD EARLIER. IT IS MOVING.

> FENELLA
Ooh, let me see!

FENELLA KNEELS DOWN BY THE BOX AND BEGINS TO OPEN IT. ANGEL POINTS ACCUSINGLY UP THE STAIRS AT HIS CAT.

> ANGEL
You! You can run but you can't hide. I'm going to see you -

THE WALL-MOUNTED PHONE IN THE HALL RINGS

>ANGEL
(RELIEVED) That'll be for me.


SCENE 11. EXT. PHONE BOX ON GUERNSEY. DAY.

WEREWOLF IS HALF-IN, HALF-OUT OF THE PHONE BOX.
GUENNOC AND HIS HEAVIES ALL HOLD PISTOLS TO HIS
HEAD AS HE SPEAKS INTO THE PHONE.

>WEREWOLF
Would that be my old and distinguished friend
Fitzroy Maclean Angel? (HE GLARES AT HIS
CAPTORS AS ONE OF THEM PRODS HIM WITH A
PISTOL) Angel, you just wouldn't believe the
circumstances under which I'm having to phone
you.


SCENE 12. INT. ANGEL'S HOUSE. HALLWAY. DAY.

>ANGEL
(ON PHONE) Oh, I just might. (HE LOOKS ON,
HORRIFIED, AS FENELLA PRODUCES KITTEN AFTER
KITTEN FROM THE BOX) What's that? You want me
to come to Guernsey? Tomorrow?

>LISABETH
(POINTING AT THE BOX) Hey, you've got
responsibilities now.

>ANGEL
(INTO PHONE) Yeah, sure. I've got nothing on.

HE WAVES A FINGER ANGRILY AT SPRINGSTEEN, STILL
KEEPING OUT OF RANGE.


SCENE 13. INT. ANGEL'S FLAT. DAY.

ANGEL IS CRASHING ABOUT IN THE KITCHEN, OPENING
CANS OF CAT FOOD AND COUNTING OUT PLATES AND
SAUCERS. LISABETH AND FENELLA STRUGGLE INTO THE
FLAT CARRYING THE BOX. AS THEY SPEAK, FENELLA
UNPACKS THE KITTENS AND COUNTS THEM.

>LISABETH
What do you mean, *we'll* have to look after
them?

>ANGEL
It's only for a day. Or two.

                    FENELLA
Angel's got to go to Guernsey. (HOLDING A
KITTEN UP) Aren't they scrumptious?

                    LISABETH
Be quiet, Binky. (TO ANGEL'S BACK) You're
going on holiday? You turn our house into a
safari park and then you go on holiday?

                    ANGEL
It's not a holiday, it's urgent business.
(SUDDENLY) 'Binky'? Where's that from?

                    FENELLA
It's her pet name for me. (WITH KITTEN) Pet
name - geddit? Actually, they used to call me
it at school. It comes from my surname:
Binkworthy. Some people seem to ... (SHE
DRIES UNDER LISABETH'S KILLER LOOK).

                    LISABETH
I said, be quiet. There'll be tears before
bedtime at this rate.

                    FENELLA
(QUIETLY AND SULKILY) Sorr - ree.

ANGEL CARRIES IN CONTAINERS OF CAT FOOD - PLATES,
CUPS, PANS, ANYTHING HE CAN FIND.

                    ANGEL
Okay, Binky, how many we got?

                    FENELLA
Five. No, six. No, wait. I'll do a proper
head count. Do you think Springsteen will get
to like them?

                    ANGEL
Only for lunch. Where is he?

                    LISABETH
At the vet's, that's where he should be.

                    ANGEL
(WORRIED) Don't say things like that, not
even in jest. He might hear you.

                    FENELLA
Do you talk to your cat like you talk to your
taxi?

                    ANGEL
(PUTTING DOWN MORE CAT FOOD) Of course.

                    FENELLA
Does that make you a sad person?

                    ANGEL
No. The people who eavesdrop on me - they're
sad. (LISABETH SNORTS IN DERISION) You'd
better keep them away from Springsteen, just
in case.

                    LISABETH
While you go swanning off on holiday.

                    ANGEL
It's not a holiday. I've been called to help a
friend.

                    FENELLA
It's one of Roy's old and distinguished
friends, Lisabeth, so he has to go.

                    LISABETH
(MIMICKING) Old and distinguished ... Does
that mean it's another scruffy musician?

                    FENELLA
Yes. He's a pop star, Angel told me. There's
six of them, by the way. Kittens, that is.

                    ANGEL
(DISTRACTED, LOOKING AT A BOOKSHELF) I said he
was with a band. He was driving them,
actually, on a tour of Europe.

                    FENELLA
Anyone famous?

                    ANGEL
(SELECTING A BOOK) A heavy metal band called
Astral Reich. (FENELLA AND LISABETH GO 'WHO?'
TO EACH OTHER SILENTLY. ANGEL DOESN'T TURN
ROUND) Yeah, I knew you'd have never heard of
them.

ANGEL TAKES A BOOK OFF THE SHELF AND OPENS IT. THE
FIRST FEW PAGES HIDE A SMALL COMBINATION LOCK BOOK
SAFE. HE OPENS IT. THERE ARE TWO PASSPORTS,
VARIOUS CREDIT CARDS AND MONEY IN THERE. HE
SELECTS ONE PASSPORT AND AN AMERICAN EXPRESS CARD,
THEN A NEW TOOTHBRUSH STILL IN ITS WRAPPING.

                    ANGEL
Well, that's me packed. I'll just go and phone
the airport. There's a flight first thing in
the morning.

                    LISABETH
You're just going? Leaving us with this lot?

                    ANGEL
What do you expect? They're not old enough to
use the can-opener themselves.

                    FENELLA
Ow! (SUCKING A FINGER) That one just bit me.

                    ANGEL
(PROUDLY) That's my boy.


SCENE 14. EXT. GUERNSEY. HARBOUR SIDE. DAY.

LOCATION ESTABLISHED AS GUERNSEY, WITH A CENTRAL
PUB OR BAR. A GUERNSEY TAX GOES BY ONE WAY, THEN
THE OTHER. ON ITS THIRD PASS IT STOPS. ANGEL GETS
OUT, ARGUES WITH THE DRIVER, AND THE CAB DRIVES
OFF. ANGEL LOOKS AT HIS WATCH - HE'S OBVIOUSLY
EARLY - THEN WANDERS OFF. HE CARRIES A SHOULDER
BAG.

ANGEL FINDS A BENCH SEAT VANTAGE POINT SO HE CAN
OBSERVE THE PUB. HE READS A BOOK, WATCHES WOMEN
GO BY, HAS AN ICE-CREAM.

GUENNOC, SUMO AND COWBOY EMERGE OUT OF THE
HARBOUR (SURPRISING ANGEL), MANHANDLING WEREWOLF
IN HIS WHEELCHAIR, AMIDST MUCH SWEARING AND
ARGUING.

ANGEL PRODUCES A PAIR OF MINIATURE BINOCULARS
FROM HIS BAG AND SEES-IN CLOSE UP SUMO HIT
WEREWOLF IN THE STOMACH. HE FOLLOWS THEM WITH THE
BINOCULARS

AS THEY HEAD FOR THE PUB, IN THE THRONG OF
BODIES, HE SEES A PISTOL UNDER ONE OF THE
HENCHMAN'S COATS.

                    ANGEL
(LOOKING THROUGH BINOCULARS) O-Oh!


SCENE 15. INT. PUB BAR. DAY.

THE SET UP IS PURE WESTERN B MOVIE. ANGEL ENTERS
THE PUB LIKE ROBERT VAUGHN IN *THE MAGNIFICENT
SEVEN*. THE CLOCK ABOVE THE BAR SAYS NOON.

WEREWOLF IS AT A CORNER TABLE, SURROUNDED BY
GUENNOC, COWBOY AND SUMO. ANGEL WALKS SLOWLY UP

TO THE BAR, IGNORING THEM.

        ANGEL
(TO BARMAN, DROPPING THE ATTITUDE) Two pints
of bitter, squire.

THE BARMAN SERVES HIM WHILE THE OTHERS WATCH. HE
PICKS UP THE BEERS, TAKES THEM OVER TO THE TABLE
AND PUTS ONE IN FRONT OF WEREWOLF BEFORE SITTING
DOWN.

        ANGEL
You ain't from around these parts, are you,
stranger?

        WEREWOLF
A lost lad, miles from home, but this isn't a
bad wee place. Cheap beer, cheap smokes. Good
place (HE LOOKS AROUND) to open a pub.

        ANGEL
(DRINKING) Oh, I wouldn't know about that.
You can get a lot of aggro from customers.

        WEREWOLF
(STRAIGHT) Who said anything about customers?
Still, it's sorely good to see you here.

        ANGEL
Bet you thought I wouldn't come, didn't you?
Go on, what odds were you giving? Three to
one?

        WEREWOLF
(CATCHING ON) Six to one, actually, but -

        GUENNOC
(RAPPING THE TABLE) Enough! This is the Angel
person?

        WEREWOLF
In person, the man you can trust to ride to
the rescue of an old and distinguished friend
in his hour of need.

        GUENNOC
Shut up.

COWBOY SAYS SOMETHING IN BRETON. GUENNOC REACTS.
THEN TURNS TO ANGEL.

        GUENNOC
My name is Yannick Guennoc.

                    ANGEL
(NERVOUS) I knew someone called Yannick once.
Someone else of course. He was a Breton too.

                    GUENNOC
(SHARP) Who said we were Bretons?

                    ANGEL
(SHRUGGING)  That  wasn't  any  French  I
understood, but, anyway, Yannick is a dead
giveaway. The one I knew married a Welshwoman
and when they had a row, he shouted in Breton
and she shouted back in Welsh. (LIMPLY) Shame
of it was they understood each other.

                    GUENNOC
(TO WEREWOLF) Is he a fool?

                    WEREWOLF
He must be to come here. (TO ANGEL) Roy, cool
it with the crap, eh? Yer man here is on a
mission.

                    ANGEL
Okay, okay, crap cooled. What's the deal?

                    GUENNOC
(TO ANGEL) I had some property in transit and
this man lost it. He tells me you can get it
back for me.

                    ANGEL
That's not exactly a detailed brief. I'd need
to know a tad more, like: what, when, where,
how and what's in it for me? I take it this
is something not likely to be handed in at a
lost property office?

                    GUENNOC
You don't need to know -

                    WEREWOLF
Yes, he does. Look, I'm not in the loop on
this at all. I was just the driver, an
innocent bystander in all this.

                    ANGEL
You're not doing much standing now.

                    WEREWOLF
Ah well, that's part of the blag, so let me
tell it. (HE TAKES BIG DRINK) We were coming
to the end of the Astral Reich tour -

ANGEL
(SLAPPING THE PLASTER CAST) The last leg, so
to speak?

WEREWOLF
(GLARES) Ha-bloody-ha. Just listen will yer?
We'd done ten days in Holland and two in
Belgium. Nothing big, mostly universities,
student gigs. And we had one last date in
France, in Rouen, before we hopped the ferry
from Roscoff to Plymouth. It's cheap this
time of year. Anyway, the gig goes down and
next morning I'm tooling down the autoroute.

ANGEL
What in?

WEREWOLF
In a bloody great Volvo artic. You know what
these heavy metal bands are like; they've got
to have three trucks of gear whether they
need it or not.

ANGEL
Are they any good, this Astral Reich lot?

WEREWOLF
Nah. Musically they're shite, but they are
loud. So there I am, doing around the ton -

ANGEL
Kilometres?

WEREWOLF
No, miles - when these two nuns on mopeds -

ANGEL
(GRINNING) Nuns? On motorbikes?

WEREWOLF
Tell me about it. Yes, two nuns pull out in
front of me, I swerve, the Volvo jackknifes
and we hit the crash barrier. I wake up in
hospital, leg in the air. 'Course, the tour's
insured and the Volvo gets shipped back to
England, but I get left in some bloody French
casualty ward. Mind you, the food's good.

ANGEL
No cops? The *flics* not interested?

WEREWOLF
They tested me and I was clean, and the nuns
stood up for me, said it was their fault. All

that was cool. Then a few days later this
bunch of hooligans turned up and said they
were taking me home. Instead, they took me -

                    GUENNOC
(REACHING INSIDE HIS JACKET) Be careful.

                    WEREWOLF
- took me to their little hideaway and
explained the facts of life to me.

                    ANGEL
Those being that they had naughty substances
stashed in the truck -

                    GUENNOC
Wait! Who said anything about drugs?

                    ANGEL
You just did. Anyway, the truck was coming
from Holland, right? Stands to reason. (TO
WEREWOLF) And you knew nothing about them,
did you, darlin'?

                    WEREWOLF
Honest, guv', not a thing.

                    ANGEL
I'll believe you; thousands wouldn't. (TO
GUENNOC) And you were going to - what? Unload
them when he stopped for a tea break? No, I
know. At the docks, before the truck got on
the ferry, that'd be it. French Customs don't
give a monkey's what goes *out*, do they?

                    GUENNOC
You do not need to know. All you need to know
is that we want our property back.

                    ANGEL
Who's 'we'?

                    GUENNOC
The Front Populaire Breton. That is who you are
dealing with.

                    ANGEL
Well, excuse me, but you are so *populaire*
I've never heard of you.

                    GUENNOC
We are not asking you to do this out of
sympathy with our cause - independence for
Brittany.

ANGEL
Not asking me to do what?

GUENNOC
Find our property for us.

ANGEL
(HORRIFIED) And just how am I supposed to
...? (LOOKING AT WEREWOLF) Oh, no ...

WEREWOLF
I told them you were The Man, Roy. You know
everybody I know in the music business and
you can operate back in England. These
cowboys would stand out a mile as soon as
they (CURIOUSLY URGENT) *got off the boat.*

ANGEL
Well, thanks a bunch for the recommendation,
you big girl's blouse. I ought to ...

WEREWOLF
(MOCK HORROR) You'd hit a cripple, wouldn't
you? Look, all you've got to do is go to the
tour agents - it's Box Pop out at Hounslow,
they set up the whole deal. Find out if the
gear from my truck has caught up with Astral
Reich's gigs back in England. Once you know
where they're playing ... aw, come on, you
know the ropes. You've been a roadie yerself
in yer time.

ANGEL
So what was in your truck?

WEREWOLF
Lights, light-show stuff, a back-up generator
and speakers. Nothing they couldn't hire in.
The stuff might have gone out with another
band or it might be in store at Box Pop, but
if anyone can find it, you can.

ANGEL
That's what you told our amateur terrorists
here, is it?

WEREWOLF
I said you were Top Man for this, Angel.
Look, you need a float, so ... (HE HANDS OVER
A PIECE OF PAPER) ... this is a number for my
brother. His name's Gearoid but answers to
Gary when the English have trouble with it.
He's got a stash of mine for emergencies
only. I reckon this is an emergency.

                    ANGEL
How come your brother can't do this?

                    WEREWOLF
You'd see if you ever met him. He's not
exactly what you'd call streetwise.

                    ANGEL
(LOOKING AT THE PAPER) Where the hell is this
number?

                    WEREWOLF
Dorset. Gearoid likes the quiet life these
days.

                    ANGEL
So do I. (WEARILY) All right, what am I
looking for?

                    WEREWOLF
They won't say.

                    GUENNOC
When you find it, you will know. Until then,
the less you know, the better.

                    ANGEL
So where do I look?

                    GUENNOC
Of that, we are not exactly sure, but you
should look in the equipment of this band,
not in the truck.

                    ANGEL
Oh well, that narrows it down. (THINKS) Won't
their gear have been sniffed by British
Customs?

                    WEREWOLF
The band will have, that's for sure, and all
the electronics are checked as routine, but I
was carrying mostly scaffolding. Nowhere to
hide anything that I can think of.

                    ANGEL
(SARCASTIC) Well that's just bleedin'
brilliant, isn't it? I don't know what to
look for or where. Terrific. Give me one good
reason I should do this.

                    GUENNOC
In five days' time we'll kill your friend.

                    WEREWOLF
(RESIGNED) Bummer, isn't it? Oh, and there's
one other thing you should know.

                    ANGEL
I'm not going to like this either, am I?

                    WEREWOLF
Astral Reich's manager was flying in from the
States to personally manage the British end
of the tour.

                    ANGEL
And who's he?

                    WEREWOLF
She. It's Lucinda.

                    ANGEL
(HORRIFIED) Lulu? Lucinda L Luger, the bitch
queen of schlock 'n roll?

                    WEREWOLF
The very same. Knew you'd be pleased.

ANGEL SITS IN STUNNED SILENCE. GUENNOC AND THE
OTHERS GET UP TO GO.

                    GUENNOC
You will stay here while we leave. We will
telephone for a report in five days' time.
Make sure you are at your number - and that
you have located our property.

                    WEREWOLF
You'll come through for me, Angel, I have no
worries on that score. (ANGEL GLARES AT HIM)
Mind you, you look like you could use a
serious drink right now.

                    ANGEL
(STILL GLARING) A bottle of Scotch, with the
top off.

SCENE 16 EXT. GUERNSEY HARBOUR SIDE. DAY.

ANGEL IS HIDING, WATCHING THE HARBOUR THROUGH HIS
BINOCULARS. HE SEES WEREWOLF'S WHEELCHAIR BEING
LOADED ONTO A FISHING BOAT BY GUENNOC'S MEN AND
THREE OTHERS - OBVIOUSLY FISHERMEN, ONE OF THEM
OLD. HE NOTES THE NAME OF THE BOAT - 'CENDRILLON'
- AND DOES A HEAD COUNT.

                    ANGEL
(TO HIMSELF) ... four, five ... six to one.
You were right there, my old friend.


SCENE 17. EXT. HEATHROW AIRPORT. EVENING.

ESTABLISHING SHOT OF ANGEL DRIVING HIS TAXI OUT
OF A CAR-PARK NEAR THE TERMINALS AT HEATHROW. A
BUSINESSMAN/TOURIST WITH SUITCASES FLAGS HIM
DOWN, THINKING HE IS A GENUINE CAB.

                    TOURIST
Can you take me to the City, please?

                    ANGEL
Sorry, squire, I'm not a ... (HE LOOKS AROUND
FURTIVELY TO MAKE SURE THERE ARE NO OTHER
CABS) ... It'd be thirty quid, this time of
the day, what with the traffic ...

                    TOURIST
That'll be perfectly all right.

ANGEL OPENS THE DOOR LIKE A CABBIE AND THE
TOURIST GETS IN. ANGEL STILL LOOKS FURTIVE, THEN
DRIVES OFF.


SCENE 18. INT. ANGEL'S HOUSE - PHONE IN HALL.
DAY.

ANGEL IS ON THE PHONE WITH THE PAPER WEREWOLF
GAVE HIM AND A ROAD MAP/ATLAS. HE DOES NOT SEE OR
HEAR LISABETH COME DOWN THE STAIRS BEHIND HIM, SO
WHEN SHE SPEAKS, SHE STARTLES HIM.

                    ANGEL
(INTO PHONE) Hello? Yes? I'm trying to
contact Gearoid, or Gary. Last name, Dromey.
I've been given this number. (LISTENS) Yes.
(BEAT) Werewolf's brother, that's right.
(PUZZLED BUT IMPRESSED) What? Sorry, it's
difficult to hear with all the music ...
Lunchtimes? He only comes in lunchtimes?
Okay. Tomorrow? Great. I'll catch him then.
Hang on a minute, exactly where are you? The
Sundial, that's a pub, right? (BEAT, LOOKS AT
MAP) Donhead St Agnes? Great. Thanks. Cheers.


                    LISABETH
I hope you're writing down that call.

                    ANGEL
(JUMPING) Jesus! Don't do that! I've used up
enough nervous energy already today.

                    LISABETH
You've just got a guilty conscience, that's
all. Now what are you going to do about them?

                    ANGEL
(ALARMED) About who? How did ...?

                    LISABETH
(POINTING UP THE STAIRS TO WHERE THE KITTENS
ARE TEARING ABOUT) About them. They're
wrecking the place. They go mad every time
they see Springsteen.

                    ANGEL
Is he attacking them?

                    LISABETH
No. (THOUGHTFUL) They seem to be ganging up
on him, but we know he's got a temper, don't
we? That's why the milkman doesn't call any
more, isn't it? Not to mention three postmen,
is it now?

                    ANGEL
Look, I've got things on my mind, stuff to
do. I've got to go away for a few days on a
mission of mercy ...

                    LISABETH
Oh no you don't.

                    ANGEL
(PLEADING) A few days only; four max. Here
... (TAKES THE MONEY THE TOURIST GAVE HIM OUT
OF A POCKET) ... here's thirty quid for cat
food and the trouble.

                    LISABETH
No way. Not Springsteen and this devil's
brood. They're going to kill each other, and
I am not letting Binky clean up after that!

                    ANGEL
Okay, I'll do a deal. I've got to go to
Dorset, see a guy. (HE WAVES THE ROAD MAP)
Now he's here, I reckon (POINTING), but *here*
I've got family.

                    LISABETH
You've got a family? You mean there are more
of you?

                    ANGEL
(IGNORING HER) It's my sweet old maiden
aunty, Aunt Dorothea. You'd like her. (SEES
HER EXPRESSION) Well, you don't have to. Let
me bell her and I'll con ... ask her to look
after Springsteen for a few days. She's into
animals. Has dogs, things like that. All you
have to put up with is the kittens. Binky
could manage that. She likes them. I've seen
her drooling.

                    LISABETH
(THINKS, THEN TAKES THE MONEY) Well, it'll be
on Binky's head then.

                    ANGEL
Attagirl!

                    LISABETH
*But* only if you take Springsteen to this aunty
of yours.

                    ANGEL
I'll ring her now.

                    LISABETH
(NOT MOVING) I'll wait and see what she says.

ANGEL KNOWS BETTER THAN TO ARGUE AND TURNS TO THE
PHONE AND DIALS.

                    ANGEL
Hello? Aunty? Dorothea, it's me, Roy. (BEAT)
No, I'm not selling anything. It's Roy.
(BEAT) Your favourite nephew. (BEAT) Fitzroy.
(BEAT) Fitzroy Maclean Angel. (PAUSE) Yes,
that's the one, but surely the insurance
covered it? (PAUSE) Yes. Okay, if you say so.
(PAUSE) Do I have to say it out loud? (BEAT)
Okay, then, this is the Scumbag calling.

ANGEL COVERS THE MOUTHPIECE OF THE PHONE AND
TURNS TO LISABETH, NODDING, CONFIDENT.

                    ANGEL
She'll do it.


SCENE 19. EXT. COUNTRY ROADS OUTSIDE LONDON. DAY.

ANGEL'S TAXI ON COUNTRY ROADS IN DARKEST DORSET. ESTABLISHING SHOT OF COUNTY SIGN?

## SCENE 20. EXT. OUTSIDE DOROTHEA'S COTTAGE. DAY.

ANGEL'S TAXI PULLS UP OUTSIDE A CLASSIC COUNTRY COTTAGE WITH ROSES ROUND THE DOOR. ANGEL GETS OUT OF ARMSTRONG AND PULLS ON A PAIR OF WICKET-KEEPER'S GLOVES TO REMOVE A CAT BASKET FROM THE BACK SEAT OF THE CAB. THE BASKET KICKS AND HISSES AS HE STRUGGLES TO CARRY IT UP TO THE COTTAGE.

>           ANGEL
> Aunty! Dorothea? Where are you?

>           DOROTHEA
> (VOICE OFF) Back garden. Come round.

ANGEL WALKS ROUND THE SIDE OF THE COTTAGE AND IS CONFRONTED WITH A LARGE WIRE CAGE. TWO HUGE DOGS STAND ON THEIR HIND LEGS AGAINST THE WIRE, SNARLING AT HIM BUT NOT BARKING. THEY ARE TALLER THAN HE IS AND HE FLATTENS HIMSELF AGAINST THE COTTAGE WALL, FRIGHTENED, ALTHOUGH HE NOTICES THAT THE CAT BASKET HAS GONE QUIET, MAKING HIS ARM ALMOST RIGID.

>           ANGEL
> Dorothea? (SOFTLY) Help!

DOROTHEA APPEARS ROUND THE CORNER.

>           DOROTHEA
> Fitzroy! Don't be such a baby, they can't hurt you, they're locked up.

>           ANGEL
> Aunty, *what* are they? Have you been seeing that strange Mr Baskerville again?

>           DOROTHEA
> God, you're ignorant. They are Akitas, Japanese attack dogs. I'm training them and breeding them.

>           ANGEL
> For pity's sake, why?

>           DOROTHEA
> For money of course. Security companies buy them to guard things.

                    ANGEL
You mean like Rottweilers?

                    DOROTHEA
(LAUGHS) These babies eat Rottweilers for
breakfast. You'd better come in, I suppose.
Is that Springsteen? (ANGEL NODS, BUT STILL
NOT MAKING ANY SUDDEN MOVES) Then bring him
round into the kitchen. He can keep Bishop
company.

                    ANGEL
(FOLLOWING HER, HIS BACK TO WALL TO GET BY
THE DOGS) Er ... The Bishop?

                    DOROTHEA
Bishop. My Labrador. He won't come outside
now these two are here.

                    ANGEL
Maybe he has a point.


SCENE 21. INT. DOROTHEA'S KITCHEN. DAY.

                    DOROTHEA
There he is, the sad hound.

THERE IS AN OLD BLACK DOG UNDER THE KITCHEN
TABLE. THERE IS A LOUD HISS FROM THE CAT BASKET.

                    ANGEL
Maybe you'd better keep Springsteen in
another room for a day or so, Aunty.

                    DOROTHEA
When I tell you how to play the trumpet, then
you can tell me how to raise animals. Now put
down that fleabag, give your spinster aunt a
kiss and tell me what you are doing down here
in God's own country. I thought your sort
weren't let out of the city without a pass.

                    ANGEL
(KISSING HER ON THE CHEEK) I've got to see a
man in a pub at lunchtime, then I've got some
business that will probably take a couple of
days.

                    DOROTHEA
Fine. Don't tell me what you're doing.

                    ANGEL
But I am. That's it. Just look after
Springsteen for me.

                    DOROTHEA
So you're not in trouble?

                    ANGEL
(CAREFULLY) No, *I'm* not. I'm doing a favour
for an old and distinguished friend.

                    DOROTHEA
Oh, one of those. I always say the trick with
old and distinguished friends is not to have
too many of them.

                    ANGEL
You are wise indeed, Aunty. Now, where's
Donhead St Agnes from here?

                    DOROTHEA
About ten miles, due west. You're not going
to The Sundial are you?

                    ANGEL
(WARY) Yes. You don't know it, do you?

                    DOROTHEA
Not really. Prat of a landlord barred me
after the last visit.

                    ANGEL
Oh. (EYES LIGHT UP) Still got your bike here?

                    DOROTHEA
Sure. (CATCHING ON)

                    ANGEL
Can I borrow it?

                    DOROTHEA
If I can borrow Armstrong. It'll scare the
bollocks off the vicar if he sees me in that.

                    ANGEL
It's a deal. I'll bring it back in one piece.

                    DOROTHEA
You'd better. It's round by the shed.

ANGEL TOSSES HER THE KEYS TO HIS TAXI AMD SHE
CATCHES THEM WITH A TRIUMPHANT 'YES!'

SCENE 22. EXT. SIDE OF DOROTHEA'S COTTAGE. DAY.

ESTABLISHING SHOT OF ANCIENT BICYCLE LEANING
AGAINST A GARDEN SHED. SUDDENLY DOORS OPEN AND
OUT RIDES ANGEL IN CRASH HELMET, FIRING UP A BIG
BMW MOTORBIKE AND RIDING OFF AS DOROTHEA HEADS
FOR THE TAXI.

SCENE 23. EXT. SUNDIAL PUB. DAY.

ANGEL, ON THE BMW, PULLS INTO THE PUB CAR-PARK
AND TAKES OFF HIS HELMET. HE HAS PARKED
UNDERNEATH A SIGN SAYING 'NO BIKERS'. HE IGNORES
IT AND GOES INTO THE BAR.

SCENE 24. INT. SUNDIAL PUB. DAY.

IN THE PUB IS GEAROID, A BROAD, DUFFLE-COATED
FIGURE AT A CORNER TABLE, PLAYING CHESS. OVER HIS
SHOULDER WE SEE ANGEL ENTER, BUY A PINT AND CHAT
UP THE BARMAID, WHO POINTS TO GEAROID. VIEWPOINT
SWITCHES TO ANGEL APPROACHING HIM. GEAROID LOOKS
UP FROM THE CHESSBOARD BEFORE HE ARRIVES.

           GEAROID
(INDICATING THE BOARD) Do you play?

           ANGEL
No. You can't deal at chess.

           GEAROID
(LAUGHS LOUDLY, IGNORING THE STARES OF THE
OTHER CUSTOMERS) You must be Angel.

           ANGEL
How did you know?

           GEAROID
Francis doesn't give out this number to many
people. Julie, behind the bar there, said it
was a man asking after me. That narrowed it
down to one actually.

           ANGEL
So you're Gearoid. That is how you say it,
isn't it?

           GEAROID
Spot on. (HE STANDS TO SHAKE HANDS) Pleased
to meet you.

AS HE STANDS, HIS COAT FALLS OPEN TO REVEAL A

LARGE WOODEN CROSS HANGING ROUND HIS NECK, OVER A MONK'S HABIT.

>                    ANGEL
> (STUNNED) Jesus Christ!

>                    GEAROID
> (COOL) Not quite, just one of his soldiers on Earth.

>                    ANGEL
> God, I'm sorry. I had no idea. When Werewolf - Francis - said he had a brother, I didn't know he meant 'Brother'!

>                    GEAROID
> (INDICATING HIS HABIT) This? Oh never mind this. To be absolutely honest, we're not proper monks, but does help the image.

>                    ANGEL
> The image?

>                    GEAROID
> Let me show you. I have some samples with me.

GEAROID PRODUCES A CARRIER BAG AND PLACES A CARTON OF MUSHROOMS, JARS OF HONEY, BOTTLE OF MEAD ETC. ON THE CHESS BOARD. ANGEL PICKS UP THE PRODUCTS ONE BY ONE, READING THE LABELS.

>                    ANGEL
> 'Monk's Hood Organic Mushrooms'. Hang on, isn't a Monk's Hood a ...

>                    GEAROID
> Yes, yes, I know. It's called marketing, apparently.

>                    ANGEL
> Monk's Hood Honey, Monk's Hood Beeswax Polish, Monk's Hood Mead. (TAKES AN INTEREST IN THIS ONE) Alcohol by volume 27%. (HE WHISTLES SOFTLY)

>                    GEAROID
> We'll try some. We do glasses as well.

HE PRODUCES TWO SMALL ENGRAVED GLASSES. ANGEL READS ONE WHILE GEAROID OPENS THE BOTTLE.

>                    ANGEL
> 'Produce of the Community of Saint Fulgentius'. That's your - er - monastery?

                    GEAROID
(POURING) Retreat; we call it a retreat. The
Church of England has always been a bit
ambivalent about monasteries. Cheers.

                    ANGEL
Cheers. So this retreat, it's Anglican?
(GEAROID NODS) But you and Francis are ...

                    GEAROID
That's right. Who'd ever think of looking
here for a good Irish Catholic like me?

                    ANGEL
(GRINNING) You're winding me up.

                    GEAROID
Maybe I am, but you didn't come here just for
the pleasure of my excellent company, did
you?

                    ANGEL
No, I didn't. Francis is in trouble and I'm
sort of helping him out of a situation. He
said you held some ... er ... cash - savings
- a sort of emergency fund ...

                    GEAROID
And this *is* an emergency?

                    ANGEL
Oh yes, you could say that.

                    GEAROID
But you're not at liberty to tell me what
sort of emergency. That right?

                    ANGEL
(WARY) You've done this before, haven't you?

                    GEAROID
Once or twice. Only with women though.
Francis must talk in his sleep sometimes. And
then, when he leaves them, as he always does,
they remember him mumbling about his brother
the monk who holds his savings.

                    ANGEL
This is genuine, Gearoid, and I won't use it
unless I have to.

GEAROID STARES AT HIM, THEN PRODUCES A THICK
BROWN ENVELOPE FROM THE FOLDS OF HIS HABIT. HE
LAYS IT ON THE TABLE IN FRONT OF ANGEL.

                    GEAROID
Francis left me three thousand pounds for
safe keeping. You'll find three thousand
seven hundred and fifty-five in there. That
was following a small investment in the Irish
Derby. Don't worry, the rest of the winnings
went to a good cause.

                    ANGEL
(REACHING FOR THE ENVELOPE) Believe me, this
will go to a good cause too.

AS HIS HAND COVERS THE ENVELOPE, GEAROID GRABS THE
BOTTLE OF MEAD AND PRESSES IT HARD, HOLDING IT,
ONTO THE BACK OF ANGEL'S HAND.

                    GEAROID
(PUTTING PRESSURE ON) I'm sure it will, Friend
Angel, but not exactly one hundred percent
sure. I think there's a lot more you ought to
be telling me; I can see it in your eyes. So
what's the story?

                    ANGEL
(EYES WATERING) You really don't want to know.

                    GEAROID
What? Because of this? (HE FINGERS THE
CRUCIFIX AT HIS NECK) Don't be put off by
this. All this means is that I've surely heard
worse than anything you're going to tell me.

                    ANGEL
(IN PAIN) I got the impression Francis didn't
want you involved.

                    GEAROID
Well we're here and he's not. (HE LIFTS THE
BOTTLE TO POUR. ANGEL MASSAGES HIS HAND).
We've got this to drink, then it's your round,
so you've plenty of time to tell me how you
intend to spend Francis's nest egg.

                    ANGEL
(LOOKING HIM IN THE EYE) I've got absolutely
no idea.

                    GEAROID
(BEAT) You're not kidding, are you? I can see
it in your eyes. (SLAPS THE TABLE) By heavens,
this is going to be good! (HE DRINKS THEN
POURS MORE MEAD) Go ahead, Friend Angel, in
your own time.

SCENE 25. EXT. OUTSIDE DOROTHEA'S COTTAGE. DAY.

A TRANSIT VAN PULLS UP. ON THE SIDE IT HAS
STENCILLED: 'The Retreat of St Fulgentius, Donhead
St Agnes, Dorset.' THEN UNDERNEATH: 'Peace and
Fulfilment - website: ...'

TWO MONKS GET OUT, ONE SHORT, FAT AND WHITE, ONE
TALL, THIN AND BLACK. THEY OPEN THE REAR DOORS AND
ANGEL AND GEAROID FALL OUT, BOTH HOLDING BOTTLES
OF MEAD. DOROTHEA'S MOTORBIKE IS IN THE BACK OF
THE VAN.

ANGEL AND GEAROID HOLD EACH OTHER UP AND GIGGLE
WHILE THE TWO MONKS UNLOAD THE BIKE.

>ANGEL
>Who are these two again?

>GEAROID
>(POINTING) That one is Brother Stephen and
>*that* one is Brother Stephen. (GIGGLES) But
>they're not twins.

>ANGEL
>They haven't said much.

>GEAROID
>Just as well. (CONSPIRATORILY) Vow of silence.
>It's not compulsory, though. They volunteered
>for it.

>ANGEL
>So what's their story then?

>GEAROID
>Don't know. They've never said!

BOTH COLLAPSE IN HYSTERICS.

>ANGEL
>Is there anything in the rules about drinking?

>GEAROID
>No! For sure no! (CONFIDENTIALLY) I checked
>the small print. Oops, time to go.

THE TWO STEPHENS HAVE WHEELED IN THE BIKE AND ARE
WAITING PATIENTLY FOR GEAROID. ANGEL HOLDS OUT A
HAND TO SHAKE BUT THEY MISS.

>GEAROID
>You're not going back to London tonight are
>you?

                    ANGEL
Not now. I'm going to crash here and get an
early start.

                    GEAROID
Then may your God go with you, as the
philosopher said. Watch yourself and let me
know if there's anything I can do.

                    ANGEL
Don't worry. (DRUNKENLY CONFIDENT) With a bit
of luck, Werewolf - Francis - is as good as
home and dry.

                    GEAROID
Good. He's depending on you, so stay lucky.

GEAROID CLAPS HIM ON THE BACK, GETS IN THE VAN
AND IT DRIVES OFF, WITH ANGEL SALUTING IT.

                    ANGEL
(ALONE) Depend on me ... course he can.

ANGEL WEAVES HIS WAY ROUND THE BACK OF THE
COTTAGE.

                    ANGEL
(TO HIMSELF) Rule of life Number One - it's
better to be lucky than good. So stay lucky.

ANGEL DISAPPEARS ROUND THE CORNER, TRIGGERING
LOUD BARKING FROM THE AKITAS. HE STUMBLES BACK
INTO VIEW, TRIPS, HITS HIS HEAD, KNOCKS OVER THE
MOTORBIKE, TRIES TO PICK IT UP, GIVES UP AND
SINKS DOWN AGAINST THE DOOR.


SCENE 26. EXT. BOX POP. LONDON. DAY.

ESTABLISHING SHOT. ANGEL DRIVES HIS TAXI INTO
INDUSTRIAL ESTATE, PASSING SIGN SAYING: HOUNSLOW
BUSINESS PARK UNIT 1-33.


SCENE 27. EXT. OUTSIDE BOX POP. DAY.

ANGEL PARKS OUTSIDE THE OFFICE/WAREHOUSE THAT
SAYS 'BOX POP TOUR MANAGEMENT'. HE OPENS THE BOOT
OF HIS CAB, TAKES OUT A SCRUFFY LEATHER JACKET
AND PUTS IT ON. THEN HE SORTS OUT THE TAXI'S TOOL
KIT, PUTTING A BATTERY CHARGER (I.E. SOMETHING
ELECTRICAL) ON TOP SO IT SHOWS. HE MARCHES INTO
BOX POP.

IN LONGSHOT WE SEE A PARKED MERCEDES SPORTS CAR
ACROSS THE ROAD. THE PASSENGER WINDOW GOES DOWN.


SCENE 28. INT. BOX POP RECEPTION. DAY.

THIS IS LIKE THE SERVICE DEPARTMENT OF A LARGE
GARAGE. JEV JEVONS (HE HAS A NAME BADGE) IS
BEHIND A COUNTER WORKING AT A COMPUTER. HE ALMOST
NEVER TAKES HIS EYES OFF THE SCREEN.

ANGEL BREEZES IN AND DUMPS HIS TOOL BAG ON THE
COUNTER.

>          ANGEL
> Morning, mate. Bleedin' Nora, you took some
> finding.

>          JEV
> (NOT LOOKING) Hmm. They all say that. How can
> we help you?

>          ANGEL
> You can't, I'm here to help you.

>          JEV
> (BORED) They all say that as well. (CAMP)
> Exactly how?

>          ANGEL
> Come to do a 'lectrical check on some gear
> you've got back in from a tour on the
> continent.

>          JEV
> And what gear would that be then?

>          ANGEL
> Stuff from the Astral Reich tour.

>          JEV
> (STILL ENGROSSED IN HIS VDU) What for?

>          ANGEL
> What for? To see if it's still kosher. It's
> for the insurance company. There's been a
> claim. Wasn't there an accident or something
> with one of the trucks?

>          JEV
> (BORED) Oh *that*. Yeah. Last time we use that
> dipshit Irishman. But I don't know nothing
> about any insurance claim. It's not on my
> screen, mate.

ANGEL
(INDIGNANT) Well, if you don't co-operate, you don't get paid, and I wouldn't fancy your premiums next year.

JEV
(HITTING KEYS) Hey, hey, don't let's twist our knickers. I said it's not on my screen. (HE TURNS THE VDU TOWARDS ANGEL) See, it's out on the road.

ANGEL
How do you make that out?

JEV
(POINTING AT SCREEN) All our equipment is coded and logged by truck. This is what Astral Reich has out on hire. One truckload - this one - is logged to a new vehicle, but it's a full quota.

ANGEL
You mean none of the gear in the accident in France was damaged?

JEV
Doesn't appear to have been. (HITS KEYBOARD) Mind you, it was mostly staging, lighting trusses, that sort of thing. Fairly solid stuff.

ANGEL
And its back in use? It's out on tour?

JEV
(HITS KEYBOARD) Yep. It's back with Astral Reich, playing Leicester Students Union tonight. Looks like they got away with nothing worse than a bust light bulb or two.

ANGEL
Good. Then you won't be making a claim, will you?

JEV LOOKS UP FOR THE FIRST TIME ONLY TO SEE ANGEL'S BACK, HEADING FOR THE DOOR.

JEV
I didn't know we were ...

SCENE 29. EXT. OUTSIDE BOX POP. DAY.

CLOSE-UP THROUGH INTERIOR OF MERCEDES SPORTS CAR.

THE DRIVER (GRONWEGHE) HAS WHAT APPEARS TO BE A
PERSONAL STEREO WITH HEADPHONES. AS THE LAST
LINES OF JEV/ANGEL DIALOGUE COME OVER THE SPEAKER
WE REALISE THAT THIS IS A 'WHISPERER' THAT PICKS
UP AND AMPLIFIES SOUND.

THE DRIVER TAKES OFF HIS HEADPHONES AND PICKS UP
A ROAD MAP. WE SEE ANGEL COMING OUT OF BOX POP
THROUGH THE MERCEDES' WINDOW AS IT CLOSES.


SCENE 30. EXT. MOTORWAY. DAY.

ESTABLISHING SHOT, ANGEL'S CAB TURNING ON TO M1,
SIGNPOSTED 'THE MIDLANDS'.


SCENE 31. INT. ANGEL'S TAXI. DAY.

ANGEL DRIVING, LISTENING TO MUSIC. NOTES THE
MERCEDES OVERTAKING HIM AT SPEED.

            ANGEL
    (IMPRESSED) Mmmm. Nice motor.


SCENE 32. EXT. CAMPUS BUILDINGS/CAR-PARK. DAY.

THE VENUE FOR THE ASTRAL REICH CONCERT,
BACKSTAGE. ANGEL PARKS HIS TAXI AND WALKS OVER TO
A ROADIE (ELVIS) WHO IS UNLOADING A LARGE TRUCK.
ANGEL AUTOMATICALLY HELPS HIM PULL SOME EQUIPMENT
OUT.

            ELVIS
    Thanks, mate. Just leave it here.

            ANGEL
    Is the boss around?

            ELVIS
    (CARRIES ON WORKING) Which on

            ANGEL
    You got more than one?

            ELVIS
    This is a metal band, man. Keep the number of
    bosses in single figures and you've got a
    result. But if you want the head roadie,
    that's Mitch and he's inside doing a sound
    check.

THERE IS A CRASH OF ELECTRIC GUITAR FROM INSIDE

AND BOTH ELVIS AND ANGEL WINCE.

                    ANGEL
     They any good, this lot?

                    ELVIS
     No, but they are fucking loud.

                    ANGEL
     Cheers.

                    ELVIS
     No sweat. Nice motor.

                    ANGEL
     Thanks.

ANGEL MOVES TO GO INTO THE CONCERT HALL, STOPS
AND LOOKS AT ARMSTRONG, THEN AT ELVIS, AND
REALISES THAT *HE* HAS BEEN LOOKING AT THE MERCEDES
SPORTS CAR PARKED BEYOND THE TAXI.

SCENE 33 INT. CONCERT HALL. DAY.

ANGEL ENTERS MAIN BODY OF HALL. THE BAND IS
SETTING UP ON STAGE AT ONE END, PEOPLE ARE
MILLING ABOUT CARRYING EQUIPMENT. ONE MAN (MITCH)
WITH A CLIPBOARD AND A HEADSET RADIO MICROPHONE
IS OBVIOUSLY DIRECTING TRAFFIC.

                    MITCH
     (INTO HEADSET) Don't come too far forward,
     for Christ's sake, we haven't got the ground
     supports in yet and I want another block
     centre stage for the slammers.

                    ANGEL
     Mitch?

                    MITCH
     You the Fire Prevention Officer?

                    ANGEL
     No.

                    MITCH
     Then go diddle yourself. (INTO HEADSET) I
     want that block reduced to six foot. No way
     are we paying out on the medical insurance
     again.

                    ANGEL
     Wondered if you needed a hand?

                    MITCH
You a student?

                    ANGEL
No.

                    MITCH
Then go diddle, we ain't hiring.

                    ANGEL
That's not a problem, I've just got some time
on my hands. I've worked Wembley.

                    MITCH
(QUICK) Stadium or Arena?

                    ANGEL
Both.  The  Stones,  Michael  Jackson  ...
Genesis.

                    MITCH
Somebody  had  to,  I  suppose.  Okay,  get  up
there  (POINTS  TO  STAGE)  and  help  them  set
that  centre  block  on  the  right  marks.  And
make sure it's secure. It's for the lemmings.

                    ANGEL
Lemmings?

                    MITCH
(PITYINGLY) This is *slam* metal, Sunshine. The
bozos  queue  up  to  get  thrown  back  into  the
audience.  Can't  have  them  breaking  their
necks, though, can we?

                    ANGEL
(CATCHING  ON)  I  heard  you  sell  tickets  to
help them jump the queue.

                    MITCH
I  don't  -  that's  Security's  perk,  and  I
wouldn't  mess  with  them  if  I  were  you.  But
then,  I'm  not  you.  I'm  down  here  waiting  for
you to get up there.

                    ANGEL
I'm gone.

ANGEL  GETS  UP  ON  STAGE  AND  STARTS  TO  HELP  MOVE
THINGS.  AT  THE  BACK  OF  THE  HALL,  A  SHADOWY  FIGURE
(GRONWEGHE)  TAKES  A  SEAT,  CLIPS  ON  HIS  'WHISPERER'
AND  STARTS  SCANNING  THE  HALL.  ELVIS  REAPPEARS,  ON
STAGE, AND SPOTS ANGEL.

                    ELVIS
Find Mitch, did you?

                    ANGEL
The guy directing the Nuremburg Rally? Yeah,
sure. Do people really pay to jump off this
thing? (HE SLAPS THE STAGING)


                    ELVIS
Oh no, they don't jump, they have to be
thrown. Wouldn't be worth a toss to be seen to
jump. These headcases have to be thrown.

                    ANGEL
Who throws them?

                    ELVIS
Whoever's nearest at the time, but mostly
Julian, the lead guitarist. Speaking of which,
here comes old glue-eyes now.

JULIAN WANDERS ACROSS THE STAGE. HE IS OBVIOUSLY
STONED OUT OF HIS MIND.

                    JULIAN
Elvis, Elvis! Speak to me, man.

                    ELVIS
Half a minute, Julian. Nearly ready. (HE
BUSIES HIMSELF PLUGGING IN A GUITAR)

                    JULIAN
Say the words, Elvis, man, say the words.

                    ELVIS
Oh, if you must. I am here, not gone, I didn't
die. My work is not yet finished and I will
return. (TO ANGEL) Don't ask, just don't ask.

                    JULIAN
The words. He said the words we've waited
for.

                    ELVIS
(HANDING HIM A GUITAR) Here you go.

                    MITCH
(OVER THE PA/RADIO) Julian on stage - fire in
the hole!]

AS JULIAN STRAPS ON THE GUITAR, ELVIS CROUCHES
DOWN NEXT TO ANGEL AND PUTS HIS HANDS OVER HIS
EARS. ANGEL DOES LIKEWISE. JULIAN HITS ONE CHORD

ON THE GUITAR AND HOLDS IT, MOVING IN FRONT OF THE AMP TO PRODUCE A HUGE BELT OF FEEDBACK.

AT THE BACK OF THE HALL, GRONWEGHE RIPS OFF HIS HEADPHONES IN AGONY.

ONCE THE CHORD DIES AWAY, JULIAN TAKES OFF THE GUITAR AND HANDS IT TO ELVIS.

> JULIAN
> Outstanding.

HE SHAMBLES AWAY. ELVIS HANDS THE GUITAR TO ANGEL.

> ELVIS
> Cop this while I check he hasn't done any lasting damage.

> ANGEL
> That was it? That was his sound check?

> ELVIS
> Sound check *and* rehearsal. (WINKS) These guys are professionals.

ELVIS BUSIES HIMSELF WITH THE AMPS. ANGEL LOOKS AT THE GUITAR AND IDLY STARTS PICKING OUT SOMETHING INCONGRUOUS (A BLUESY 'GEORGIA ON MY MIND' SAY). JULIAN WALKS BACK ON STAGE AND UNPLUGS THE GUITAR AS ANGEL IS PLAYING IT.

> JULIAN
> This guitar doesn't do melodies.

HE MARCHES OFF, LEAVING ANGEL SPEECHLESS.

SCENE 34. INT. CONCERT HALL STAGE. DAY.

ANGEL IS MINGLING WITH THE OTHER TECHNICIANS, MITCH IS STILL DIRECTING OPERATIONS. ELVIS IS NOT AROUND.

ANGEL DOES NOT NOTICE LULU COME ON STAGE UNTIL SHE STARTS HITTING ONE OF THE MICROPHONES, DISTORTING THE PA SYSTEM. THEN HE LOOKS UP AND SMILES IN RECOGNITION. LULU IS VERY TALL AND DRESSED OUTLANDISHLY IN ZEBRA-STRIPED MINISKIRT, COWBOY BOOTS AND STETSON,

                    LULU
(INTO MIKE) It's ass-kicking time! Let's go
for it! Get some lights on me here, you know
I love it!

ANGEL COMES UP BEHIND HER, MAKING A GUN OUT OF
TWO FINGERS AND PUSHING THEM INTO HER BACK.

                    LULU
This is not a drill! This is the full *son et
lumière*, so let's get sweaty, people.
I want this timed better than an orgasm. I
want clockwork precision to make the Swiss
bitch. I want ...

                    ANGEL
(IN HER EAR) This is the fashion police.
You're under arrest.

LULU'S FACE LIGHTS UP AND SHE SWINGS ROUND, PUTS
A BEAR HUG ON ANGEL AND LIFTS HIM OFF HIS FEET.

                    LULU
Angel! The ultimate party animal!

THEY KISS UNTIL LULU NOTICES THE ROADIES ARE
DOING NOTHING EXCEPT WATCH THEM.

                    LULU
Show's over, boys. (SHE PUTS ANGEL DOWN)
There's nothing to see. Give the man some
air. Move along. Get back to your homes -
(SHOUTS) and *jobs*! (TO ANGEL, SOOTHING) Now,
baby, just what the hell are you doing in
town?

                    ANGEL
(STRUGGLING FOR AIR) I need a favour, Lulu.

                    LULU
I was always yours to command; it's just you
never did, Angel honey.

                    ANGEL
Well I need to call one in now, Lulu, a big
one.

                    LULU
(SMILING) How big, big boy?

                    ANGEL
Down, girl. I need to talk. Is there somewhere
we can go *and just talk*?

           LULU

With three hours to go to showtime and these
zombies screwing up on me? (THINKS) Sure, why
not? (SHE GRABS THE PA MIKE) Mitch! You out
there? Your ass is on the line. I'm going to
be in conference with my old and distinguished
friend Mr Angel, in the nearest bar. You copy?

           MITCH

(OVER TANNOY) That's a big 10-4, Mean Momma.

LULU DOES A DOUBLE-TAKE AT THAT BUT LETS IT GO.
SHE LINKS ARMS WITH ANGEL AND THEY JUMP OFF THE
STAGE.

IN THE BACK OF THE HALL, GRONWEGHE LEAVES HIS SEAT
WITHOUT ANYONE NOTICING.


SCENE 35. INT. HOTEL BAR. DAY.

ANGEL AND LULU ARE SAT IN A CORNER, THEIR TABLE
ALREADY COVERED WITH EMPTY BEER BOTTLES. IN
ANOTHER PART OF THE BAR, MEMBERS OF ASTRAL REICH
ARE TRYING TO PLAY POOL, THOUGH ONE OF THEM IS
CHALKING THE CUE AN AWFUL LOT, VERY NEAR HIS NOSE.

           LULU

(SOFT LOW WHISTLE) The Wolfman really is in
deep doo-doo. Are the guys holding him
serious?

           ANGEL

Worse than serious - they're amateurs, which
means they're dangerous. If they'd been pros,
they would have come looking themselves, or
not let the stuff get out of France in the
first place.

           LULU

So what do we do?

           ANGEL

Clear it with your guys so I can get access
to the gear that was in Werewolf's truck.

           LULU

Do you know what you're looking for?

           ANGEL

No, but it's got to be dope of some sort.

                LULU
(INDICATING THE BAND) And you think it would
be a good idea to tell them that?

                ANGEL
I get your point. Okay, then, you're the
boss, right?

                LULU
Sure.

                ANGEL
Then get me a job with the crew. Just for
tonight.

                LULU
Doing what? Security's pretty tight
backstage. Believe it or not, these boys have
a following.

                ANGEL
Only in the sense of a pursuing army ... Oh
yeah, I'm sure they have. Look, I've snooped
around the amps and the staging and there's
nothing I can find. The only other thing that
was part of Werewolf's cargo was the lighting
trusses.

                LULU
The flying trusses, above the stage? (ANGEL
NODS) Well you could always go up there with
a hand-held spot. I can say its something new
I'm trying out. How's your head for heights?

                ANGEL
Pretty good.

                LULU
It'll need to be. Why not wait until the guys
do rip-down at the end of the show?

                ANGEL
Because the guys will be all over the place,
that's why. Too many witnesses, and I'll bet
the gear gets stowed away in the trucks,
right?

                LULU
Right. We place Noocassle tomorrow night, so
it's an early start.

                ANGEL
And the trucks'll be locked and alarmed,
right?

                    LULU
You bet.

                    ANGEL
So at least let me check out the lighting
trusses tonight, huh? If there's nothing
there we'll have to think of something else.

                    LULU
Okay then, Angel honey, but you watch that
cute little ass of yours. I don't want you
crashing down on to the stage in the middle
of one of Julian's solos.

                    ANGEL
Would anybody notice?

                    LULU
Probably not. Think it was part of the act.
Hey, if we got a stunt man in, it could be.

                    ANGEL
Don't even think it, Lulu.

                    LULU
Aw shucks. Anyway, we got the Plan, so you'd
better come up to my room and help me change.

                    ANGEL
(SUSPICIOUS) Into what?

                    LULU
Into my costume. I come on and introduce the
band. (CONFIDENTIAL) They have trouble
remembering their names.

                    ANGEL
(LOOKING AT WATCH) There's still two hours to
showtime.

                    LULU
(SMILING SWEETLY) We'll think of something.


SCENE 36. EXT. CAR-PARKS/TRUCKS. NIGHT.

TRUCK PARK, OUTSIDE CONCERT. GRONWEGHE CREEPS UP
TO ONE OF THE BAND'S TRUCKS AND USES A LOCK GUN
TO OPEN THE REAR DOORS.

HE IS INSIDE, LOOKING AROUND WITH A TORCH, WHEN
THE DOOR IS OPENED BY ELVIS. GRONWEGHE SHINES HIS
TORCH FULL IN ELVIS'S FACE.

SCENE 37. INT. HOTEL ROOM. NIGHT.

LULU IS SITTING IN HER UNDERWEAR AT A DRESSING
TABLE, PUTTING ON HEAVY MAKE-UP. ANGEL EMERGES
FROM HER BATHROOM HALF DRESSED, CARRYING A
HANDFUL OF TOILETRIES.

          ANGEL
I've raided the soap and shampoos. Anything
in the mini-bar?

          LULU
(APPLYING EYE MAKE-UP) Help yourself.
Somebody'll pick up the tab.

ANGEL PUTS HIS HAUL IN HIS SHOULDER BAG AND
STARTS SELECTING VODKAS ETC FROM THE MINI-BAR.

          ANGEL
Want anything?

          LULU
Uh-huh. You can get my costume though. It's
hanging in the closet.

ANGEL OPENS THE WARDROBE DOOR, JUMPS BACK IN
SURPRISE, THEN PULLS OUT A RUBBER SUIT (LIKE
BATMAN'S) ON A HANGER.

          ANGEL
Er ... Lulu ... Somebody's shot a large seal
and left in here to dry.

          LULU
Coolski, huh? I designed it myself.

          ANGEL
(TO HIMSELF) Good of you to admit it. (IN THE
MIRROR, TO LULU) How do you get into it?

          LULU
With the help of a friend and (SHE HANDS HIM
A TIN) lots of talcum powder.

ANGEL EXHALES IN WONDER.

          ANGEL
What does it take to get you *out* of it?

          LULU
(BEAT, MISCHEVIOUS) A large tequila usually.

SCENE 38. EXT. TRUCK PARK. NIGHT.

CONCERT IS UNDERWAY AS ANGEL AND LULU COME OUT OF
THE BACK OF THE HALL AND WALK TO ANGEL'S TAXI,
PASSING THE TRUCK. THEY ARE BOTH WEARING
'SECURITY' BADGES, AND LULU HER RUBBER SUIT.

                    ANGEL
  (WALKING) The support band are quite good.
  What're they called?

                    LULU
  The Support Band - that's what they call
  themselves.

                    ANGEL
  Mmmm. Ambitious.

LULU REACHES ANGEL'S TAXI AND SPREADS HER ARMS
OVER IT AS IF HUGGING.

                    LULU
  Armstrong, good buddy, great to see yer! Have
  I had some memorable times in the back of
  you!

                    ANGEL
  (QUIET, PATTING THE BOOT) Sorry, Armstrong, I
  should have warned you.

ANGEL OPENS THE BOOT AND RUMMAGES FOR HIS TOOL
KIT. HE TAKES OUT A SMALL HACKSAW AND A PENCIL
TORCH AND PUTS THEM IN HIS JACKET POCKETS.

                    LULU
  (TO ARMSTRONG) Now, don't you worry about
  Angel; Lulu will take care of him. (ANGEL IS
  SHAKING HIS HEAD) And if he falls, Lulu will
  be there to catch him.

                    ANGEL
  Lulu, I have done this before. When I worked -

BEHIND THEM, THE DOOR OF THE TRUCK BURSTS OPEN AND
ELVIS FALLS OUT. HE IS BADLY BRUISED AND DAZED.

                    LULU
  Elvis! Shit!

THEY RUN TO HELP HIM.

                    LULU
  What happened? Who did this to you?

                    ELVIS
(SLURRED) Dunno, he didn't say. Found him in
the truck, then he hit me.

                    ANGEL
(LOOKING TO WHERE THE MERCEDES HAD BEEN) Was
it the guy in the flash car? The Merc?

                    ELVIS
Could be - I'm not sure - Happened too fast ..

                    LULU
(HOLDS UP ONE FINGER) Elvis, how many fingers
can you see?

ELVIS COUNTS THEM SILENTLY, ONE, TWO, THREE

                    ELVIS
Seven.

                    LULU
That does it. You're going to hospital for a
check up.

                    ELVIS
(PROTESTING) I'm okay. I'm fine. You can take
the fingers away now. (HE FLAPS AT NOTHING IN
FRONT OF HIS FACE). Got to do the follow spot

                    LULU
No way, Elvito. (THINKS) Angel can do that.

                    ANGEL
Do what?

                    LULU
The follow spot, from up on the lighting
trusses. (SHE DOES A THUMBS UP) Mitch can
radio instructions. We only use it twice in
the show.

                    ANGEL
Oh yeah, sure. I'm up for it.

                    LULU
There we go. You're hired; on the team; in
the gang; with the crew.

SHE GIVES ANGEL A HIGH FIVE, DROPPING ELVIS'S
HEAD ON THE GROUND IN THE PROCESS.

                    ELVIS
(SITTING UP) And another thing. He had a gun.

                    LULU
Who? The guy who bushwhacked you?

                    ELVIS
(SNAPPY) No, the sodding milkman. Of course,
the guy searching the truck.

                    LULU
So he's armed?

                    ANGEL
(SHRUGS) Well, we already knew he was
dangerous.


SCENE 39. INT. ASTRAL REICH CONCERT. NIGHT.

ANGEL IS CRAWLING ALONG ONE OF THE 'FLYING'
LIGHTING TRUSSES (THE METAL STRUCTURES FROM WHICH
HANG SPOTLIGHTS). HE IS THIRTY FEET ABOVE THE
STAGE. BELOW HIM, ASTRAL REICH ARE PLAYING FULL
BELT.

AS THEY PLAY, MEMBERS OF THE AUDIENCE ARE ALLOWED
ON STAGE AND THEN THROWN OUT INTO THE AUDIENCE
('SLAM METAL') BY THE SECURITY BOUNCERS. ANGEL'S
JOB IS TO SHINE A HAND-HELD 'FOLLOW SPOT' ON THE
SLAMMERS. HE RECEIVES INSTRUCTIONS OVER A HEADSET
FROM MITCH.

                    MITCH (ON RADIO)
[*Red* filter, I said red, not blue!}

                    ANGEL
(INTO MIKE) Sorry. I'll get the next one.

                    MITCH
[Left! left! Follow through!]

                    ANGEL
(STRUGGLING WITH SPOTLIGHT, SWEATING) Sorry
again. Christ, it's hot up here.

                    MITCH
[Get ready. Come on. Track this one out into
the audience. See where he lands.]

                    ANGEL
(LOOKING DOWN) Oops! Wasn't somebody
supposed to catch him?

                    MITCH
[Kill the spot for now. We'll have to see if
that one can still walk.]

                    ANGEL
Do you need me anymore?

                    MITCH
Doubt it. You're not making much of an
impression.

                    ANGEL
(TAKES OFF HIS HEADSET) Thanks a bunch. I'm
being microwaved up here.

ONCE HIS HEADSET IS OFF, IT IS IMPOSSIBLE TO
HEAR HIM. THE REST OF THE SCENE IS PLAYED TO THE
BACKDROP OF THE BAND. ALL DIALOGUE IS MOUTHED OR
SIGNED, NOT HEARD.

ANGEL CRAWLS ALONG THE TRUSS UNTIL HE COMES TO
THE END, THEN HE PUTS AN EAR TO THE METAL, ONE
HAND OVER HIS OTHER EAR, AND BEGINS TO TAP THE
TRUSS WITH HIS HACKSAW.

LULU'S HEAD APPEARS AT THE BACKSTAGE END OF THE
TRUSS, STARTLING HIM.

                    LULU
(INDICATING EARS - WHAT'S HE DOING?)

                    ANGEL
(MIMES TAPPING ON THE TUBULAR FRAME - THEY
SHOULD BE HOLLOW.)

                    LULU
(THUMBS UP - SHE'S GOT THE IDEA AND WILL DO
THE BACK ONE.)

THEY CRAWL OFF AT RIGHT ANGLES TO EACH OTHER,
THE BAND PLAYING ON BENEATH THEM. ANGEL IS
HORRIFIED TO SEE LULU PRODUCE A FLICK-KNIFE WITH
WHICH SHE BANGS THE PIPING.

ANGEL COMES TO THE END OF HIS TRUSS, TURNS RIGHT
TO GO DOWN THE NEXT. HALF WAY ALONG, HE STOPS,
KNEELS UP AND BEGINS TO CUT INTO THE METAL WITH
THE HACKSAW.

                    LULU
(LOOKING UP, MOUTHS 'FOUND SOMETHING?)

                    ANGEL
(CAN'T HEAR. POINTS. SHRUGS.)

LULU CRAWLS OVER TO HIM. BY THE TIME SHE GETS
THERE, ANGEL HAS CUT A 'V' SLICE OUT OF THE
METAL. HE HOLDS HIS TORCH BETWEEN HIS TEETH. WHEN

LULU GETS TO HIM, HE MIMES WITH STABBING MOTIONS
THAT HE WANTS TO BORROW HER KNIFE.

WITH THE POINT OF THE FLICK-KNIFE, ANGEL DIGS
INTO THE METAL AND PULLS OUT A STRIP OF PAPER OR
TAPE WITH TABLETS EVERY INCH OR SO.

LULU PICKS UP THE TAPE, PULLS A LENGTH OUT, AND
RIPS OFF A TAB, OPENING IT AND LOOKING.

> LULU
> (MOUTHING - 'Eeee'.)

SHE PULLS THE STRIP OUT. IT KEEPS ON COMING, YARD
AFTER YARD. JUST AS LULU SPEAKS THE BAND STOPS
SUDDENLY.

> LULU
> Bingo!

BELOW THEM, THE AUDIENCE BURSTS INTO APPLAUSE.

SCENE 40. INT. CONCERT HALL. NIGHT.

ANGEL, LULU, MITCH AND ELVIS ARE IN A HUDDLE. THE
CONCERT IS OVER AND ROADIES ARE 'RIPPING DOWN'
WITH IMPRESSIVE SPEED.

> MITCH
> So what you're saying is the guy who duffed
> up Elvis is gonna come back, that it?

> ANGEL
> Seems reasonable. He didn't get what he
> wanted first time round.

> ELVIS
> What *did* he want?

> ANGEL
> Dunno. Maybe this way we'll find out. Can you
> fix it?

> ELVIS
> (SHRUGS) Sure, if I can take a cable from the
> main junction box here.

> LULU
> That's cool, I've checked.

> ELVIS
> Then okay. I'll get on it.

                    MITCH
What if the guy doesn't show?

                    ANGEL
Then he doesn't show, and we've all lost a
night's sleep.

                    LULU
Come on, Mitch, it's worth it to see if we
can flush this guy out. We don't want him
following us around on the tour. Let's get it
done.
                    MITCH
Fair enough, you're the boss.

                    LULU
(SURPRISED) Yes I am, aren't I.

                    MITCH
(STANDING TO GO) I'll start loading the
truck. (TO ANGEL) You'll be okay locked in
there?

                    ANGEL
I'll take a book or something. Keep myself
occupied.

MITCH AND ELVIS LEAVE THEM.

                    LULU
(SUGGESTIVE) I could come in there and keep
you company ...

                    ANGEL
Oh no. I need to conserve my strength and,
anyway, I'll need you on the outside on one
of the walkie-talkies.

                    LULU
You sure there's nothing I can get you?

                    ANGEL
There is one thing - a suitcase. I'm going to
be busy packing.

                    LULU
(QUIET) How many tabs do you reckon are in
those things?

                    ANGEL
(RESIGNED) A lot.

# ANGELS IN ARMS: THE SCRIPT

SCENE 41. INT. BACK OF TRUCK. NIGHT.

ANGEL, WEARING GLOVES AND WORKING BY TORCHLIGHT,
IS PULLING LENGTH AFTER LENGTH OF STRIPS OF
TABLETS FROM THE LIGHTING TRUSSES PACKED IN THE
TRUCK. HE PACKS THEM IN A BIG SPORTS BAG.

THE BACK OF THE TRUCK IS CRAMPED, FULL OF
EQUIPMENT AND A STACK OF SPOTLIGHTS.

ANGEL HAS THE RADIO HEADSET ON AND LULU'S VOICE
COMES OVER IT.

>           LULU
> [How's it going, Angel honey?]

>           ANGEL
> I'm guessing, but counting by the yard, we
> are talking several thousand tabs here.

>           LULU
> (GIVES A LOUD WHISTLE, MAKING ANGEL GRAB HIS
> HEADSET) Riders on the storm or what! Street
> value?

>           ANGEL
> (STILL COUNTING) Who knows? A lot of dosh.

>           LULU
> [Is that dosh in dollars?]

>           ANGEL
> Pounds.

>           LULU
> [Yee-ha! We're rich, honey child. Hey, hold
> it down, we've got Indian sign out here.]

ANGEL SCURRIES THINGS AWAY.

>           ANGEL
> Is it him?

>           LULU
> It's somebody, and he's heading your way.

>           ANGEL
> You got the Security guys with you?

>           LULU
> Three of them, and they're all big boys. We
> can take him.

                    ANGEL
Just wait. See what he does.

                    LULU
He's coming. He's almost on you. You set?]

                    ANGEL
Yeah - if Elvis has done his stuff. Signing
off.

ANGEL TAKES OFF THE HEADSET AND HIDES BEHIND A
SPEAKER. HE PICKS UP A CABLE WITH A LARGE SWITCH
THEN TURNS OFF HIS TORCH.

THERE IS A WHIRRING NOISE (THE LOCK GUN) AND THE
DOORS OF THE TRUCK OPEN. A TORCH BEAM LIGHTS UP
THE INTERIOR BUT CAN'T PICK OUT ANGEL.

SOUND OF SOMEONE CLIMBING IN.

ANGEL HITS THE SWITCH HE IS HOLDING AND THE BANK
OF MEGAWATT SPOTLIGHTS COME ON.

THE INTRUDER SCREAMS, STUMBLES BACKWARDS AND
FALLS OUT OF THE TRUCK.

FROM OUTSIDE, HE IS ON THE GROUND, ANGEL STANDS
IN THE BACK OF THE TRUCK. LULU AND THREE LARGE
SECURITY MEN (SEEN EARLIER AT CONCERT) RUN UP AND
STAND OVER HIM. THEY ARE ALL WEARING DARK GLASSES
AGAINST THE LIGHT SHOW.

                    ANGEL
(HANDS ON HIPS, LOOKING DOWN) Let's go to
work.

THEY DESCEND ON GRONWEGHE, TYING HIM UP WITH
YARDS OF GAFFER TAPE. THE SECURITY MEN LIFT HIM
UP INTO THE TRUCK. LULU AND ANGEL GET IN WITH
HIM. THE SECURITY MEN SHUT THE DOOR AND STAND
GUARD.

INSIDE THE TRUCK:

                    LULU
(HANDING ANGEL A PISTOL) He had this on him,
velcroed to the inside of his jacket. Neat.

                    ANGEL
(SHYING AWAY) No thanks. Get rid of it. I saw
enough of those on Guernsey. They seem to be
a fashion accessory.

                    LULU
(EXPERTLY UNLOADING IT) It's a Walther P-38,
an old one. Nazi issue but in immaculate
condition. Worth something to a collector.

                    ANGEL
Not in this country. Get rid of it. (READING
FROM AN EU PASSPORT) His name is Paul
Gronweghe - 'Groanvegge' - if that's how you
say it.

                    LULU
If that's the real McCoy.

                    ANGEL
(AGREEING) If that's the real McCoy. He's
Dutch. That figures. It must be the start of
the pipeline Werewolf interrupted. Watch it,
he's coming round.

GRONWEGHE WAKES UP, TAKES IN HIS SURROUNDINGS
CALMLY, MAKING HIMSELF COMFORTABLE. DESPITE LULU
WAVING THE GUN OVER HIS HEAD, HE IS TOTALLY COOL.

                    GRONWEGHE
(TO ANGEL) So, do I do a deal with you (BEAT)
or with her?

                    ANGEL
Well, well, an equal opportunity gangster.
You deal with me - and be grateful for that.

                    GRONWEGHE
Then you are not as stupid as I first
thought.   (ANGEL   REACTS.   LULU   GRINS.)
Therefore I will deal with you. Give me my
property and let me go.

ANGEL AND LULU EXCHANGE LOOKS. LULU SHRUGS.

                    ANGEL
*That's* a deal?

                    LULU
Dream on, Mr Shit-for-Brains. Do you know who
you are dealing with here?

                    ANGEL
(WARNING) Lulu ...

                    LULU
We are the roughest, toughest duo this side
of the Pecos. We are the *law* here. We taught
Judge Roy Bean jurisprudence. We are the ones

holding the gun.

                    GRONWEGHE
(SHAKING HIS HEAD) I was wrong. You *are*
idiots.

                    LULU
(WAVING GUN) Smile when you say that,
stranger. You ain't from around these parts,
are you?

                    ANGEL
Lulu, we've established that. Now let's do a
reality check on this deal, shall we? We give
you everything and you go away and leave us
alone. Is that it?

                    GRONWEGHE
Yes. Good. I was speaking slowly enough.

                    LULU
Hey! Has he got a smart mouth or what? Can I
hit him now?

                    ANGEL
(IGNORING HER) Then what happens to our
friend.

                    GRONWEGHE
(THROWN FOR THE FIRST TIME) What do you think
(SLY) should happen?

                    LULU
Hey, we're talking the Wolfman here. And old
and distinguished ...

                    ANGEL
(TO LULU) Shut it! (TO GRONWEGHE) You don't
know, do you? Guennoc didn't tell you. You're
just (TAUNTING) the messenger boy sent to
keep me on track, aren't you.

                    GRONWEGHE
Guennoc is a moron! And so are you! You have
no idea what is going on, do you?

                    LULU
Can I kick him?

                    GRONWEGHE
(REALISING) They don't either, do they? The
ones outside. They don't know what you've
found. (LOOKING AT ANGEL'S BAG) You haven't
told them have you? (LOUD, SHOUTING AT THE

233

DOOR) Hey, you outside! There's enough drugs in here to make you rich! Do you know what your bitch boss is hiding from you?

                    ANGEL
(REACHING FOR HIS BAG) Now, Lulu.

                    GRONWEGHE
She's not going to cut you in. She and her boyfriend -

LULU STAMPS ON HIS CHEST WITH HER COWBOY BOOTS, BUT HE CARRIES ON AS THEY STRUGGLE.

                    GRONWEGHE
Enough for all of you to be rich. They're hiding from you and its a safe deal, untraceable, no comeba ck -

                    LULU
Can I kick him again?

                    ANGEL
Hold him.

ANGEL HAS TAKEN SOMETHING OUT OF HIS SHOULDER BAG AND UNWRAPPED IT. HE SHOVES IT INTO GRONWEGHE'S MOUTH.

                    ANGEL
Gaffer tape - quick.

LULU GRABS A ROLL, RIPS OFF A STRIP AND PLASTERS IT ACROSS GRONWEGHE'S MOUTH. HE BUCKS THEN GOES ALMOST RIGID.

                    LULU
(STANDING BACK) Whatever that was, Angel honey, it did the trick. Hey, is he foaming at the mouth?

                    ANGEL
Probably. He's eating soap.

                    LULU
Soap?

                    ANGEL
One of the ones I nicked from the hotel. He's just worked out it's easier to keep his mouth shut and breathe through his nose.

                    LULU
Coolski! Where d'you learn that one?

ANGEL

Don't ask. (TO GRONWEGHE) Now listen, Paul, if that's your name. I'm taking the stuff and cutting out of here. The band know nothing. You hang around them and they'll turn nasty. You won't find me. (TO LULU) Take the gun and his passport to the nearest river.

LULU

It's done. Missing them already.

ANGEL

Can your Security boys carry him to his car? (GOING THROUGH GRONWEGHE'S POCKETS UNTIL HE FINDS CAR KEYS) It can't be far away.

LULU

Sure. Then what?

ANGEL

Leave him in it, but lose the keys.

LULU

Do you want me to tell them he was the one who zapped Elvis?

ANGEL

(BEAT) Yeah, why not?

SCENE 42. TRUCK PARK. NIGHT.

ANGEL AND LULU STANDING BY TRUCK, ANGEL HEFTING OUT LARGE BAG. LULU'S SECURITY MEN ARE (ROUGHLY) MANHANDLING GRONWEGHE OUT OF SHOT.

LULU

Now what?

ANGEL

I'm out of here. I've got a date with the Popular Front of Brittany.

LULU

I thought they gave you five days?

ANGEL

They'll be early. They always are. Amateurs can never wait.

LULU

Amateurs or not, this bitch boss reckons you need help. (PUTS HER ARM ROUND HIM) So I'm riding along with you on this one, pardner.

ANGELS IN ARMS: THE SCRIPT

                ANGEL
Oh no you're not. What about the band?

                LULU
Screw them. They won't even notice I've gone.
Werewolf's a friend of mine, too, you know.

                ANGEL
(DOUBTFUL) Well okay, but what I intend to do
is turn the stuff over to this Guennoc guy
and get Werewolf back. Straight arrow, okay?
No tricks. (TO HIMSELF) Famous last words.

                LULU
What if this Dutch guy comes after you?

                ANGEL
He doesn't know me from Adam.

                LULU
He's seen you (IDEA) and he's seen Armstrong.

                ANGEL
(JEWISH) So he's going to come looking for a
black cab in London?

SCENE 43. EXT. MOTORWAY. DAY.

ANGEL'S CAB ON MOTORWAY. VOICE OVER.

                LULU
(V/O) Doesn't this thing go any faster?

                ANGEL
(V/O) Shut up and keep the pedal to the
metal, you're making me lose count. 8,231.
8,232. 8,233 .

SCENE 44. INT. ANGEL'S FLAT. DAY.

CLOSE UP ON LULU'S FACE - RAPTURE.

                LULU
You're glad I came, aren't you? You love me,
I can tell. Oh, you animal!

CUT AWAY TO LULU HOLDING ONE OF SPRINGSTEEN'S
KITTENS.

                ANGEL
Stop that, you'll go blind. Or he will.

236

HE HANDS HER A BOTTLE OF BEER. SHE HAS THREE OR FOUR KITTENS IN HER LAP.

> LULU
> What was the count?

> ANGEL
> Nearest I could make out, somewhere over 15,000 tabs.

> LULU
> (WHISTLES) Value?

> ANGEL
> (SHRUGS) Depends on your distribution and market forces, but you could clear £150k to £160k.

> LULU
> Shitski! That's a quarter of a million dollars in real money.

THEY BOTH LOOK AT THE BAG OF DRUGS.

(BEAT.)

> ANGEL
> (THOUGHTFUL) Lot of hassle, getting into street sales.

(BEAT.)

> LULU
> (DREAMY) Yeah, hassle city, dealing that quantity.

(BEAT.)

> ANGEL
> Wouldn't know how to spend the money anyway, would we?

(BEAT.)

> LULU
> Oh, I don't know ... (BEAT) Still, we've got to think of Werewolf, ain't we?

> ANGEL
> (BEAT) Werewolf who?

LULU DOES A DOUBLE-TAKE, THEN IS ABOUT TO LAUGH WHEN THE PHONE (DOWNSTAIRS) RINGS.

                    LULU
(NERVY) Is that them?

                    ANGEL
I knew they'd be early. I knew they couldn't
wait. They're amateurs.

                    LULU
Hadn't you better answer it?

                    ANGEL
(JUMPING UP) Stay calm, stay cool. Let *them*
sweat.

                    LULU
Yeah, good advice, but answer the goddam
phone first, huh?

                    ANGEL
Sure, on my way. Cool. Stay cool.


SCENE 45. INT. HALLWAY, ANGEL'S HOUSE. DAY.

ANGEL EMERGES FROM HIS FLAT, BREAKS INTO A RUN
AND TAKES THE STAIRS IN TWO JUMPS, SWINGING ON
THE BANNISTER, ALMOST FALLING AND ENDS UP
CRASHING INTO THE WALL PHONE, GRABBING THE
PHONE, DROPPING IT ...

                    ANGEL
(BREATHLESS) Yes ... Yes it is, and before
you ask, yes I have. (BEAT) What? Are you
wearing your head on right today? (BEAT) No
way, Yannick, baby, you go - (BEAT) (LULU
COMES AND SITS ON THE STAIRS BEHIND HIM)
Monday? Give me a break. How the hell do -?
(BEAT) Oh, like that - *just* like that? Sod
you, you nasty little turd, you can -

HE LOOKS AT THE RECEIVER IN DISBELIEF, THEN
REPLACES IT.

                    LULU
(SURPRISING ANGEL) So how's Mr Total Cool?
Ice-water calm and in control?

                    ANGEL
(NOT LOOKING ROUND) Ever been to France,
Lulu?

SCENE INT. ANGEL'S TAXI. EAST LONDON. DAY.

> LULU
> So we're going to see a drunk to buy a car?

> ANGEL
> Duncan the Drunken. It's his name. He's usually sober when he's working, though. (BEAT) Sometimes.

> LULU
> Why him? Why not go in Armstrong? (SHE HUGS HER SEAT) Bet the French ain't seen anything like this.

> ANGEL
> Exactly. Anonymous in London but would stand out like a McDonald's with a Michelin star in France. And another thing: if they catch drug runners these days, they confiscate their vehicles, so I want a back up.

> LULU
> So you're gonna do it, huh? You're gonna re-smuggle all that E back to France?

> ANGEL
> Looks like it. (THINKS) Where did the 'we' thing go all of a sudden?

> LULU
> Hey, hey, Angel honey, I ain't quitting on you now. We're gonna ride down there to get Werewolf 'cross the border ... Whatever. We'll ride into town and shoot the place up ...

> ANGEL
> (SUDDEN) You did get rid of that gun, didn't you?

> LULU
> Yeah, yeah. Relax-ski. So maybe we don't shoot the place up. We ride into town and say 'I've come for ma boy'.

> ANGEL
> *What?*

> LULU
> Well, you know what I mean. We're the good guys aren't we?

> ANGEL
> (RESIGNED) If you say so, Lulu, if you say so.

THE CAB PULLS INTO AN EAST END GARAGE WITH WORKSHOP.

SCENE 47. INT. DUNCAN'S GARAGE. DAY.

DUNCAN IS WIPING HIS HANDS ON AN OILY RAG, SHOWING ANGEL AROUND THE FIVE OR SIX CARS IN HIS GARAGE, BUT MOSTLY LEERING OVER LULU.

> DUNCAN
> So, then, young Angel. You're looking for a nice little runabout to impress this beautiful lady, are you?

LULU GIGGLES AND PUNCHES HIM ON THE ARM.

> ANGEL
> No, I want something cheap, semi-legit and with a few extras.

> DUNCAN
> (EYEING LULU) Something with a lot of leg room, eh?

> LULU
> Hey - are you upfront or what?

LULU PUNCHES HIM ON THE ARM. IT HURTS.

> ANGEL
> I'm not after a passion wagon, Duncan. Four wheels and an engine that'll keep going for a week will do me.

> DUNCAN
> Going far, then? Nothing wrong with Armstrong, is there?

> ANGEL
> No, just need a one-off for a one-off job.

> LULU
> In France. We're going (SHE SEES ANGEL'S KILLER LOOK) ... to France ... to do some shopping.

> DUNCAN
> So these optional extras you mentioned. They'd be things like Green Card insurance documents maybe?

> ANGEL
> Yup.

                DUNCAN
What name this time?

                ANGEL
Roy Maclean.

                DUNCAN
What, from the old Southwark address?

                ANGEL
Yeah, Redcross Street.

                LULU
(CATCHING ON) Roy ... Maclean ... Hey, hold
it. Fitzroy Maclean Angel ... Roy Maclean. I
get it.

                ANGEL
And sometimes Fitzroy Angel, or Mac Maclean
Angel.

                LULU
You could turn it around and call yourself
Angel F M, like a radio station

                ANGEL
Thanks, Lulu, we really value your input.

                LULU
(LOOKING AT BOTH OF THEM) You've done this
before, haven't you?

                DUNCAN
You'll learn, my lass, you'll learn. Young
Angel changes his names more often than I
change me socks.

                ANGEL
Thank you for sharing that with us, Duncan,
but is there any chance of getting some
wheels out of you before my eyesight goes?

                DUNCAN
How about the Ford? (HE INDICATES A BASIC
FORD SALOON) You know where you are with a
Ford. Anything goes wrong, it's easy to get
at, easy to fix.

                ANGEL
I don't want anything to go wrong, Dunc.

                DUNCAN
It'll be fine. I've given it one of my
special 70,000 mile services.

                    ANGEL
      How many has it done?

                    DUNCAN
      95,000 - but it's a good runner.

                    LULU
      What? One little (SHE TOWERS OVER DUNCAN) old
      lady driver?

                    DUNCAN
      (EYEING HER) Something like that.

ANGEL WALKS AROUND THE FORD, KICKS THE TYRES,
OPENS A DOOR, TRIES THE WHEEL, ALL VERY
PERFUNCTORY.

                    ANGEL
      How much?

                    DUNCAN
      Three grand.

                    LULU
      Pounds? Get real!

ANGEL INDICATES THAT SHE SHOULD STAY OUT OF IT.

                    ANGEL
      With documents?

                    DUNCAN
      Do 'em for you now. Not worth the paper
      they're crayoned on though.

                    ANGEL
      Buy-back?

                    DUNCAN
      Give you a grand if it's back in one piece in
      a week.

                    ANGEL
      One other extra.

                    DUNCAN
      Thought there might be.

                    ANGEL
      A spare set of plates.

                    DUNCAN
      In the cupboard, help yourself while I get
      the paperwork.

ANGEL OPENS A METAL CUPBOARD. THERE ARE DOZENS OF
NUMBER PLATES. HE GOES THROUGH THEM.

LULU
(MYSTIFIED) Angel ...?

ANGEL
Excellent! This is a bonus. (HE HOLDS UP AN
ORANGE PLATE) Dutch plates.

LULU
How do they help?

ANGEL
(FROWNS) Not sure, but you never know, it
could be a bit more insurance.

LULU
Insurance? We've got a fake car and fake
papers - isn't that enough?

ANGEL
You can never have too much.

LULU
(LOOKS ROUND, DROPS VOICE) So you've worked
out how we hide the drugs?

ANGEL
No, not yet, but at least we've got
transport.

LULU
Oh come on, Angel honey, you must have
thought of something. (WHISPERS) Is it the
car? Does this guy Duncan sell cars with
secret compartments?

ANGEL
No, Lulu, it's just a car.

LULU
You must have *some* idea. We're in this
together, Angel honey. You can tell me. Where
you gonna stash the stash?

ANGEL
Honest, I don't ... yes, I do. (IDEA HITS)
You've just said it.

LULU
I have?

ANGEL

Yes, Lulu-honey!

HE KISSES HER AND GOES TO PLAY WITH THE FORD, LEAVING LULU SHAKING HER HEAD.


SCENE 48. EXT. DORSET. DAY.

ANGEL AND LULU IN THEIR 'NEW' FORD ARRIVING AT GEAROID'S RETREAT. THEY DRIVE THROUGH A GATE. THE SIGN SAYS:

The Community of
St Fulgentius of Ruspe.
Peace in Body and Soul.
Registered for VAT.
Monk's Hood Organic Products Ltd.


SCENE 49. EXT. COMMUNITY GARDENS. DAY.

GEAROID, LULU AND ANGEL HOLDING A COUNCIL OF WAR, DRINKING 'TEA' OUT OF PLASTIC CUPS. OTHER 'MONKS' ARE GARDENING, FLOATING BY TO LOOK AT LULU.

> GEAROID
> When you phoned, I assumed Francis's war chest had run out.

> LULU
> (TO ANGEL) Francis?

> ANGEL
> Werewolf. (TO GEAROID) Well it has in one sense, but that's not why we came.

> GEAROID
> Did you find what you were looking for?

> ANGEL
> Yes.

> GEAROID
> How?

> ANGEL
> You don't want to know.

> GEAROID
> You keep saying that, but there's nothing you could say that would shock me.

> LULU
> (COY) Bet I could ...

                    GEAROID
(COOL) No doubt about that, Lucinda. Wouldn't
even give you odds. But Angel here can't tell
me anything I haven't done, seen, tried,
forgotten or been arrested for.

                    LULU
(TO ANGEL) This guy's a *monk*?

                    ANGEL
Okay. These Popular Front for Brittany people
holding Werewolf - sorry, Francis - were
buying ecstasy tabs from a Dutch supplier.

                    GEAROID
How may tabs?

                    ANGEL
Around 15,000, give or take an overdose or
two.

                    GEAROID
(THOUGHTFUL) Why didn't they smuggle powder?
Easier to move - and it takes effect quicker.

                    LULU
(POINTING) Does this monk know his stuff or
what?

                    ANGEL
It wasn't supposed to come here. It was
headed for France, ready processed and
wrapped.

                    GEAROID
And how was this supposed to help the Front
Populaire de Breton?

                    ANGEL
Not at all. That's a con. This is someone out
to make a bucket of dosh.

                    GEAROID
Is there a drug scene in France? In Brittany?

                    ANGEL
Search me. Mind you, with this lot you could
start one. Target one of the big university
scenes there.

                    GEAROID
Professional gig?

                    ANGEL
(THINKS) At the Dutch end, maybe, but the
French side are a bunch of cowboys.

                    GEAROID
And you have to get the stuff back to these
guys by when?

                    ANGEL
Monday morning. There's an overnight ferry
from Portsmouth.

                    GEAROID
So you're going to St Malo?

                    ANGEL
They want to meet in a café called Le Biniou.

                    GEAROID
'Bagpipes'. (TO LULU) It's a traditional
Breton instrument. Will they have Francis
with them?

                    ANGEL
Doubt it. They'll string us along like
they've seen in the movies.

                    GEAROID
How many of them are there?

                    ANGEL
There's a head honcho called Guennoc and two
heavies plus three locals with a fishing
boat. They may or may not be on the team.

                    GEAROID
Assume they are. That's six on to one.

                    LULU
(STROPPY) Two. Six on two. My kinda odds.

                    GEAROID
(SIGHS) That's what General Custer used to
say. You want back up?

                    ANGEL
No, I want some honey. As many jars as you
can spare. Look on it as an export drive.

GEAROID THINKS ABOUT THIS. LOOKS AT HIS EMPTY
CUP.

                    GEAROID
Anyone for more gooseberry and camomile tea?

THE OTHERS SHAKE HEADS. GEAROID PRODUCES A HIP
FLASK OF WHISKEY FROM THE FOLDS OF HIS ROBES.

                    GEAROID
    Can't blame you, it is pretty foul, isn't it?
    Here (POURING), take the taste away. Let me
    tell you the flaw in your plan.

                    ANGEL
    I was hoping you would.

                    GEAROID
    Customs officer, nosey policeman - whichever
    - comes along and goes 'Ah honey, I love it',
    opens a jar and dips a finger in for a taste
    and gets a real blast instead.

                    ANGEL
    There is that. So what's *your* plan?

                    LULU
    Hey - out of order, Angel. This guy's a monk,
    you can't expect ...

                    GEAROID
    *My* plan is the better one. You cut out the
    honey, go to the source.

                    LULU
    What? Source of what?

                    GEAROID
    The bees.

                    LULU
    The bees?

                    ANGEL
    (IMPRESSED) Top man, Brother G. Don't you get
    it, Lulu? How many Customs officers or nosey
    cops are gonna stick their fingers in a
    beehive?

SCENE 50. EXT. MONASTERY BEEHIVES. DAY.

GEAROID, LULU AND ANGEL ADVANCE ACROSS A FIELD
TOWARD THE ST FULGENTIUS' BEEHIVES. THEY ARE
WEARING FULL BEEKEEPING KIT, MAKING THEM LOOK
ALMOST LIKE ASTRONAUTS. GEAROID CARRIES A
'SMOKER'. ANGEL AND LULU MOVE CLUMSILY AND
UNGAINLY.

                    GEAROID
Now you'll be remembering what I told you?

                    LULU
Don't flap at the bees. Don't flap at the
bees, no matter what.

                    ANGEL
(EQUALLY NERVOUS) And don't sweat. They don't
like that.

                    LULU
Yeah, great. Don't flap and don't sweat. (TO
ANGEL) *This* is good advice?

ANGEL SHRUGS, HIS MOVEMENTS RIDICULOUS IN THE BEE
SUIT. GEAROID IS OPENING A HIVE AND USING THE
SMOKER TO CLEAR THE BEES.

                    GEAROID
Just don't flap around and the bees won't
sting you. Ow! You little bugger!

                    LULU
You've been stung? (PANIC) What happens when
you get stung?

                    GEAROID
Ach, nothing. I'm immune by now. Happens ten
times a day.

                    LULU
And what happens if you're *not* immune?

                    GEAROID
Nothing much. Stings a bit but it's not
serious unless you're one of the two percent
of the population who are allergic.

                    LULU
What happens *then*?

                    GEAROID
(CASUAL) Oh, I think you die. Now stand still
and look in here.

HE REMOVES THE TOP FROM A HIVE, PUFFING SMOKE AT
THE BEES.

                    GEAROID
Right, downstairs we have the queen in her
brood chamber, along with the drones. They
make up about ten percent of the colony and
do nothing except mate with the queen. The

other little darlings are the workers.

                LULU
Er ... how may are there in here?

                GEAROID
In the middle of summer, there could be 60,000 in this hive, but this time of year, maybe 35,000.

                LULU
Wow ...

                ANGEL
And exactly how many hives do you have?

                GEAROID
Thirty-two.

LONG SHOT OF HIVES STRETCHING INTO DISTANCE.

                LULU
That's ...

                ANGEL
A million bees, give or take.

                LULU
Jesus! I'm in the middle of a million bees.

                GEAROID
Don't flap!

                ANGEL
Don't sweat!

                LULU
(BREATHING DEEPLY) Okay, okay, I can handle this.

                GEAROID
Good, now look. This is a Hoffman self-spacer. (HE HOLDS UP A HONEYCOMB 'FRAME') Or it can be called a 'super'. You slot these in with a sheet of wax over them so the bees can make themselves at home making a honeycomb, which they then let us steal. Now you've got 11 spacers here. See them?

                ANGEL
(NOT MOVING) I can see fine from over here.

                LULU
I'll take your word for it. For anything.

                    GEAROID
Now when we export bees ...

                    LULU
You export them?

                    GEAROID
Sure    we    do.    We    supply    half    a    dozen
monasteries  and  farmers  in  France  alone,  but
we can send them anywhere. For that, we use a
nucleus hive, which is smaller than this but
the  principle's  the  same.  You  put  one  of
these  spacers  in  for  a  queen,  to  keep  the
others   quiet,   then   you   have   bees   on   the
spacers  at  each  end.  The  ones  in  the  middle
...

                    ANGEL
We  hollow  out  and  fill  with  ecstasy  tabs.
It's brilliant.

                    LULU
What if the bees eat the tabs?

                    ANGEL
Even better. No Customs man is going to put
his   hand   into   a   hive   full   of   thousands   of
bees smashed out of their tiny bee brains ...

                    GEAROID
They won't touch it. Be like eating chalk to
them.  But  a  clever  Customs  man  wouldn't  put
his  hand  in  anyway,  he'd  *weigh*  the  nucleus
hive. So we'll have to make sure the weight
of the tabs isn't more than the weight of the
bees we're replacing.

                    ANGEL
Will we need any paperwork?

                    GEAROID
No. The retreat here has a health certificate
under  the  Bee  Diseases  Control  Act  -  don't
laugh, it's true. And if you're exporting to
one end destination in France, you don't even
need a transit certificate.

                    ANGEL
Do we have an end destination?

                    GEAROID
I've thought of that. A colleague of mine, a
monk   called   Frostin   -   a   real   monk   from
Normandy. He'll take them off our hands. You

get the bill though.

                    ANGEL
How much?

                    GEAROID
Coupla hundred for the bees, plus the petrol
and costs for taking one of the St Fulgentius
vans across on the ferry.

                    ANGEL
With you along as a sort of bee consultant?

                    GEAROID
You could say that.

                    LULU
He's coming with us?

                    GEAROID
I've done the St Malo run many a time. No-
one's likely to stop me.

                    ANGEL
I don't know if this is a good plan.

                    LULU
Hey, Angel, it'll cut the odds if there are
three of us.

                    GEAROID
(POINTING AT THE HIVE) Actually, there'll
probably be around 28,003 of us.

                    LULU
Coolski. We're not a posse anymore, we're an
invasion force.

                    ANGEL
(TO GEAROID) You're beginning to enjoy this,
aren't you?

                    GEAROID
Yes, I'm afraid I am.


SCENE 51. EXT. ST MALO FERRY TERMINAL. DAY.

A DOCKED CAR FERRY DISGORGING VEHICLES. THE ST
FULGENTIUS TRANSIT ROLLS OFF WITH GEAROID AT THE
WHEEL, FOLLOWED BY ANGEL AND LULU IN THE FORD.
BOTH ARE WAVED THROUGH BY THE FRENCH CUSTOMS.
LULU WAVES AT THEM.

SCENE IS CLEARLY ESTABLISHED AS FRANCE - SHOTS OF
FRENCH FLAGS ON CITY WALLS AND, IDEALLY, THE
BRETON 'ERMINE' FLAG AS WELL.

## SCENE 52. LE BINIOU CAFÉ/BAR IN ST MALO. DAY

ANGEL IS SITTING AT A TABLE DRINKING COFFEE,
FACING THE DOOR. THE COWBOY, ONE OF GUENNOC'S
HENCHMEN, ENTERS AND LOOKS ROUND FURTIVELY, THEN
APPROACHES ANGEL'S TABLE. HE PULLS A MAP FROM HIS
BACK POCKET AND LAYS IT IN FRONT OF ANGEL.

> COWBOY
> Be here, where we have marked. (HE POINTS TO
> A RED CIRCLE DRAWN ON THE MAP). At two
> o'clock. Bring our property.

> ANGEL
> So 'X' marks the spot, eh? This is where we
> do the exchange?

> COWBOY
> Be there.

> ANGEL
> I'll find it.

> COWBOY
> Two o'clock.

> ANGEL
> I can hardly wait. (AS COWBOY LEAVES) Missing
> you already.

GEAROID HAS BEEN SITTING NEARBY HIDING BEHIND A
FRENCH NEWSPAPER. HE LOWERS IT TO SPEAK TO ANGEL.

> GEAROID
> Was that this Guennoc chappie, then?

> ANGEL
> No, just one of his gophers. He left us our
> instructions.

GEAROID LOOKS AT MAP.

> GEAROID
> Port a la Duc ... the coast road. That's a
> pretty isolated spot he's picked. Will he
> have Francis with him?

                    ANGEL
I doubt it. I think he wants to play the
tough guy.

                    GEAROID
So we might need the bees then?

ANGEL
We very well might. But don't say anything to
Lulu. I'd like to leave her out of it.

                    GEAROID
Understood. Anyway, I only brought two bee
suits with me. Where is she, by the way?

                    ANGEL
You know what they say. When the going gets
tough ...

                    GEAROID
... the tough go shopping.

                    ANGEL
Got it in one. We'll keep her in reserve. She
can be the cavalry and come riding to the
rescue if we need it.

                    GEAROID
God help us if we do.

                    ANGEL
*That* is your department.


SCENE 53. EXT. ISOLATED FRENCH COUNTRY
ROAD/TRACK. DAY.

ANGEL AND GEAROID ARE PARKED IN THE TRANSIT VAN.
THEY ARE WEARING BEEKEEPING SUITS, THOUGH NOT
(YET) THE HELMETS.

                    GEAROID
Are we on time?

                    ANGEL
We're early. Are you sure this is the right
place?

                    GEAROID
I can read a map. Just make sure you can tell
the time.

                    ANGEL
Don't get ratty, it'll only upset the bees.

                    GEAROID
Yeah, sure. (BEAT) Which way do you think
they'll come? Down the road or up behind us?

                    ANGEL
(LOOKING IN WING MIRROR) Both.

TWO CARS APPROACH THE TRANSIT, STOPPING TWENTY
YARDS OR SO AWAY. GUENNOC GETS OUT OF ONE, COWBOY
AND THE OTHER (LARGE) HENCHMAN, SUMO, OUT OF THE
OTHER. ALL THREE PRODUCE PISTOLS (ALL THE SAME
TYPE). ANGEL OPENS THE TRANSIT WINDOW TO TALK TO
THEM.

                    GUENNOC
Do you have our property?

                    ANGEL
I'm not convinced it's yours, but yes, we
have it. Where is our friend?

                    GUENNOC
In a safe place. He will be released once we
have our property.

                    ANGEL
Not good enough. We need to see him here and
now or there's no trade.

GUENNOC SHOUTS TO THE TWO HENCHMEN, SPEAKING IN
BRETON. ANGEL TURNS TO GEAROID.

                    GEAROID
He's telling them to get ready for trouble.

                    ANGEL
Do you think he means it?

                    GEAROID
How the bloody ...? Yes (SNAPPY) I think he
means it.

                    GUENNOC
(IN ENGLISH) I don't think you are in any
position to make a deal. You have ten seconds
to produce our property otherwise we shoot.
If you try to start your engine, we will
shoot. If you ...

                    ANGEL
All right, all right, we get the picture.

                    GUENNOC
One ... two      ...

ANGEL AND GEAROID EXCHANGE GLANCES BUT SAY
NOTHING. AS ONE THEY OPEN THE DOORS OF THE VAN
AND GET OUT, TURNING TO WALK TOWARD THE REAR
DOORS. GUENNOC SEES THE BEEKEEPING SUITS FOR THE
FIRST TIME.

> GUENNOC
> ... three ... *Qu'est-ce que* ...? What are you
> ...?

> ANGEL
> (TURNING, BELIGERANT) You said you'd give us
> ten.

THEY CONTINUE TO THE BACK OF THE VAN. GEAROID
CROSSES HIMSELF. AS THEY OPEN THE DOORS, THEY
WHISPER.

> GEAROID
> I've loosened the lid on all three boxes. One
> good kick should do it. Get ready with your
> hood.

ANGEL NODS AND GINGERLY PICKS UP ONE OF THE
NUCLEUS HIVES, CARRYING IT TOWARD GUENNOC. ALL
THREE BRETONS HAVE MOVED IN CLOSER.

> GUENNOC
> Stop there. What is this?

> ANGEL
> Your property. About 15,000 ways of making
> your party go with a swing. Course, you'll
> have to fight the bees for them.

> GUENNOC
> (DISBELIEF) Bees? What are you talking about.
> (HE SNAPS AT THE OTHER HENCHMEN, WHO ARE
> JABBERING IN BRETON) What do you think you
> are doing?

> ANGEL
> Giving you your goods. That's what you
> wanted, wasn't it? Or did you really want to
> count up to ten? (HE FLIPS ON HIS HOOD,
> SHOUTING TO GEAROID) Showtime!

ANGEL KICKS OFF THE LID OF THE HIVE AND PUTS HIS
(GLOVED) HANDS IN TO PULL OUT A 'SPACER'.

> ANGEL
> They're in here somewhere ...

THE BEES SWARM OUT AND GUENNOC, SUMO AND COWBOY

PANIC, FLAPPING, BEING STUNG, RUNNING AND FALLING
BACK TO THEIR CARS, COWBOY DROPS HIS GUN, WHICH
GEAROID PICKS UP.

ANGEL AND GEAROID LOOK AT EACH OTHER, HARDLY
BELIEVING THAT THE BAD GUYS HAVE RUN AWAY.
GEAROID GOES OVER TO SUMO'S AND COWBOY'S CAR,
WHERE THEY ARE FLAPPING AND SHOUTING INSIDE,
CLEARLY TERRIFIED. GEAROID TAPS THE PISTOL ON THE
BONNET OF THE CAR, UNLOADS IT EXPERTLY, THROWING
THE BULLETS AWAY AND CASUALLY TOSSING EMPTY GUN
AND EMPTY MAGAZINE ONTO THE ROOF OF THEIR CAR.
ANGEL WALKS TO GUENNOC'S CAR, WHERE GUENNOC IS
FLAPPING AT REAL OR IMAGINERY BEES. HE LOCKS THE
CAR DOORS AS ANGEL APPROACHES. ANGEL LEANS OVER
AND KNOCKS POLITELY ON THE WINDOW.

>ANGEL
You don't want them then? (HE OPENS HIS
GLOVED HAND TO SHOW GUENNOC A PILE OF
TABLETS). We can get rid of the bees for you,
but it could take a while. They seem a bit
hacked off for some reason.

>GUENNOC
(STILL FLAPPING) Get them away!

>ANGEL
And I get to see my friend Francis?

>GUENNOC
Yes, yes. I'll take you to him now, but you
get *them* away first.

>ANGEL
I knew we could do a deal. Back up the track
about a hundred yards. Sorry, metres to you.
I'll tell my friend to start rounding up our
little friends.

GUENNOC GLARES AT HIM, STARTS HIS CAR AND FLASHES
HIS LIGHTS AT SUMO/COWBOY, WHO START THEIRS. BOTH
CARS RETREAT DOWN THE TRACK. ANGEL WALKS BACK TO
GEAROID.

>ANGEL
I'm going with them to check up on Francis.
Can you round up the bees?

>GEAROID
They're not likely to come if I whistle. We
just have to wait for them to calm down.

                ANGEL
Wait here for me. If Francis checks out, I'll
reschedule the exchange for tomorrow, so you
can start unpacking the stuff.

ANGEL TURNS TO WALK BACK TO GUENNOC'S CAR.

                GEAROID
Hey, Angel, you be careful.

ANGEL RAISES A HAND AND KEEPS ON WALKING.

                ANGEL
I'll be okay. You know me. (HE DOES A SHUFFLE
AS HE WALKS) Float like a butterfly, sting
like a bee.

GEAROID WATCHES AS HE GETS NEAR THE BRETONS'
CARS. ALL THREE JUMP OUT AS ANGEL FLIPS BACK HIS
BEEKEEPER'S HOOD. COWBOY AND SUMO GRAB HIM, WHILE
GUENNOC PUNCHES HIM IN THE STOMACH. AS HE GOES
DOWN ON HIS KNEES, THEY TIE HIS HANDS BEHIND HIM
AND PUT TAPE OVER HIS EYES BEFORE BUNDLING HIM
INTO THE BACK OF GUENNOC'S CAR.

                GEAROID
(SHAKING HIS HEAD, TO HIMSELF) Oooh, I bet
that hurt ...


SCENE 54. EXT. GUENNOC'S FARM. DAY.

THE CARS ENTER A FARMYARD COMPLEX THAT HAS AN
OBVIOUS GATEWAY. SITUATION IS NEAR THE SEA ON
CLIFF TOPS.


SCENE 55. EXT. FARMYARD. DAY.

THERE IS AN OLD MAN (CADIC) AND TWO YOUNGER ONES
(HIS GRANDSONS) STANDING GUARD. THE YOUNG BRETONS
ARE ARMED WITH P-38 PISTOLS, BUT THEY ARE
OBVIOUSLY CLUMSY AND ILL-AT-EASE WITH THEM.

CADIC BEGINS TO ARGUE IN BRETON WITH GUENNOC AS
SOON AS HE GETS OUT OF THE CAR. GUENNOC, COWBOY
AND SUMO ARE ALL SUFFERING FROM BEE STINGS.

GUENNOC PULLS ANGEL FROM THE BACK OF HIS CAR AND
RIPS OFF THE BLINDFOLD TAPE. HE PRODUCES A KEY
AND PUSHES ANGEL TOWARD ONE OF THE OUTBUILDINGS
IN THE COURTYARD, UNLOCKING THE DOOR.

                    GUENNOC
Your   friend   is   in   there.   You   have   five
minutes; no more.

HE PUSHES ANGEL INSIDE.


SCENE 56. INT. FARM/STABLE. DAY.

ANGEL STUMBLES INTO WEREWOLF'S CELL. WEREWOLF IS
IN HIS WHEELCHAIR, LEG OUT, STILL IN PLASTER. HE
IS DRINKING FROM A LARGE BOTTLE.

                    WEREWOLF
Angel!  About  time.  It's  your  round.  (HE
NOTICES  THE  BEEKEEPER  SUIT)  Bloody  hell,  how
did you get here? Space shuttle?

                    ANGEL
It's a long story and we don't have time - or
enough booze.

                    WEREWOLF
Oh, we've got plenty of booze. (HE INDICATES
A LARGE PILE OF BOTTLES) If you like cider,
that is. Hang on. (HE MOVES HIS CHAIR FORWARD
AND SNIFFS ANGEL'S SUIT). I know that smell.
Bees. Hey, top man! You brought the stuff
over in a beehive. Outstanding! I wish I'd
thought of that.

                    ANGEL
Me too ...

                    WEREWOLF
Then who  ...? Oh-ho. You  went  to  see  my
brother, didn't you?

                    ANGEL
He's here, on the team.

                    WEREWOLF
(SIGHS) Keep an eye on him for me, Angel. He
needs looking after.

                    ANGEL
He's  doing  okay  so  far.  And  anyway,  we've
both got Lucinda watching over us.

                    WEREWOLF
(GROANS) Oh God. Is there any *good* news?

                    ANGEL
Not a lot. We're in a sort of Mexican stand-
off. They don't trust me and I don't trust
them. Have you found out anything?

                    WEREWOLF
Sure. I've kept my mouth shut - mostly - and
not let on that I can understand what they're
saying.

HE PASSES OVER THE BOTTLE AND HE NOTICES ANGEL'S
HANDS ARE TAPED.

                    WEREWOLF
Do you want me to get you out of that?

                    ANGEL
Don't bother; they'll be taking me back to
Gearoid in a minute. Go on.

                    WEREWOLF
Okay. From what I've picked up, these jokers
had a deal going with a Dutch firm.

                    ANGEL
(WRY) Yeah, I've met one of them, and he's
one bad dude.

                    WEREWOLF
Well, the Dutch end supplied the stuff - -
what was the stuff, anyway?

                    ANGEL
E - 15,000 tabs of it.

                    WEREWOLF
Shiiiit! I'm surprised you didn't go into
business yourself and leave me to rot.

                    ANGEL
(ANGELIC) The thought never crossed my mind.

                    WEREWOLF
(SUSPICIOUS) I'll bet. So, anyways, they did
a trade. Drugs for guns. But of course the
dope got rerouted to England and everyone
starts smelling a double-cross.

                    ANGEL
Whoa! Stop there and rewind. Guns? Drugs for
guns?

                    WEREWOLF
Hadn't you noticed all the pistols these boys
are packing?

                    ANGEL
Well, yeah, but ...

                    WEREWOLF
So this guy Guennoc, he inherits this farm,
right? Old, run-down place, and he knows
diddly about farming. So he starts to do it
up for holiday homes - gîtes, you know. Out
in one of the barns - digging a new cess pit
or something - he discovers a crate of
Walther P38s. A hundred, maybe more, all in
their factory packing, greased up and in full
working order.

                    ANGEL
And totally untraceable.

                    WEREWOLF
Exactly. So that was the deal: guns for E.
Interesting thing is, though, that old man
Cadic doesn't know. He thinks Guennoc is
selling the guns outright to raise funds for
the cause.

                    ANGEL
Cadic? Who's he?

                    WEREWOLF
The old Breton guy outside. The two younger
lads are his grandsons. He's the one with the
fishing boat. They've got it tied up at the
foot of the cliffs. He still thinks this is
all in aid of the Popular Front for Brittany.

                    ANGEL
Is that the entire army?

                    WEREWOLF
Yes, and Cadic and his boys sleep on the
boat, so there's usually never more than
three here. They must think I can't do a
runner. You planning something?

                    ANGEL
We're going to reschedule a trade for
tomorrow, you for the E. So just be ready for
anything. At any time.

                    WEREWOLF
Whatever you say, boss. You're in charge.

ANGEL
(SHAKING HEAD) If only ... if only ...


SCENE 57. EXT. OVERLOOKING GUENNOC'S FARMYARD.
DAY.

LONG SHOT OF FARMYARD THROUGH BINOCULARS. ANGEL
IS SEEN BEING BLINDFOLDED AGAIN AND PUSHED INTO
THE BACK OF GUENNOC'S CAR.

PAN BACK TO SECOND PAIR OF BINOCULARS WATCHING
THE FIRST OBSERVER, WHO IS LYING IN THE SCRUB
WATCHING. IT IS SEEN TO BE GRONWEGHE, THE
DUTCHMAN, BUT WE DON'T SEE THE SECOND WATCHER.


SCENE 58. COUNTRY ROAD/TRACK. DAY.

GUENNOC'S CAR HURTLES DOWN THE TRACK TOWARD
GEAROID AND THE TRANSIT VAN AND SCREAMS TO A
HALT. GUENNOC AND COWBOY PULL ANGEL FROM THE BACK
AND THROW HIM ON THE GROUND. THEY KICK HIM HALF-
HEARTEDLY AND THEN DRIVE OFF. GEAROID COMES TO
HELP ANGEL UP.

GEAROID
Did that hurt?

ANGEL
Not really.

GEAROID
This will.

HE RIPS THE TAPE BLINDFOLD OFF.

ANGEL
Oww! Thanks a bunch.

GEAROID
Where did they take you?

ANGEL
(DRILY) I wasn't able to enjoy the scenery.
How long have I been gone?

GEAROID
'Bout half-an-hour.

ANGEL
So it's within ten minutes' drive and it's by
the sea; a sort of farmhouse converted into
holiday cottages.

                    GEAROID
Then we'd better get rid of the bees and try
and find the place before nightfall.

                    ANGEL
They want another meet. Back here tomorrow,
same time.

                    GEAROID
Do you trust them?

                    ANGEL
No, but what's the alternative?

                    GEAROID
Pay them a visit and get Francis out of
there.

                    ANGEL
(REALISING) You don't want them to have the
drugs, do you?

                    GEAROID
Can't say I'm keen on the idea.

                    ANGEL
It won't be easy, they ...

THEY HEAR A CAR COMING TOWARD THEM. IT IS LULU,
DRIVING THE FORD, WAVING A COWBOY HAT OUT OF THE
DRIVER'S WINDOW. SHE PARKS VIOLENTLY UP CLOSE TO
THEM.

                    LULU
Hey, is this weird or what? Driving on the
right side of the road with the wheel on the
wrong side. Bizaaaaaare! It really does your
head, man.

                    ANGEL
Where've you been? We were worried about you.

                    LULU
Sho' didn't look like it to me, Angel honey.
Looked to me as if you had other things on
your mind when you went calling on our French
friends.

                    ANGEL
How do you know where I've been?

                    LULU
(AS IF TO A CHILD) Because I followed you.
You said I had to watch your back and that's

just what I did.

                    ANGEL
You saw where they took me? Where Francis is?

                    LULU
(HAMMING IT UP) Honey, I saw *everything*. (SHE
OPENS THE BOOT OF THE FORD AND PRODUCES A
PAIR OF BINOCULARS) I told you I was going
shopping.

                    ANGEL
So you can find it again?

                    LULU
Sho' thing, boss.

                    ANGEL
Lulu, it's true what they say about you.
You're magic.

                    LULU
(PINNING ANGEL'S ARMS) There's a downside to
this, though.

                    ANGEL
There is?

                    LULU
'fraid so. I wasn't the only one watching you
at the farmhouse. Our Dutch friend, the one
with the smart mouth, he was there too,
scoping the place.

                    ANGEL
(THINKING) Oh dear. That's not good.
Definitely not good. Maybe you were right,
Brother G. Maybe we should (HE TURNS TO
GEAROID, WHO IS TRANSFIXED, LOOKING INTO THE
BOOT OF THE FORD) pay them a visit before
anyone else does.

                    GEAROID
Lulu - (BEAT) - What's this? (HE BENDS OVER
AND PULLS A PUMP-ACTION SHOTGUN FROM THE
BOOT).

                    LULU
I told you I went shopping. There was this
really sweet salesman, wanted to practise his
American. (CHEERFUL) You know how easy it is
to buy a gun here if you say you're going
hunting?

GEAROID AND ANGEL SHAKE THEIR HEADS SLOWLY.

>           GEAROID
> Lulu, dear, you can't just go round shooting
> people.

>           LULU
> Yes I can, I'm American.

>           GEAROID
> This isn't the Wild West.

>           ANGEL
> If the Dutchman goes in there before we do,
> it could be.

>           LULU
> So it's up to us to head 'em off at the pass.
> Right, boss?

>           GEAROID
> (POINTING AT GUN) Do you know how to use one
> of them?

>           LULU
> Hell, yes. I can load and shoot faster and
> more accurately than any man.

>           ANGEL
> Just as long as she's got her contacts in.
> Come on, let's get the bees.

LULU SHOUTS AFTER THEM, THEN DOES A DOUBLE-TAKE.

>           LULU
> That's right. As long as I've got my lenses
> in ... Hey!

SCENE 59. INT. RESTAURANT/HOTEL DINING ROOM. NIGHT.

ANGEL AND LULU ARE AT A TABLE DRINKING. GEAROID IS AT THE BAR TALKING IN FRENCH ON A PHONE. HE FINISHES AND JOINS ANGEL.

>           GEAROID
> It's done. I've booked us rooms here for
> tonight and paid up front. Told them we were
> going to be leaving early.

>           ANGEL
> And the bees?

GEAROID
That's settled. My contact, Frostin - the real monk - he'll be over here in the morning to pick them up and take care of the van. I'll leave the keys here.

LULU
(WHISPERS) And the E?

GEAROID
I'll need an hour in the back of the van to transfer it. The bees will be fairly dozy now. It shouldn't be a problem.

LULU
Did you lose many?

GEAROID
A few. Most of them came back to the queens. They're very loyal. (THOUGHTFUL) That's why I like them.

LULU
(TO ANGEL) So what's the plan, boss-man?

ANGEL
Normally, I'd say wait and do a deal with Guennoc tomorrow. I don't trust him, but I can't see him massacring all four of us in broad daylight.

LULU
(UPBEAT) We can shoot back now.

ANGEL
You can; I won't. Gearoid?

GEAROID
I think it might (HE RAISES HIS EYES TO HEAVEN) be frowned upon. I have to put my faith in the Lord. It says so in my contract. But I agree, we can't trust the Bretons.

ANGEL
So the alternative - Plan B - bee, geddit? Oh, never mind. The alternative is to go in and get Werewolf out. They won't be expecting us.

GEAROID
I say we go in early; before breakfast.

ANGEL
If that psycho Dutchman is about, the sooner

the better. I'll go along with a dawn raid.

                    LULU
Dawn raid ... I like the sound of that,
*compadres*. Now, can we order some food? I'm
so hungry I could eat a horse.

                    GEAROID
(DEADPAN, PICKING UP A MENU) I'll check the
menu.

                    LULU
(TO ANGEL) He's kidding, isn't he?

ANGEL SHRUGS NON-COMMITTALLY.


SCENE 60. EXT. OUTSIDE HOTEL. DAWN.

ANGEL IS FIXING THE FAKE NUMBER PLATES TO THE
FORD. LULU IS CHECKING THE SHOTGUN. GEAROID IS
CARRYING A PLASTIC DUSTBIN (THE DRUGS) AND A CAN
OF PETROL.

                    ANGEL
(STANDING UP) I'm done.

                    LULU
(SLINGING THE RIFLE ACROSS HER SHOULDERS) And
I'm loaded for bear. Why the Dutch plates?

                    ANGEL
It might just give us an edge. Anyone round
here sees us, they'll remember the Dutch
number and hopefully not that it's a right-
hand drive British wreck Also, it might make
the Bretons think twice, if they think
they're opening up on their partners.

GEAROID DUMPS THE DRUGS AND THE PETROL CAN IN THE
BOOT OF THE FORD.

                    ANGEL
What's that for?

                    GEAROID
(WEIGHING THE CAN) If this works, we won't
have to hand over these tablets. In which
case, nobody gets them.

                    ANGEL
(TO LULU) Okay with you?

LULU
(HESITATES) O ... kay ... But only if you let
me shoot somebody. (GRINS INSANELY)

GEAROID
(TO ANGEL) Now *she's* kidding, isn't she?

ANGEL
(WINKING AT LULU) Seems reasonable ...

SCENE 61. INT. FORD. DAY.

INTERIOR OF CAR, ANGEL DRIVING, GEAROID IN
PASSENGER SEAT WITH MAP, LULU IN BACK WITH SHOTGUN
ACROSS HER LAP. SHE IS LEANING OVER, POINTING AT
THE MAP.

LULU
There's this little village up ahead - yeah,
here we are - and once through it there's a
sharp right, and a mile or so down there, we
take a left down a track ...

GEAROID
(AGITATED) Slow down. Whoa. Pull over.

ANGEL
What's up?

GEAROID
Look down the street, outside that
*boulangerie.*

(POINT-OF-VIEW DOWN STREET. THERE IS A SMALL
BAKER'S SHOP AND PARKED OUTSIDE IS A 50CC MOPED)

GEAROID
It's the one with the cowboy boots. One of
Guennoc's men.

ANGEL
You sure?

GEAROID
Look for yourself.

COWBOY COMES OUT OF THE BAKER'S WITH TWO LONG
FRENCH LOAVES UNDER HIS ARM. HE DOES NOT LOOK DOWN
THE ROAD, JUST GETS ON THE MOPED AND SETS OFF.

ANGEL
They've sent him on the breakfast run ...
(THINKS) After this village, are there any
other houses, Lulu?

                    LULU
Nope. Like I said, he'll hang a right fairly
soon, and that's clear all the way to the
farm place.

                    ANGEL
Good. (HE FASTENS HIS SEATBELT. GEAROID DOES
THE SAME) One down, two to go.

                    GEAROID
May the Ford be with you.

                    LULU
What are you two ... Yeouww! (SHE IS PUSHED
BACK IN HER SEAT AS ANGEL SLIPS THE CLUTCH)

THE CAR ACCELERATES AND FOLLOWS COWBOY AS HE
TURNS OFF THE MAIN ROAD. ON A NARROW COUNTRY
TRACK, ANGEL SPEEDS UP TO COME UP RIGHT BEHIND
THE MOPED. AS HE IS ABOUT TO OVERTAKE IT, HE
WINDS DOWN HIS WINDOW.

                    ANGEL
(OVER HIS SHOULDER TO LULU) And now to
demonstrate one of the advantages of a *right*-
hand drive car in a *left*-hand drive country
...

AS THE FORD COMES LEVEL WITH HIM, COWBOY TURNS
AND SEEMS TO NOTICE IT FOR THE FIRST TIME,
RECOGNISES ANGEL AND IS OBVIOUSLY TERRIFIED. AS
THE FORD PASSES, ANGEL REACHES OUT AND PUSHES HIM
HARD ON THE SHOULDER. THE MOPED SWERVES OFF THE
ROAD, THROWING COWBOY INTO A FIELD.

ANGEL STOPS THE CAR AND LULU IS THE FIRST TO JUMP
OUT.

                    LULU
Way to go!

SHE IS THE FIRST ONE OVER TO COWBOY'S INERT BODY,
THEN GEAROID, WITH ANGEL HANGING BACK.

                    LULU
(DISAPPOINTED) He's still breathing!

                    ANGEL
No, you can't shoot him, Lulu.

                    LULU
Awww ... Hey look. (SHE BENDS OVER AND PULLS
A WALTHER PISTOL FROM COWBOY'S JACKET) He
would have shot us.

                    ANGEL
I doubt it.

                    GEAROID
And he's not going anywhere on that thing
anymore. (HE INDICATES THE MOPED WITH A
BUCKLED FRONT WHEEL). Has he got a mobile
phone on him?

                    LULU
Nope.

                    GEAROID
Then leave him. We'll be in and out before he
comes round.

                    LULU
(SULKING) Aw phooey. Girls don't get to have
fun. (SHE OFFERS BOTH OF THEM THE PISTOL) You
want this?

                    ANGEL
Oh no; I've done my bit.

                    GEAROID
No thanks. (HE SHOWS HER THE CRUCIFIX ROUND
HIS NECK) I've got this.

LULU SHRUGS AND STUFFS THE PISTOL INTO HER BELT.

                    LULU
Then let's go.


SCENE 62. EXT. GUENNOC'S FARMYARD. DAY.

THE FORD IS PARKED IN THE FARM COURTYARD OUTSIDE
THE MAIN BUILDING. ANGEL STANDS BY THE DRIVER'S
DOOR. LEANS THROUGH THE WINDOW AND BLASTS THE
HORN. THERE IS NO SIGN OF LULU AND GEAROID.

                    ANGEL
Anybody home? This is Ecstasy Express.
Delivery for Monsieur Guennoc ...

(DIFFERENT POINT-OF-VIEW. SUMO BURSTS OUT OF THE
HOUSE AND GEAROID, HIDING BEHIND THE DOOR,
CATCHES HIM WITH A PERFECT RIGHT CROSS AND HE
GOES DOWN. AS GUENNOC EMERGES, HALF-DRESSED, LULU
SPRINGS UP FROM BEHIND THE FORD AND WORKS THE
SLIDE ON THE SHOTGUN.)

                    LULU
(SHOUTS) Don't move an eyebrow, dog's breath!

                    ANGEL
     She's been dying to say that. I'd pay
     attention if I were you.

GUENNOC PUTS UP HIS HANDS. GEAROID HOLDS HIS
RIGHT FIST AND CAREFULLY UNWINDS THE CRUCIFIX AND
CHAIN HE HAD WRAPPED AROUND IT.

                    GEAROID
     (HOLDING UP CRUCIFIX) See, told you it
     worked.

HE REACHES BEHIND GUENNOC AND TAKES A PISTOL FROM
HIS BELT THEN PUSHES HIM FORWARD.

                    GUENNOC
     (TO ANGEL) What do you want?

A BOTTLE COMES SMASHING THROUGH THE WINDOW OF
WEREWOLF'S PRISON AND LANDS NEAR THEIR CAR.

                    WEREWOLF
     (FROM INSIDE) Lulu! I love you! Come here and
     let me ravish you!

                    LULU
     (NOT TAKING HER EYES OFF GUENNOC) Keep it
     warm for me, Wolfman, but don't start without
     me. With you in one crucial minute.

                    ANGEL
     (TO GUENNOC) *She's* come for her boy. I want
     the keys to all the outbuildings.

GUENNOC HANDS OVER A BUNCH OF KEYS.

                    GUENNOC
     You won't get very far.

LULU WALKS OVER TO GUENNOC'S AND SUMO'S CARS AND
FIRES THE SHOTGUN, BLOWING UP THE FRONT TYRE OF
EACH.

                    LULU
     Needed to shoot something. (SMILES)

                    ANGEL
     Glad that's out of your system. (TO GUENNOC)
     Come on you.

ANGEL LEADS THEM OVER TO A BARN-LIKE BUILDING AND
FINDS THE KEY. GEAROID DRAGS/PUSHES SUMO. SUMO
AND GUENNOC ARE LOCKED IN.

                    ANGEL
  Let's get Werewolf.

THEY CROSS THE COURTYARD AND LET WEREWOLF OUT.

                    LULU
  Wolfman!

SHE STRADDLES THE WHEELCHAIR TO GET CLOSE ENOUGH
TO KISS HIM.

                    GEAROID
  I take it they've met before.

                    ANGEL
  Looks like it.

                    WEREWOLF
  (STRUGGLING UNDER LULU) You were taking a
  risk, Angel. Did my mad brother talk you into
  this?

                    GEAROID
  And it's good to see you again too, Francis.

                    LULU
  (PLAYFULLY PUNCHING HIM) Hey, lighten up,
  Wolfman. Your brother's pretty cool for a
  monk. We couldn't have done it without him.
  Now we got you *and* we got the dope.

                    WEREWOLF
  You've got ...? Where are the bad guys?

                    ANGEL
  We locked them over there in the barn.

THEY ALL REACT AS THEY HEAR GLASS BREAKING.

                    WEREWOLF
  Oh you dipsticks! (A SHOT FLIES OVER THEM)
  *That's* where they've got the guns stashed.

THERE ARE MORE SHOTS. LULU SCRAMBLES TO GET THE
SHOTGUN.

                    ANGEL
  Inside!

HE DIVES FORWARD AND PUSHES WEREWOLF IN HIS
WHEELCHAIR BACK INTO THE COTTAGE. GEAROID AND
LULU FOLLOW. LULU TURNS TO FIRE AT THE BARN, THEN
THEY GET THE DOOR SHUT. BULLETS CRASH THROUGH THE
WINDOWS, SO THEY DUCK DOWN ONTO THE FLOOR,

PULLING WEREWOLF OUT OF HIS CHAIR.

                    WEREWOLF
     You know, I think I was better off before you
     rescued me.

                    GEAROID
     You ungrateful little ...

                    ANGEL
     Now, boys, let's not panic. We can work this
     out. Things could be worse.

LULU HAS CRAWLED TO ONE OF THE WINDOWS AND
SMASHED OUT SOME GLASS SO SHE CAN LOOK OUT AND
USE THE RIFLE.

                    LULU
     Hey, Mastermind, I've got news for you. It
     just *has* got worse.


SCENE 63. EXT. TRACK OUTSIDE GUENNOC'S FARM. DAY.

ABOUT 200 YARDS FROM THE FARM, GRONWEGHE AND
THREE OR FOUR HEAVILY-ARMED MEN ARE ADVANCING
TOWARD THE GATEWAY. GRONWEGHE HAS A SUB-MACHINE
GUN AND IS PUSHING A LIMPING COWBOY IN FRONT OF
HEM. THEY START SHOOTING AT BOTH ANGEL AND
GUENNOC.


SCENE 64. EXT. FARMYARD. DAY.

                    LULU
     (DUCKING DOWN) These guys mean business. I
     don't think they intend to leave any
     witnesses.

                    GEAROID
     (PATTING WEREWOLF'S LEG) See, Francis, we got
     here just in time.

                    WEREWOLF
     Gee, thanks. Are you qualified to do
     funerals?

                    LULU
     Hey, don't talk like that. It ain't gonna
     come to that. (TO ANGEL) Is it?

                    ANGEL
     No, it isn't. I have another plan.

                    GEAROID
          I knew you would.

                    WEREWOLF
          We can hardly wait. And I mean that!

                    ANGEL
          (BEAT) Let's run away.


SCENE 65. EXT. FARM COURTYARD. DAY.

POINT-OF-VIEW ABOVE COURTYARD.

LULU SHOOTS REPEATEDLY AT ANGEL'S FORD UNTIL THE
PETROL TANK RUPTURES AND PETROL FLOWS OUT.

CLOSE UP OF ANGEL WITH A MAKESHIFT TORCH. GEAROID
POURS WHISKEY FROM HIS HIP FLASK OVER IT. ANGEL
LIGHTS IT AND THROWS IT INTO THE PETROL STREAM.
THE PETROL IGNITES AND THE TANK GOES UP, FILLING
THE COURTYARD WITH THICK BLACK SMOKE.

LULU STEPS OUT UNDER THE SMOKESCREEN, HOLDING TWO
PISTOLS TO COVER THEM. GEAROID CARRIES WEREWOLF
PIGGY-BACK STYLE AND WEREWOLF POINTS TOWARD THE
CLIFFS, AWAY FROM THE GATE.

ANGEL IS LAST, BUT HAS TO GO BACK TO PULL LULU
(WHO IS TRYING TO GET A SHOT OFF) BY THE BELT TO
MAKE HER COME.

AS THEY REACH THE EDGE OF THE CLIFF, THE SMOKE
CLEARS. THERE IS A PATHWAY DOWN THE CLIFF TO THE
SEA.

LULU CANNOT RESIST FIRING A COUPLE OF SHOTS.
ANGEL PULLS HER TO THE GROUND.

                    ANGEL
          That's enough!

                    LULU
          Aw hell, I couldn't hit anything in all this
          pollution.

                    ANGEL
          Don't worry, it's unleaded.

                    LULU
          Hey, have I just torched all that lovely E?

                    ANGEL
          Yes you have. Feel good about that?

                    LULU
Am I supposed to?

                    ANGEL
I think Gearoid would say ...

                    GEAROID
He would say what now? We've got to get down
this cliff before the boat goes without us.

                    LULU
Won't they have heard the Gunfight at the OK
Corral up here?

                    WEREWOLF
Maybe not; not down there on the sea. But
they'll sure as hell see the smoke.

                    ANGEL
Lulu, can you run on ahead and persuade them
not to leave without us?

                    LULU
Can I ...? (SHE HOLDS UP THE PISTOLS)

                    ANGEL
No you can't. Somebody has to sail the boat.

                    GEAROID
Go with her, Angel. I'll carry Francis.

                    ANGEL
You sure?

                    GEAROID
Yeah - he's my brother.

                    WEREWOLF
(SINGING) And he sure is heavy!


SCENE 66. EXT. CLIFF PATHWAY. DAY.

GEAROID CARRIES WEREWOLF PIGGY-BACK DOWN THE CLIFF
PATH WHILE LULU AND ANGEL RUN AHEAD.

AS THE FISHING BOAT COMES INTO SIGHT, CADIC AND
THE CREW SEE LULU AND ANGEL. CADIC JUMPS ONTO THE
ROCKS TO UNTIE THE BOAT.

LULU OUTSKIPS ANGEL, GETS CLOSE ENOUGH, THEN
STOPS, RAISES BOTH PISTOLS AND FIRES RAPIDLY,
PUTTING BULLETS ABOVE CADIC'S HEAD AND NEAR HIS
FEET. HE FREEZES.

                    LULU
(SHOUTS) Touch that rope, dog's breath, and
I'll shoot your frigging eyes out!

ANGEL STAGGERS UP TO HER, WHEEZING, OUT OF BREATH.

                    LULU
(STANDING, MENACING) Translate it for them,
Angel.

                    ANGEL
(CATCHING HIS BREATH) I think they got the
message ...


SCENE 67. EXT. ON BOARD *CENDRILLON*. DAY.

LULU HOLDS CADIC AND ONE GRANDSON AT GUNPOINT, THE
OTHER SON STEERS THE BOAT. GEAROID AND WEREWOLF
LAY IN A HEAP ON A PILE OF NETS. ANGEL IS LOOKING
BACK AT THE COAST.

                    ANGEL
I reckon we're clear. There's somebody on the
cliff top, but we're out of range.

CADIC SAYS SOMETHING IN BRETON.

                    GEAROID
He wants to know where to go now.

                    ANGEL
Can this thing get us across the Channel?

                    LULU
I'll ask. (SHE WAVES A GUN AT CADIC)
Angleterre?

CADIC NODS.

                    ANGEL
That's settled then, we go home.

              ANGEL/GEAROID/WEREWOLF
(ALL POINTING IN DIFFERENT DIRECTIONS) That
way.


SCENE 68. EXT. ONBOARD *CENDRILLON*. DUSK.

THE ATMOSPHERE HAS CHANGED. GEAROID, WEREWOLF AND
CADIC ARE SHARING A BOTTLE. LULU IS IN THE
STEERING HOUSE, CRACKING JOKES WITH THE
GRANDSONS.

                    GEAROID
Hey, Angel, did you know this fine man kept
bees and made mead? (DRINKS) Of the finest
quality!

                    WEREWOLF
And if we'd told him Lulu was American at the
off, he'd have laid on a better boat. He was
liberated by the Yanks back in 1944.

                    GEAROID
And he never really trusted Guennoc. You were
right. He didn't know about the drugs-for-
guns deal.

                    ANGEL
So where's he going to take us?

                    GEAROID
Dorset, would you believe? He can get us into
Weymouth or West Bay and dump us if the tide
is right, then turn around and head back home
before Customs or Immigration even notice. I
can ring the retreat and get the Brothers
Stephen to come and pick us up.

                    WEREWOLF
Good idea of yours, Angel. You picked the one
French fishing boat that didn't mind being
hi-jacked by a bunch of armed hooligans.

                    ANGEL
It's better to be lucky than good, I always
say. (THINKS) But I'd better start the
disarmament negotiations.

ANGEL GOES OVER TO THE WHEELHOUSE, WHERE LULU IS
TEACHING THE YOUNGER CADICS LINE DANCING, AND
PULLS HER GENTLY ON DECK.

                    ANGEL
A quick word, sweetie.

                    LULU
I'm all yours, Angel honey. (TO THE CADICS)
Back in a moment, boys. Keep the beat.

                    ANGEL
Just in case we are noticed getting ashore,
it would be best if you weren't carrying any
artillery.

# MIKE RIPLEY

LULU
What? Strip a girl of her six-guns? (HAMMING
IT) Hey, stranger, smile when you say that to
me.

                    ANGEL
I'm serious, Lulu.

                    LULU
(PATTING HIM ON THE CHEEK) Relax. I threw them
overboard hours ago when one of the boys asked
me if I could get Bruce Springsteen's
autograph.

                    ANGEL
(RELIEVED) Good; great. (BEAT) What did you
tell him?

                    LULU
(CROSSING HER FINGERS) I said me and the Boss
were like that.

SCENE 69. INT. ST. FULGENTIUS RETREAT. DAY.

ANGEL, GEAROID, WEREWOLF (ON CRUTCHES) AND LULU
ARE STANDING AROUND A REFECTORY TABLE LOOKING AT
A SMALL PILE OF BRITISH AND FRENCH MONEY.

                    WEREWOLF
Is that it then?

                    ANGEL
'fraid so.

                    GEAROID
Hate to mention this, but somebody owes us
for some bees.

                    LULU
And a shotgun, pair of binoculars, an
American passport and all the clothes I lost
when you blew up the car.

                    ANGEL
When I blew up ...?

                    WEREWOLF
I'm sorry, Lulu love, but I gave Angel all my
cash. Trusted him with it ...

                    ANGEL
Oh yes, I might have known it would all be my
fault. Well, I'm out of pocket too, you know.
And I've still got to go and collect

Springsteen from Aunt Dorothea's.

THE OTHERS GO QUIET, SHOCKED.

                    WEREWOLF
     Ah yes, Angel, well, you'll be on your own
     there.


SCENE 70. EXT. DOROTHEA'S COTTAGE. DAY.

ANGEL GETS OFF A COUNTRY BUS AND WALKS INTO
DOROTHEA'S COTTAGE GARDEN. HE REMEMBERS THE
AKITAS AND AVOIDS THE SIDE OF THE HOUSE.

                    ANGEL
     Aunty! (LOOKING ROUND) Aunty!

A DOG BARKS AND HE FLINCHES, BUT IT'S BISHOP, THE
OLD BLACK LABRADOR, WHO TROTS UP TO GREET HIM.

                    ANGEL
     Hello, Bishop old boy. You were really
     depressed last time I saw you. Where's
     Dorothea and her hell hounds? (BENDS TO
     WHISPER) And where is Springsteen?

DOROTHEA APPEARS AT THE SIDE OF THE COTTAGE.

                    DOROTHEA
     Stone me, Dr Bloody Dolittle, talking to the
     animals. Well the 'do little' bit's right
     anyway. Had a good holiday?

                    ANGEL
     Holiday? I haven't been on ...

                    DOROTHEA
     Just come and see what your moggy's done.

ANGEL IS PUZZLED, LETTING HER LEAD HIM AROUND THE
COTTAGE TO THE PEN WHERE THE ATTACK DOGS ARE.

                    ANGEL
     What? What?

                    DOROTHEA
     Look.

THERE IS NO SIGN OF THE AKITAS.

                    ANGEL
     Where are they?

DOROTHEA
In the back there, in their kennels. (SHE
POINTS INTO THE DARKNESS) They won't come out
while he's there.

DOROTHEA POINTS UPWARDS. ON THE WIRE ROOF OF THE
CAGE, SPRINGSTEEN IS LYING ASLEEP, HIS TAIL
HANGING DOWN INTO THE AKITAS' CAGE.

ANGEL
I don't ...

DOROTHEA
He terrifies them. They've had a nervous
breakdown, and there's no way they are going
to breed now. I don't know what he did, but
after the first night they've just run back
there quivering whenever he strolled by.

ANGEL
Aunty, I couldn't have known ...

DOROTHEA
He's a killer, that's what he is. He's
psyched out the biggest guard dogs you can
get - without genetic engineering, that is -
and he just sits there and taunts them. My
whole breeding programme's gone pear-shaped.
Who's going to buy a guard dog that's afraid
of a cat?

ANGEL
Look, I'm sure they'll recover once I take
him away. I just need to borrow the train
fare and ...

DOROTHEA
(THOUGHTFUL) Maybe I ought to breed from him.
Ever thought of that? A new generation of
guard cats?

ANGEL
(THINKS, RELAXES, PUTS HIS ARM ROUND
DOROTHEA'S SHOULDERS) Now, funny you should
mention that, Aunty    ...

FADE OUT

END CREDITS.

# About The Author

Mike Ripley is the author of 19 novels, including the award-winning Angel series of comedy thrillers, a dozen short stories and the non-fiction memoir *Surviving a Stroke*. He was a scriptwriter on the BBC series *Lovejoy* and the crime fiction critic for the *Daily Telegraph* and the *Birmingham Post*, reviewing more than 950 novels over 18 years. In the 1990s he was the co-editor, with Maxim Jakubowski, of the three *Fresh Blood* anthologies, showcasing new crime-writing talent such as Ian Rankin, Lee Child, Ken Bruen and Denise Mina. He has appeared at many literary festivals and conventions, developed a creative crime writing course for Cambridge University and devised and produced 'An Audience With ...' stage shows for Colin Dexter and Minette Walters.

After a 25-year career in journalism and public relations, latterly for the Brewers' Society, he became an archaeologist specialising in Romano-British sites in East Anglia until he suffered a stroke at the age of 50. He sat on the government's Stroke Strategy Committee and currently supports both the Stroke Association and the Blood Pressure Association.

He wrote one hundred monthly Getting Away With Murder columns for *Shots Magazine*, is part of the obituary writing team at the *Guardian*, and is the series editor for the imprints Top Notch Thrillers and Ostara Crime. Working with the Margery Allingham Society, he completed the novel left unfinished on the death of Youngman Carter in 1969, which was published in 2014 as *Mr Campion's Farewell*. A second 'continuation' to feature Allingham's famous detective, *Mr Campion's Fox*, is published in 2015.

# COPYRIGHT DETAILS

ANGELS

'Smeltdown' © 1990 Mike Ripley. First published in *A Suit of Diamonds* (Colins Crime Club).

'Lord Peter and the Butterboy' © 1991 Mike Ripley. First published in *Encounters with Lord Peter* (Dorothy L Sayers Society)

'Calling Cards' © 1992 Mike Ripley. First published in *Winter's Crimes 24* (Macmillan)

'Brotherly Love' © 1994 Mike Ripley. First published in *Royal Crimes* (Signet)

'Angel Eyes' © 1999 Mike Ripley. First published in *Fresh Blood 3* (Do-Not Press)

'Ealing Comedy' © 2015 Mike Ripley. Previously unpublished – original to this anthology.

OTHERS

'The Body of the Beer' © 1988 Mike Ripley. First published in *Brewers' Guardian* (Advantage Publishing).

'Gold Sword' © 1989 Mike Ripley. First published in *Brewers' Guardian* (Advantage Publishing).

'Our Man Marlowe' © 1991 Mike Ripley. First published in *Crime Waves 1* (Gollancz)

'The Trouble With Trains' © 1991 Mike Ripley. First published

APPENDIX

# OTHER TELOS TITLES

SAM STONE

THE JINX CHRONICLES
1: JINX TOWN
2: JINX MAGIC (Autumn 2015)
3: JINX BOUND (Autumn 2016)

KAT LIGHTFOOT MYSTERIES
1: ZOMBIES AT TIFFANY'S
2: KAT ON A HOT TIN AIRSHIP
3: WHAT'S DEAD PUSSYKAT
4: KAT OF GREEN TENTACLES (Autumn 2015)

.

THE DARKNESS WITHIN: FINAL CUT
ZOMBIES IN NEW YORK AND OTHER BLOODY JOTTINGS

GRAHAM MASTERTON
RULES OF DUEL
THE DJINN

RAVEN DANE
ABSINTHE & ARSENIC
DEATH'S DARK WINGS

**TELOS PUBLISHING**
**Email: orders@telos.co.uk**
**Web: www.telos.co.uk**

To order copies of any Telos books, please visit our website where
there are full details of all titles and facilities for worldwide credit
card online ordering, as well as occasional special offers.